Standing in the Shadows

K. L. Worsfold

All the characters in this book are fictitious, and any resemblance to actual persons living or dead is purely coincidental.

To my family, for all your love and support.
For Ruth, because there's no such word as can't.

Prologue

The tiny hairs on the back of Eve's neck stood to attention as she woke with the cold draft. Her eyes winced from the light of the fluorescent tube as it flickered. Trying to move, she realised her hands had been bound together tightly; the sharp plastic of the cable tie biting her wrists. She lifted her shaking hands to her head and probed her scalp, finding the matted, sticky hair which was likely the cause of the throbbing. Clenching her jaw, Eve pushed herself upright. Her mouth uttered a small sob before her brain could stop it. She had to stay quiet.

Eve closed her eyes, trying to piece together the events of the last twelve hours, but the pain in her head hindered her focus. Her last memory was of her and Ryan in the safe house waiting for contact. A year ago, she would never have found herself in this situation. She was secure, unaware, content. Now events were in motion that couldn't be stopped. Her stomach lurched as she saw the time on her watch through its cracked screen. Time was running out. She had to move, but the hard fists of her captors had ensured she was not going anywhere fast.

Her prison was below ground level. Light flooded in from above through the grey, shattered windows, illuminating piles of rubble and sodden paper boxes that littered the room. In the corner lay a damaged wooden chair. Her body flinched as she remembered its solid legs collapsing beneath her during the beating, a punishment for her refusal to reveal information. As her body awakened, numbness was rapidly replaced by sharp pains attacking her limbs. Suddenly, a loud bang came from above. Eve was not alone.

She attempted to stand, but the heaviness of her legs collapsed her immediately. Eve knew her hands had to be released if she had any chance of escape. Scanning the room in desperation, her heart raced. Her body understood the urgency. Then, her eyes caught sight of the solution. Behind her stood a metal shelving unit, its rusty plinths hanging off from neglect, exposing sharp edges. After dragging herself along the concrete by her bloodied elbows, Eve reached out to touch the shelf. A grateful tear rolled down her cheek. She rechecked her watch.

Amicus. *Tick, tick, tick.*

She was devastated that Ryan had abandoned her, after everything they'd been through. He had delivered her to torturers and walked away. His betrayal was unforgivable and their trust had been eroded in a moment. They had waited in the safe house together for the call. Now her mind began to contemplate his involvement. This was a safe house suggested by a contact Ryan knew well. Had he orchestrated this? "How could I have been so stupid?" she berated herself. Eve began to question everything they had done together.

Evidently she should have known better than to put her faith in someone who, up until recently, she would never have trusted.

Like an adrenaline shot, her mind flashed back. She remembered. At the safe house, she had drunk a glass of water and within moments, her head had started spinning, before she fell to the floor.

Eve snapped back to reality, but the memory had shaken her. She reached out her hands to steady herself on the shelf but had underestimated its stability. As if in slow motion, it toppled like a redwood, smashing against the concrete and creating a din that echoed around the walls. A cloud of dust and dirt filled the air as the room shuddered. There was no doubt that whoever was above her would swiftly arrive to investigate. Despite her lungs drowing in dust, Eve knew she had to free herself quickly. Frantically rubbing the cable tie against the jagged edges of the shelf, she tried to sever the plastic. It was more gruelling than she'd anticipated; droplets of sweat emerged as her temperature rose. She was nearly there—just another minute and she would be free. The faint clatter of running steps became increasingly louder and faster, duplicating the speed of the palpitations in her chest.

Oh God! she thought, terrified by the prospect of a further beating.

Pausing in the doorway, a dark figure surveyed the room like a predator. Although relatively short in stature, his bulky shoulders and wide neck were evidence enough of his ability to easily overpower her. His cold eyes fixed on her as she furiously attempted to slice the cable tie. Within seconds he was upon her, viciously grabbing a handful of her hair. As he yanked her sharply, the last fibres of the cable tie split. Eve cried out as she was dragged from the floor before he hurled her across the room like a rag doll.

"Woken up now, have we?" he grunted.

Panicking, Eve searched the ground for a potential weapon. Her hands fumbled across a small brick, which she concealed behind her back. The thug stalked over and crouched down to grab her. Eve swung her arm towards his head and landed a dull blow to the left side of his face. He stumbled back, holding his bloodied nose, stunned by her attack. She scrambled to her feet, seizing the opportunity to flee while he was momentarily incapacitated.

"You little bitch, you broke my nose!" he roared, trying to stem the bleeding. There were many things she wanted to say in reply, but she valued her freedom too much to hesitate.

Trying to stifle her moans, Eve reached for the wall to steady herself. Stopping was not an option. Ahead was a flight of stairs which appeared to be her only route of escape. Eve grasped the rusty handrail and hauled herself to the top step. Over her shoulder, the thug had significantly closed the gap between them. She staggered into the vast space in front of her which looked like a bomb site, its roof emitting light through gaping holes. The sudden commotion startled a group of pigeons, their wings clicking as they departed. Her eyes scoured for an exit.

Then she saw it: a gap in the wall where a sliver of light revealed a gateway to freedom. She looked at her watch again. *Amicus!* Time was running out.

As she hobbled towards the opening, a tall figure entered, blocking her escape. The man slowly stepped towards her, knowing she was cornered. Eve knew the silhouette. It was him, it was Ryan.

Questions raced through her head. He had left her for dead—why was he coming back now? Was he finally coming to kill her in revenge? Behind her, the thug slowed as he saw Ryan.

Ryan froze. There was a silent recognition between the two men; she realised they had met before. All three were still. This was it. Amicus would be lost forever. Unsure of whom to look at, she remained motionless. Both men glowered at each other, neither flinching for a second. Unable to hold back her despair, Eve's eyes filled with tears, but she managed to contain the sound.

It was over.

After everything she'd been through, she had failed. Eve had done things she was ashamed of and so many people had suffered as a result of their association with her, but circumstances had pushed her to her limits.

Seconds seemed to pass like minutes, and in her quiet contemplation, Eve made a decision. It would not all be for nothing; Amicus was *not* going to be lost. Taking a deep breath, catching both figures off guard, she sped towards the opening. With no idea what was going to happen, she knew she had a better chance of survival running towards the exit than heading back into the lion's den.

Ryan retrieved a revolver from the waistband of the back

of his trousers. Firm in his stance, he raised his weapon, both hands curled expertly around its hilt. Despite the impending danger, Eve continued, hoping the pressure of the moment would affect Ryan's aim.

"Stop!" he yelled. His fingers squeezed the trigger, then the chamber released its bullet. The blast reverberated around the shabby walls, piercing the air. Eve fell to the ground with a heavy thud. Her body finally yielded. As her head dropped, it ricocheted against the hard floor before settling. Pain returned. Her eyes slowly closed.

Chapter 1

Five Days Earlier

Eve Blake inhaled deeply. Beneath her calm exterior, her heart was pounding. She was sure the jury would see the beads of sweat lining her neck, if it weren't for her gown and wig. This was it. Everything she had worked towards her entire life had led to this critical moment in her career. The failed relationships, working until all hours of the morning, everything had been sacrificed. Failure to secure a conviction would be unthinkable.

Eve had to remain focused. She couldn't let the weight of the occasion or her surroundings rattle her. She had been to the Old Bailey numerous times. The magnificence of its mahogany panelling and high ceilings had never made her feel small before—until now.

Eve turned and faced the jury, ready to deliver the concluding part of her closing statement. Her eyes targeted members of the jury she was sure would be swing voters. Her manner was resolute. "The facts of this case are clear.

Members of the jury, your role is not to make judgements based on your personal feelings towards the defendant. Your judgements must be formed purely on the facts that have been presented. Our justice system is based on a fundamental principle, proving beyond all reasonable doubt that the defendant is guilty. From the indisputable evidence, and I repeat this to you, the indisputable evidence that cannot be denied, there is no doubt that the defendant is guilty. The prosecution, therefore, asks that you return the verdict, the only appropriate verdict in this case, guilty as charged of attempted murder."

Eve's last words hung in the air. All eyes were fixed on her, with the silence only broken by the creak of the mahogany bench as she lowered herself. Exhaling slowly, she dared not reveal her inner disquiet. Sitting alongside her in court, Tom, her junior, subtly nodded his head in support. He often said how he admired her eloquence and how fortunate he was to be in a position to learn from her.

However, Eve focused her gaze only on what was in front of her. She heard the hushed whispers of the defendant's barristers and imagined their strained faces as they tried to appear unaffected by her delivery. Her eyes then moved to the accused, Tony Taylor, his face expressionless, as if he were completely numb to the drama of his predicament. She had seen this look many times before; it was reserved for those whom she believed had their fate sealed, something the defendants also knew. Taylor looked like most of the other criminals she had encountered, he was nothing special. Although not the brightest of men, when forced into a corner, Taylor would not go down without a fight. He was a survivor and fiercely loyal. But what he knew and could reveal about his employers, the Wheeler family, that was what made him the prize. The irony of his cheap, ill-fitting suit was not lost on her. The Wheelers had secured the expensive services of defence barrister Oliver Rees-Philips in an attempt to keep Tony out of prison. Still, Eve imagined that he would face another kind of justice on his return to freedom, understanding the capabilities of the Wheelers.

Directed by the presiding judge, the Honourable Mrs Justice Aiza Rahman, all stood for the jury as they left the courtroom, the weight of their decision etched on their faces. Nothing more could have been done. This was a legal system in which Eve believed profoundly, one she trusted to return the right result.

Eve stood in the robing chambers in solitude and removed her wig. Her mind was full of nothing else but the secret deliberations. She reached for her phone as it buzzed.

"Hi, Dad," she said in relief.

"How did it go?"

"Put it this way—I left them with no doubt that he did it. It's whether or not they fell for the sob story that his defence gave them."

"Darling, there is no-one who can present the facts better than you, and if I were him, I'd be preparing for the worst. I have no doubt that you'll get your guilty verdict." Unwavering in his support as ever.

"Thanks, Dad. Look, I've got to go. I'll call you later, okay?"

"Of course. Try and get some sleep tonight if possible. This is going to be one hell of a week. Love you, Eve."

"Love you, too, Dad."

*

It was two days before the phone call came. Eve had barely slept, replaying the action of the case over and over in her mind. Finally, she was recalled to the court. The jury had taken longer than she had expected to consider their verdict, but professionally speaking, she was confident that the result was likely to be in her favour. Not only was a conviction in the best interests of society, but securing a positive result would ensure she would be recognised as a suitable candidate to be appointed to the Queen's Counsel. An appointment to QC was a symbol of professional excellence that only the finest barristers achieved. Eve had consistently demonstrated the quintessential tenacity, expertise, and zeal to be considered for Silk. This was her ultimate goal, and one wrong move could set her back years or even end her dream entirely.

Eve was the first to arrive in the courtroom. She was always first. She liked to sit quietly to contemplate the possible outcomes and her responses. Her quiet reverie was interrupted by the arrival of her opponent, Oliver Rees-Philips, one of the vilest men she had ever encountered. Oliver came from a long pedigree of barristers before him, including his father, Mr Justice Nicholas Rees-Philips of the High Court. Eve often thought that he relied upon his family name and moderately good looks, both were poor substitutes for his lack of wit and charm. The heavy thud of his polished shoes announced his entrance like a military procession. His sharp features were matched by his crisp Savile Row suit, which he wore with pride and conceit. Oliver relished the opportunity to use his height and enormous ego to intimidate; however, Eve was unaffected by his stature or attitude. She knew his methods and ethics were reckless and highly questionable. As a result, he had carved a reputation within the criminal underworld as the man to procure to avoid a custodial sentence.

"On your own again, Blake? Thinking about what you'll do when you lose? I hear the appeals process is delightful." He postured as he took his place in the courtroom.

"I'm so glad you have confidence in abundance, Oliver. It will be useful when you need to console yourself that you weren't quite good enough to get the better of me." His smug grin was swiftly wiped from his face.

As the gallery filled, the air of anticipation was almost suffocating. Tom, her junior, fastidiously arranged their files as Eve attempted to steady her heartbeat. Finally, the clerk stood. The courtroom felt more extensive and grandiose than ever. This was it. Oliver leaned over and whispered, "You're going to lose, Blake. Don't cry too hard when you finally get what you deserve."

Chapter 2

Smith's phone vibrated, announcing a text. *The Old Bailey, Taylor trial, as discussed.* Replacing the phone in his pocket, there was no need to respond with a pleasantry. It was a business arrangement. Smith was in already London, waiting. He was used to staying in hotel rooms. They all blended into one, only the brand of the bathroom toiletries denoting the quality of the establishment. This place was no different. Smith had a simple routine: get up, get dressed, pack his bag, go. Some would say that he was lonely, closed off, but he preferred the solitude.

Finally, he was ready to leave. The bin was empty, the cups untouched, and the bed was made with military precision. Any maid coming in might think the room had not been used; however, the card hanging from the door saying *Please service this room* would suggest otherwise. There was neither a print nor a fibre left behind, such was his meticulousness. Smith was unremarkable in his appearance, which was perfect for his line of work, since he was quickly forgotten. At just under six foot with an athletic build, Smith did not stand out amongst the crowd. As the door closed behind him, he pulled his baseball cap down over his face to avoid the CCTV in the hotel corridors. His journey through the lobby was uncomplicated. The bustle of new guests checking in ensured a safe passage as he slipped out unnoticed by the hotel staff. A smooth transition and an excellent start to the day.

To anyone watching him, Smith was simply a commuter heading into the city to work. Unbeknownst to them, his backpack contained the deadly tools of his trade. Although Smith waited for commissions, he thought of himself as self-employed. His portfolio of work, a catalogue of assassinations that left behind barely a trace of their architect. Smith had developed quite a reputation for his services. He was in high demand and, as such, commanded a substantial price tag. As he walked out of the front door of the IBIS in Shoreditch, Smith glanced at his watch, assessed his surroundings to verify he was not being followed, then began his journey.

He knew that a professional of his stature would not go unnoticed forever, and at some point, he would register on someone's radar. Scrupulousness was therefore vital to ensure his operations were flawless, leaving nothing that could lead directly back to him or his client. Yet as he crossed Commercial Street, a shadow began following his every move.

Chapter 3

"All rise," the clerk of the court commanded. Eve noticed Tom's hands as they trembled by his side. The rest of the courtroom stood to receive the judge and jury. The twelve jury members appeared solemn and pensive, all averting their eyes from both the defence and prosecution barristers. This was not unusual. Eve had seen juries behave this way many times; however, it did nothing to calm her nerves. Eventually, when the jury had taken their places, the judge seated herself, followed by the rest of the courtroom. The Honourable Mrs Justice Rahman had a long-established reputation for integrity, an incredible eye for detail, and unmovable adherence to the law. In court, she was tough and showed no tolerance for showboating, much to the annoyance of Oliver, who had felt her wrath on numerous occasions during the trial.

As she waited, Eve's stomach muscles tightened. The silence in the room was charged with expectation. The shuffling of the judge's papers as she prepared herself was the only sound. In her head, Eve was hurrying her along, but

Justice Rahman seemed to be content in taking her time and moved at her own pace.

At last, she was ready. Eve's breathing quickened. The courtroom was motionless, as if they had all been frozen in time.

"Would the defendant please stand," the clerk asserted. Eve's gaze turned to Tony Taylor, who rose to his feet. The imposing police officer positioned behind him carefully scrutinised his movements. Taylor then surprised Eve. Throughout the trial, he had not paid much attention to the gallery. But today, he markedly turned to his wife before focusing on his son, Ryan.

The clerk then turned to the jury. "Would the foreman please stand."

A tall, dark-haired man wearing a charcoal jacket and tie slowly stood. His face was ashen. He did not look at Taylor. Instead, he focused on the judge, a move that was echoed by the eleven other jurors.

Looking up from her papers, the judge finally questioned, "Has the jury reached a verdict upon which you are all agreed?"

"No, Your Honour." A gasp echoed through the gallery.

Eve's perturbed expression betrayed her bewilderment. It was true that the defence had created an incredible sob story of wrong place, wrong time, but he *was* guilty. His fingerprints and DNA evidence were present at the scene.

"Then have you reached a verdict upon which the majority have agreed?"

"Yes, Your Honour."

"On the single charge of the indictment, attempted murder, do you find the defendant guilty or not guilty?"

There was a pause, almost a hesitation from the foreman. The whole courtroom was on the edge of their seats, hanging off his every word.

"Not guilty, Your Honour."

The cacophony of cheers and roars was deafening. Eve was dumbfounded. How had this happened? She was stunned that a verdict of not guilty had been returned, to Eve, the case was clear-cut. The congratulating and posturing coming from Oliver and his team was distasteful and arrogant, not that it that surprised Eve.

It was almost like an out-of-body experience. Eve listened as Justice Rahman dismissed the charges, but the noise of the courtroom seemed to blend into a loud din as Eve felt her entire career crumbling. For the first time in her life, she was entirely lost. Tom appeared equally stunned, and she could see his disappointment as he hung his head. The courtroom slowly emptied, leaving Eve and Tom alone.

"I'm so sorry, Miss, I really thought we had it. I don't think anyone saw this coming." His words offered no consolation, but his heart was in the right place. Tom carefully packed away his documents, then touched her gently on the shoulder. "I'll see you back at Chambers."

Once again, Eve sat alone in the courtroom, desperately trying to fathom what had just happened. She had presented the facts of the case clearly; she knew she had. Eve had spent weeks analysing every angle of the evidence to ensure it was irrefutable. Taylor had a motive, and the opportunity, not to mention the overwhelming physical evidence of his DNA and fingerprints found at the scene. The defence had concocted an absurd notion that this evidence had resulted from a previous visit and that its presence was therefore reasonable. Pain began to burst in her brain.

Suddenly the double doors behind her flew open. Tom rushed over to Eve, his expression grave. "Thank God you're okay." he gasped.

"What on earth is going on? Are you all right? Breathe, will you," Eve implored, trying to calm him.

"You are not going to believe this. Tony Taylor has just been shot."

Chapter 4

Twenty Minutes Earlier

Assured of a not guilty verdict, Smith had secured a location overlooking the Old Bailey, which facilitated close proximity to the target and a covert entrance and exit. The target was to be executed upon exiting the building, sending a clear message to the Wheelers as well as the Taylor family. Smith accepted the commission, demanding his most substantial fee to date as compensation for the increased risk.

Situated directly opposite the Old Bailey was a row of established buildings with a parade of shops and bars underneath. Above their brightly coloured awnings and kerbside tables and chairs were privately owned flats. Most of them housed residential tenants, but there were a small number available for short-term let. Smith had rented a flat weeks before the case concluded. The large window in its front room faced the Old Bailey, the perfect vantage point to take aim. He had decided not to stay there, to avoid familiarity with any of the other tenants. There was one main entrance to the flat, but at the rear of the property, there was a fire escape which he used to enter and exit. The rental arrangements had been taken care of by his employer, so there was no direct trail back to him.

During his journey to the flat, Smith detected a shadow. The shadow had made itself visible almost as soon as Smith had left the IBIS. He was not concerned and he allowed the shadow to tail him. Smith would choose the location and moment to handle the situation, so he made his way through the back alley up to the flat and started to position the rifle he had deposited during an earlier visit. It was only minutes before he heard the soft tread of footsteps heading towards him.

"You shouldn't be here," he uttered calmly. He listened to the click of a firearm safety catch; he did not turn his head.

"*You* need to stop," the female voice retorted.

"We both know that's not going to happen. You should leave while you still can," he asserted, remaining with his back to her.

"Place the rifle on the floor slowly and slide it away from you," she demanded.

There was a moment of silence; then Smith carefully placed the rifle on the floor. He slowly rose to his feet before turning to face her, a wry smile spread across his face. She seemed unnerved by his reaction. He delighted in watching her refocus. Smith imagined that a little tete-a-tete would be entertaining; however, time was of the essence. Within seconds, Smith skilfully disarmed her, spinning her around and fixing her in a headlock. Smith held her tightly against his chest as he whispered, "You're looking in the wrong place. The answers are closer to home."

The tight squeeze of his muscular arms against her windpipe worked quickly, and she passed out. Smith did not want to needlessly murder. He wasn't about to kill another professional, especially someone who had gone to such pains to track him, and attracting unnecessary attention was undesirable, with the potential to betray his location and intentions. Patting her down quickly, he found there was no identification on her person. Despite searching her, Smith didn't need to see her ID. He knew exactly who she was. He took a photograph on his phone to inform his employer, Amicus, of her exact identity. He admired her tenacity. Few had ever come close to discovering him. The only thing left of hers was the Glock that had been pointed at him, MI6 standard issue. He had wondered when their paths would cross again.

Her approach did not unsettle Smith; such was his confidence. He moved her unconscious body over to one side, out of the way. As she lay on the floor, strands of hair fell gently over her eyes. She intrigued him, especially since they had never been in such close quarters before, but getting distracted was not an option; he had a job to do.

There were never face-to-face interactions between Amicus and Smith. They knew each other after being associates in a previous life. Meeting in person would only serve to raise the stakes; it would create unnecessary exposure. Amicus provided Smith with all the intel that he needed for a job; his dealings with Amicus were purely transactional. Information and instructions with 50 percent of his fee up front, followed by a final payment upon completion. This arrangement kept things simple. He liked simple.

Smith finally manoeuvred himself into position, lowered his head, then stared through the sight of his rifle and waited. It wasn't long before the message came through to Smith's phone: *Not guilty*. Within fifteen minutes, the doors were flung open, and crowds of people flooded the street—the sound of congratulating and cheering filled the air. Smith's SAS training in Iraq and Afghanistan had made him an expert marksman. Despite the crowds and furore, he focused on the target. As soon as he had a clear shot, he squeezed the trigger.

Tony Taylor fell to the ground. The broad smile plastered on his face diminished instantly as the bullet pierced his heart. Assignment complete. Smith knew he would have a limited window before the chaos ensued—the screams of onlookers served as his warning siren. Now to leave. He checked that the agent, whom he had earlier disarmed, was still unconscious in the corner of the room before disengaging his rifle, quickly wiping it down and collecting the shell casing and his backpack. Smith then swiftly headed towards the fire exit to leave the building.

Like all of his other commissions, Smith's departure route and timing had to be exact. He expertly descended the fire escape and pulled down his baseball cap once again to mask his face. After a final assessment of the area, he headed towards the end of the alleyway. He emerged casually before crossing the road towards St Sepulchre's Church, then into Smithfield Market, where he immersed himself within the crowd.

Smith opened a new message on his phone and typed *Complete.* He then looked at the photograph of his female adversary. Shame. In another time and place, he could have engaged her in conversation. It might have made the proceedings more interesting, but she had come too close. Unless he controlled the situation, it could become dangerous. He sent the photo to Amicus with the caption, *Someone that needs to be dealt with.*

Chapter 5

The Goring Hotel in Belgravia was the place Amicus stayed when she was in London. Adele Davenport preferred to be known by her alias, Amicus, and the anonymity had served her well. Her clientele, upon first communication, were more receptive when assuming that they were working with a man. She no longer lived in London and hadn't for many years. Not since she had been ejected from the Secret Service. Europe was now her home, and she moved around the numerous houses she owned across the continent, depending on the circumstances of her business. The refinement of the Goring provided quiet and calm surroundings, which she knew thoroughly due to her countless visits. She had also developed a rapport with the personnel, many of whom had worked there for years, knowing she could rely on their discretion. Its clientele, like herself, were abundantly wealthy. She had often watched wives and mistresses deposited in the lounge while their husbands attended to business. These women had no interest in making new acquaintances or engaging in conversation, which suited

Amicus perfectly. She was not in the habit of making friends.

The lounge had a quiet hubbub that Amicus favoured. She always selected the same table, which was reserved by the concierge for the duration of her stay. Amicus was a highly valued client. Her seat was situated at an angle that gave her the most comprehensive view of the room to scan its occupants. This habit had been ingrained since her MI6 training and, in her line of work, was a necessity. She knew every entry point and had a clear route to the vast garden outside. Her detailed inspection of the grounds had identified several viable exits if required. Amicus preferred the gentle hum of the lounge to the confinement of her room. She liked noise; the silence was uncomfortable.

However, the position that Amicus had built and earned had not always been the status quo. In her youth, Amicus was a protege of a senior intelligence official at MI6 who recognised her potential. She had embarked on a career in the Secret Service in the linguistics division. An honours degree in Russian and Politics alongside her natural propensity to absorb languages created the perfect combination of skills. Her father had been a colonel in the British Army and had commanded units across Europe. This lifestyle provided the ideal conditions to learn a variety of languages and immerse herself within diverse cultures, experience that would become invaluable later in her life.

Occupying her preferred spot, Amicus's solitude was disturbed by the gentle shaking of the marble tabletop. A message from Smith. It contained one word: *Complete.* A term that she was used to receiving from him, such was their arrangement. Excellent, she thought as she lifted a cup of coffee to her Chanel-coated lips. As she replaced the phone on the table, it buzzed again—Smith. This was unlike him to send two messages. This time, it was an image. The photograph was of a young woman lying on the ground with her eyes closed. At first glance, Amicus thought she was dead; however, as she knew Smith was not in the habit of unnecessary murder, it was more likely he had incapacitated her. She raised her eyebrow; indeed, this was something to be dealt with.

Amicus selected the first number on her speed dial and lifted the phone to her ear. "Meet me in my suite immediately. We have a situation," she instructed without waiting for her associate to respond. She was not frightened by the message, more annoyed. This was an issue that needed to be resolved, and quickly, in order to prevent the operation from being jeopardised. Amicus had a long and varied client list that included numerous wealthy and influential figures in the Western world. The privacy of her suite would now be a more appropriate location from which to conduct affairs and meet her associate, Butler.

Amicus was aware of the observer watching her from the other side of the room. She had come across men like him before, looking to see if she was joined by a husband or partner, trying to work out whether or not she was wearing a wedding ring. She had no interest in their attention. Amicus often felt pity for the women they had left behind, who were unaware that their husbands regarded their own wedding rings as without jurisdiction. Amicus had always attracted attention, particularly early in her career in MI6. Her talents had been utilised during her postings in Moscow and Berlin, where she developed an aptitude for recruiting and handling assets.

Briefcase in hand, Amicus started towards the lobby. She knew her observer was not a threat; working as a field agent for years had taught her that. She had become an expert at reading people and situations and was not at all perturbed by his attention. As she passed the bar on her way out of the room, the man rose to his feet, a clean white smile stretched across his face.

"I've been watching you all afternoon. Coffee is okay, but if you'd like to join me for a real drink, give me a call."

This was followed swiftly by an expensive-looking business card pushed gently into her briefcase with a raised eyebrow.

"Perhaps," she replied, turning on her heel. She imagined him watching the red soles of her black heels as she left the room.

As Amicus walked through the lobby towards the lift, the stranger's business card was removed from her briefcase and handed to one of the footmen. "Bin this for me, would you," she said in amusement as the lift doors opened, and she was returned to her suite.

Chapter 6

Jo Hunt awoke with a gasp, desperate for air. She was still on the floor after Smith had immobilised her. She could feel the carpet under the palms of her hands as she lay on her back. The breeze from the open window was making the discoloured muslin panels flap and sway in the empty room. Her eyes searched for evidence of him, but as expected, he was long gone. Two parallel lines drawn in the carpet led to her feet, explaining why she awoke in a different position. She had obviously been dragged to one side so Smith could finish the job. It had all happened so fast. One moment she had pointed her gun at him; the next, he was crushing her windpipe. She reached for her throat in an attempt to soothe the discomfort, but the real pain she felt was exasperation. Hunt had failed in the purpose of approaching Smith, which was not to apprehend him, because she knew she couldn't, but to seek answers.

Hunt was more than capable of handling herself in high-pressure situations, but not against Smith. He was in a different league. She had been trying to track and find Smith for months, then three days ago, he had appeared on her radar. Undeterred by the fact that he could kill her in seconds, she had to speak to him. Hunt was not afraid of Smith, which had made her reckless in her eagerness to confront him alone. She also knew the pursuit of Smith was unsanctioned by her superiors at MI6, which would lead to further consequences.

Hunt rolled onto her side so she could push herself from the floor. She froze as the words, "Armed police!" were bellowed from the floor below. These were swiftly followed by Special Firearms Officers who moved into position, standing over her, their weapons pointed at her head.

"Lie on your front, hands behind your head!" came the command, which she followed without hesitation.

"Is there anyone else here?" one of them shouted.

"No, it's only me," she croaked, the pain in her throat making it difficult to speak clearly.

"Suspect on the ground appears unarmed. All clear." The rest of the army of black rubber boots pounded towards her. Their owners, clothed head to toe in black overalls and combat helmets, carried standard issue MP5SF submachine guns. SCO19 had arrived. Hunt was surrounded.

She knew any attempt to explain her presence would be pointless until they had ensured she did not present a danger. Her hands were then manoeuvred to the base of her back, where they were cuffed. Another SFO had located her discarded Glock and secured it, therefore eliminating any further threat. The apparent lead SFO then tilted his head to one side as he used his radio. "Victor Charlie four-four, suspect in custody. Safe to proceed."

Hunt was left lying on the ground, the synthetic carpet fibres irritating her cheek. There were only two SFOs with their firearms pointed at her now as the rest of the unit seemed to be deep in conversation with the man who appeared to be in command. She wanted to release the discomfort in her shoulders, but they were waiting for something before attempting to question her.

The static of the commander's radio crackled, "He's on his way up." The clatter of his feet preceded the man whom she assumed was an officer from the Met, most likely from Counter Terrorrist Command SO15. His grey overcoat flapped behind him as he strode across the room. Seconds later, he was followed by two other suited men who appeared to be waiting for direction. He looked tall in comparison with the SFOs and had an abundance of mousy brown hair, which softened his features. His expression, however, was not soft. This was no run-of-the-mill drive-by. This was a targeted assassination, and the Met would send no-one less than their best. As he moved closer, he slowed his pace. She watched him as he surveyed the scene. He finally made eye contact with Hunt. She watched his expression change to confusion; was he not expecting a woman?

"I'm DCI Brian Walker of the Metropolitan Police, and I am arresting you on suspicion of the murder of Tony Taylor. You do not have to say anything, but it may harm your defence if you do not mention when questioned something which you later rely on in court. Anything you do say may be given in evidence. Do you understand?"

"Yes," Hunt confirmed, still feeling groggy. "I'm unarmed. Look, I'm MI6, I haven't got my credentials on me, but if you call it in, I'm Joanna Hunt. Ask for Peter Ashford. He'll confirm what you need to know."

"What the hell are you doing here?" Walker replied tersely.

"If you let me move from the floor, I can talk," she hissed.

"Leave her there," he barked at the SFOs. He swiftly turned on his heel, gestured for the suited men to follow him, then stalked out of the room. Still on the floor, Hunt couldn't stop thinking about the words Smith had said to her before she fell to the ground. What the hell did he mean? Look closer to home for the answers?

Walker's return forced her back into the moment. "Stand down!" he demanded, and the armed officers complied. He gestured to the commander to hand him the key, then knelt down to remove the handcuffs. Walker firmly lifted her shoulders so that she was in an upright position. Hunt coughed, then moved her hand to her throat, hoping to soothe the pain. She then pushed herself from the floor but stretched out her hand to prevent Walker from assisting her. She could get up by herself.

"I will repeat. What the hell are you doing here? I spoke to your commanding officer, Ashford, and he confirmed who you were but didn't tell me anything else. He may not have told me what you were doing here, but to say Ashford is pissed off is an understatement!"

"It's classified. I can't tell you. If you want to know, you'll have to go through the proper channels."

"Don't pull that bullshit with me," Walker sneered. "I'm looking for a sniper who's just shot a nasty little toe rag and is potentially tearing around London picking off new targets. I need to find him, and you're going to help me."

Chapter 7

It was inevitable Smith's movements would be recorded via CCTV, but he had undertaken rigorous reconnaissance to avoid a facial image capture. With his job complete, Smith was ready to return to his European base.

Tony Taylor had been a clean kill. Smith had carried out the contract without emotion or further contemplation. It was his job. He lived in a constant state of heightened awareness, such was his training within the SAS. Relaxation was an alien concept, but Smith was ready to return to familiar ground. For a moment, he allowed himself to muse about his female adversary and how she had added an unexpected dimension to his assignment. Smith preferred the solitude of his job but was intrigued by her boldness. He was almost flattered; however, this was a fleeting thought. He was not interested in making new acquaintances. Smith had a modus operandi that worked perfectly, and any deviation from this could lead to mistakes that could get him killed, or even worse, caught.

Before exiting the country, Smith needed to alter his appearance. This was necessary to navigate the British side of border control, although when he had travelled through certain European countries, the border security was laxer. Smith was sure the woman would now be awake and halfway through explaining his identity to the Met. He had never seriously concerned himself with the prospect of being caught, not because he thought himself infallible but because no-one had ever come close before. Smith always knew at some point that he would have to retire, preferring retirement to death. However, over the years, he had created an insurance policy, one he hoped would never be used.

Smith knew that within hours his profile would appear on Interpol's radar. The time had come for him to go underground indefinitely and had generated enough in commissions to retire very comfortably. Money had never been his motivating force, but it provided him with enough means never to have to worry again. Just then, his phone buzzed with a message from Amicus.

It hadn't taken long for Amicus to respond to Smith's text. She had access to vast resources with a range of influential contacts at her disposal. He knew that finding out about his "shadow" would not be a difficult task. It was more for her benefit rather than his. He knew exactly who she was—it was the MI6 agent who had been tracking him. An old associate contacted him to say that someone had been asking questions and trying to unpick his movements. She wanted answers, answers that he was not ready to give.

Up until now, she had always been one step behind. Was this why he had been followed? Was she looking for revenge? he wondered.

Smith had marked her as he moved across London and decided to let her get close so she could follow him into the flat. This location was the perfect place to disarm her quietly and cleanly to minimise disruption. He had expected her to be easy to disable, and he was correct.

Although now he was being tracked by government organisations, Smith often wondered how he'd arrived at this juncture. How killing had become his employment and death the norm. He didn't believe himself to be an entirely coldhearted bastard; the people he dispatched deserved it. They were usually men whose demise was justified, so removing their last breath was a service to humanity. Their actions threatened and contributed to the suffering of innocent people. Smith had his own unique moral code: no women or children, and nothing unnecessary. He did not have in-depth knowledge of the rationale behind his kills, but he had known Amicus for a long time and trusted her.

His phone buzzed again. It was another message from Amicus: *Funds transferred.* Just as he was about to put his phone back into his pocket, it rang. He recognised the number immediately.

"Are you okay? I said to only call me in an emergency," Smith snapped.

"It is! I went to the shops 'cos I needed some bits, and a weird man kept staring at me—I'm sure he was following me. I tried to lose him, and I thought I had until I saw him again near the garage. Now there's a strange car parked down the street with blacked-out windows. I'm scared—I don't know what to do!"

"Calm down. It's probably nothing. Get some things together quickly and leave the house. Get in your car and go to a hotel. Call me when you're safe."

"Okay, I'll go and do it now. Oh God! Someone is trying to get in through the back door, Danny, help me—"

The sound of banging and scraping ensued as Smith desperately tried to hear what was going on.

"Zoe? Zoe! Hello!" Smith shouted.

The line went dead.

Chapter 8

Jo Hunt sat on the back steps of an ambulance with a blanket draped around her shoulders. Walker had sent her for medical attention after her run-in with Smith. The steam from her tea slowly danced in spirals against the air like smoke signals. The warm liquid soothed her aching throat, which did not appear to be suffering any lasting damage. The paramedic had told her she needed to rest after the ordeal. Rest—what was that? It was not a part of her vocabulary and was certainly not a consideration when there was an assassin at large.

She could see Walker, who was standing to one side, keeping a close eye on her. He was talking to one of the other paramedics in hushed tones, clearly not wanting her to hear their conversation. She sipped her tea slowly, her mind regurgitating the words that Smith had said before the attack. She had no intention of working with Walker. He would only slow her down, and she needed to try to locate Smith before he went underground. As she glanced at Walker, he took out his phone and turned his back to her.

That was her chance. She turned to the paramedic completing his paperwork in the ambulance. "I feel okay now, but I just need to go to the toilet."

"Are you sure? You need to go to the hospital to get yourself looked at. You could have a concussion."

"Really, I'm fine. But you're right. I'll head to A and E to get checked out afterward."

Hunt removed the blanket from her shoulders, placed her tea behind her, then carefully slipped around the side of the ambulance. There was no traffic, just numerous police vehicles strewn across the street, as the immediate surrounding area was in lockdown. She crossed into a nearby greasy spoon. It was refreshing to see a traditional cafe that served mugs of tea, coffee, and bacon butties, not focaccia and Americanos. As she opened the door, she was flooded by the aroma of cheap bacon sizzling on the plate and hot buttered toast. Had she been hungry, she might have indulged.

The worn tables and faded leather seats gave the cafe an unintentional shabby chic. There were two waitresses with similar features, who Hunt assumed were family. The large window at the front flooded the place with light, but as the cafe stretched further back, booths supplied pockets of privacy. There were several quiet customers, some facing but not looking at each other, none seemed interested in Hunt's presence. An old man sat in the corner reading the paper, engrossed in the latest rhetoric between Labour and the Tories. He shook his head in disgust as he loudly recounted the details of the most recent scandals to an unshaven, swarthy-looking man with a gut and an apron. He appeared to be in charge and lifted his head up to acknowledge her as she moved towards the counter.

"Are you okay, love? Lord knows what's going on out there. We've all had a good look, but we can't see nothin'. What can I get you?"

"Just a cup of coffee to go, please. Is the ladies' out the back?"

"Yeah, go through, watch the step at the end."

Hunt made her way past the kitchen. Although it was clean, she wasn't sure her stomach could cope with anything right now. The toilet occupied a tiny room with a cheap yellow paint job, a small sink, and a mirror on the wall. She locked the door and leaned forward on the basin, exhaling as she stared at her reflection. She had definitely looked better. Her eyes were puffy, and her neck was swollen; red marks and bruising were beginning to appear where she had been gripped. "What the hell were you thinking?" she said to herself. "What a bloody idiot!"

Hunt turned on the tap and splashed her face. The cold water prickled her skin, awakening her senses so she could decide her next move. Smith's words repeated like a mantra in her head: *The answers are close to home.* Did Smith know who she was? Was he talking about the murder of her friend or something else? She just wanted to speak to him again, to ask Smith what he meant, but she knew the chances of that happening again were slim. He wasn't going to hang around after what he'd just done. She needed to find him before he went off the grid.

Hunt knew she had to lose Walker. She had no time to

explain herself. There might be an exit round the back to avoid him entirely. Perhaps he might think she had gone to A&E—maybe the paramedic had recounted their conversation. She dried herself off and straightened her clothes before unlatching the door. Just as she approached the kitchen, she saw Walker standing there, waiting, his expression vexed.

"Nice try," he said.

Walker was a large man; however, his stature did not intimidate Hunt. She was more than capable of handling herself and had proved it on numerous occasions. Except for today. Today was different. She had never been choked before, and she had paid a heavy price for her recklessness with Smith. Walker gestured to a vacant booth, out of earshot of the cafe staff, where they could talk. They each took a different side of the table and sat opposite each other as opponents in a game, waiting for the other to strike first. "You know you can't leave. You need to explain yourself," he demanded. "Listen, I want to catch this bastard, and I *know* you know who he is. I need your help."

"I told you before, the information is classified, and I'm not authorised to disclose it to you or anyone else. Look, I can't sit here, I need to move."

"We are both on a deadline, darlin', but we're not moving until you tell me exactly what's going on." He leaned back against the booth with his arms folded.

Hunt hadn't noticed his northern accent until now, which seemed to become more prevalent with his assertiveness. The cafe owner broke the tension by delivering their coffees. As he turned to leave, Walker uttered, "Two rounds of that buttered toast to go, please, mate." Hunt glared at him in annoyance.

"I can't think on an empty stomach, and the smell of that buttered toast is really starting to get to me," Walker mused. Just then, his phone rang. "Walker. Yeah, okay...any other CCTV? Right. Keep on it. I'm following up on a lead. I'll call you back. Keep me posted."

Now that she was sitting opposite him, Hunt realised that Walker was actually younger than she had first thought. It must have been his five o'clock shadow and long overcoat that made him look older than his years. As she sipped her coffee, Hunt felt resentful that she would have to work alongside someone else.

"So, who is he? And let's cut the crap, shall we? Ashford as good as confirmed that you know exactly who he is. We can't afford to waste any more time."

"All right, I'll tell you, but not here."

Chapter 9

Eve was stunned. Not only was her own life imploding, but there was a professional sniper on the loose. Why had Taylor been executed? What did he know that had secured his death? Her head pounded as her thoughts swirled. She needed air, she had to get some space and leave the building. The police were concerned for her safety, but Eve was sure that anyone wanting to kill Taylor wouldn't want to harm the person who was trying to put him away. Once the area had been thoroughly swept and the police were satisfied, she was free to go. She decided to head back to her office in Blackwell Chambers. There was one person who would provide the solace she needed.

Eve hated losing, especially when she knew she was right. The very thought of walking through those hallowed doors that she had worked so hard to get to made her sick to her stomach. There were so many eager to take her place, to stab her in the back for their own promotion. She knew they would be celebrating her defeat and hoping that this would be the beginning of her demise. There would also be a contingent that would display the condescending head tilts and comments of commiseration, sentiments that she desperately wanted to evade. Then there were the senior partners, Richard Arden and Alistair Ferguson. She knew they would be waiting for her back at Chambers and would require a debrief. They were not going to be happy. Taking a deep breath, she tiptoed up the white marble steps, then swiftly passed through the foyer. Martha, the receptionist, caught Eve's eye with concern. Martha was about to speak, but Eve's vehement shake of the head silenced her. Eve quietly then began the short journey to the office at the end of the corridor, careful to not make too much noise.

Fiona Saxby had been her mentor, therapist, relationship expert, and surrogate sister ever since she had joined Blackwell. Having been without her own mother since she was six years old, Eve looked up to Fee and leaned on her in times of uncertainty. Fee was her constant, she always had Eve's back. Fee peered over the dark rims of her glasses as she watched Eve enter the room. Eve had never been so grateful to see her. Fee moved from behind her mahogany desk and hugged her friend. At one point, Eve thought she might burst into tears, but she managed to hold it together. Fee passed her a half-drunk gin and tonic without saying a word. Eve was not perturbed that Fee had already been drinking it. The cliché would be to knock back a glass of whisky, but Eve was not a hardened drinker—wine, gin, and the occasional champagne usually did the trick. Eve unceremoniously dropped her briefcase on the floor, kicked off her shoes, and slouched into the leather sofa behind her.

"What the hell was that? Only you could screw up your chances of getting Silk, see your defendant murdered, and put your own life in danger all in the same day. Well done—that's good going!" Fee scoffed.

"I have no idea what just happened. It was so clear-cut. How the hell did the jury find him not guilty? I think I'm still in shock. In fact, I know I'm in shock." Eve took a large gulp of the gin before finishing it off in one go.

"Steady on, I don't want to have to carry you to a cab. Although let's be honest, I'm well practised at that when it comes to you," she remarked, trying to lighten the moment.

"Are Richard and Alistair pissed off? God, what a mess. I hate letting people down."

"You haven't let anyone down. It just wasn't your day today, there was nothing else you could have done. I reviewed everything with you, remember? Naturally, as senior partners, they're disappointed to lose any case, but they'll get over it." Fee was always the voice of reason, but Eve couldn't help but think there was more to it.

"But what did I miss? Something caused the jury to have doubts. I need to go through my files again."

"Not tonight you're not. You are exhausted and probably about to get shit-faced by the way you've just knocked that gin back. You need to go home and try and get some rest because I know you won't sleep."

"I just wish I knew why they let him off. You're right, I know you're right. I'll go home and try and look at this tomorrow with a clear head."

"Of course I'm right, I'm always right. That's why you

love me so much. Oh, and your dad called—you haven't been answering your mobile. Please let him know you're still breathing. You know he'll be panicking."

Eve felt a pang of guilt. She knew her father would be worried that she hadn't been in touch, and the shooting was undoubtedly going to make the news. Eve also knew he'd be thinking the worst, dredging up old memories of when her mother had died. She couldn't put him through that again. "God, I never thought. My phone was on silent. I'll definitely call him later."

Eve dragged herself to her feet, put on her black shoes, and picked up her briefcase between her fingers. "Can you put the seniors off for twenty-four hours? I haven't got the energy to go through it all again."

"Don't worry, I'll smooth things over with them. They can't expect you to be coherent today, not after what has just happened," Fee reassured her.

"Thanks. I don't know what I'd do without you."

"You'd get yourself up to your neck in trouble. Now go home and rest, and no staying up till all hours rereading the case files."

Eve walked towards the door before turning to Fee. "Whatever you say, boss."

Chapter 10

Hunt was not comfortable sharing the intelligence she had gathered about Smith with Walker, but she could tell from Walker's attitude that he wasn't going to let her get away without divulging the truth. She'd spent months and months gathering intelligence and analysing information to get her this far. As they walked away from the Old Bailey in silence, Hunt felt pressure from Walker as he stared at her expectantly, despite her attempts to avoid his glare. When she could no longer bear his persistence, she relented.

"His alias is John Smith, but officially his name is Daniel Cooper," she whispered in exasperation. "He's ex-SAS, and he's been operating as a gun for hire for the last five years. He's managed to evade detection that entire time."

"So how the hell have you managed to pick him up and nobody else has?" Walker questioned.

"If you didn't know his MO, you'd be fooled into thinking some of his targets died as the result of accidents or natural causes. He's never even come close to being caught. Unless you know what to look for, his contracts have never been connected until now."

"But how do you know all of this? You're not telling me something, because when I spoke to Ashford, he was infuriated that you were on the scene. He said he had no idea that you were there."

Hunt took a deep breath. She found it difficult to talk about her partner, Nick. Even though it had happened twelve months ago, she still felt raw.

"He killed one of our agents, who was also my friend and one of the best agents I've ever worked with. Nick got in the way of one of Smith's contracts and was shot and bled to death. He called Ashford before he died." A sudden sadness washed over her. It had been a while since she had said Nick's name.

"If Smith is so good at his job, why did he leave him to bleed out? Is he just a sadistic bastard?"

"No. Smith sees this as a job. He doesn't needlessly murder. I think he wounded Nick so he could escape." It was cathartic to talk about Nick; she hadn't shared her grief over his death with anyone at all. "After it happened, I went back to Nick's desk and tried to find out why he was there. Obviously, there was nothing, He hadn't told me or anyone else where he was going. I went to his wife, Ali, to see if we could make sense of it, and she let me look at his personal laptop. When I started to look through it, there were loads of encrypted files, some I managed to break, others I didn't. He'd been cataloguing Smith's work, starting to piece together his movements and linking them to suspicious deaths. We trusted each other implicitly, so the only reason for him not telling me must have been that he didn't want to put me in danger."

"Why didn't you share this with anyone else? Trying to tackle this guy by yourself clearly didn't work out, did it?" Walker replied sarcastically.

"If Nick didn't share it, it was because he thought he couldn't trust anyone. Working on the same principle, I could end up getting myself killed if I'd shared what I'd found out."

"Hang on a minute." Walker seemed confused. "So how were you able to find him today if he was so difficult to track?"

"I was looking at surveillance footage for something else, and I spotted him coming through Dover security. It was pure chance, and I nearly missed him. He hadn't been in England for a year. As soon as I saw Smith, I knew that this could be my first and last chance to get face-to-face and ask him what happened. I wasn't planning to confront him at that moment, but as soon as I saw him setting up for the kill, my instincts took over, and I made a mistake."

"So he let you get close enough to him, in a private, enclosed space, before he knocked you out? And instead of waiting for backup, or even running it by your own boss, you decided to go off and play the hero." Walker paused, shaking his head in irritation. "You're right. He's not stupid. However, you were—you're a bloody liability. He could have killed you."

"I know. But I wasn't thinking about that. I just wanted answers."

"So why has he come out of the woodwork now? Why such a high-profile job?"

"I don't know. This is extremely unlike Smith. All his other jobs have been covert. I just wanted to ask him about Nick, and I thought it might be my only chance."

The sound of their footsteps was now in sync as they made their way along the cleared high street. Hunt stopped as she considered Smith's reproach. "When I confronted him, he obviously knew I'd been following him. He told me to leave, but I refused. Then he said something that has been bothering me since. It only took a split second for him to disarm me and knock me unconscious, then I woke up, which was about thirty seconds before you lot arrived."

"So, what did he say?" Walker demanded.

"He said that I should be looking for answers closer to home."

"Clearly he knows who you are if he said that. He must be talking about your partner, or what else could it be about?"

"I really don't know, but I've got to find out."

"Well, he now knows that you're not intimidated by him, and he also probably realises that he's not seen the last of you." Hunt watched Walker as his brain seemed to be whirring. "I don't think we need to share this with anyone else, not till we work out what he meant. It could be nothing—he could be playing with you."

"I don't think he was. He seemed serious in his tone. And why say anything at all? He could have just knocked me out straight away."

"Ashford has authorised our working together. The top brass have colluded because they know how important it is to catch this sniper. That's what I was on the phone about when you conveniently disappeared." Walker stopped and turned to face her, his expression sincere. "Is there anything else that I need to know? Now is not the time to be holding back—we need to act fast."

Hunt regarded him first with hesitation, then decided that if she had any chance of getting to the bottom of this, she would need Walker's help. "The strange thing is, when Smith first came back into the country, I lost him after only a few hours. He disappeared somewhere, I'm not sure where. He was gone for two days, and I couldn't pick him up anywhere. It must have been important, because from all the intelligence Nick collected about him, we know Smith only ever focused on one job at a time. He never deviated from his routine. Then, amazingly, he showed up back in London, and he continued as usual. That's how I was able to follow him and track him to the Old Bailey job."

"We need to find out where he went and what he did. It's obviously important and could explain everything else. Let's not waste any more time."

"Okay." Hunt paused, contemplating whether her next move was the right one. "I think I need to show you something."

Chapter 11

Smith had manoeuvred himself into a narrow side street away from the bustling crowds. He needed space to think. Along its graffiti-covered walls were piles of discarded cardboard boxes and black bin bags that spilt out of wheelie bins overflowing with rotting food and plastic bottles. Metal pipes weaved in and out of the walls, and power lines swung lazily in the breeze. The dull hum of the air conditioning units was occasionally punctuated by the sirens and horns of the nearby traffic. Smith was already feeling sick to his stomach from the phone call he had just received from Zoe; however, the stench of greasy food sent him over the edge, and vomit spewed from his lips. The acidic taste in his mouth burned as he propped his back against the wall in an attempt to steady himself, but his knees gave way before he slid to the ground.

For the first time in years, Smith was unable to think clearly. The horror of the phone call replayed in his head. He felt powerless. He tried in vain to call Zoe back, but each time he dialled, the phone failed to connect. He had no control. Smith was too far away to reach her quickly and unable to contact anyone who could help her directly. He should have known she was a target. The distance between them, alongside the lack of contact, was designed to protect Zoe's identity from his enemies, but he was wrong. Going to see Zoe when he arrived back in England had been his undoing. Of course, he could have been watched, why did he honestly think his past wouldn't catch up with him? Her shrill screams still echoed in his head, knowing what they would be doing to her to extract information. The thought of the woman he loved, suffering at his hands again, was unbearable.

Smith gathered himself. He needed to refocus. He closed his eyes tightly with his fingertips pressed firmly against his forehead and played out different scenarios in his mind. There were a limited number of people who knew about Zoe and Smith's past, and Amicus was one of the only ones who knew the entire story, outside of their families. Whoever had taken Zoe had to have been informed by someone who knew the connection. It could only have been Amicus that led Zoe's abductors directly to her, he realised that now. But why? The arrangement between him and Amicus had been built over many years and had been mutually beneficial. Why did she want to jeopardise it now? Amicus knew Smith well enough to know the consequences of an attack on his family, so she would have anticipated his reaction. If this was how Amicus wanted this to play out, Smith was ready to oblige. He finally took a deep breath and opened his eyes. He felt a sudden sense of clarity. Smith took out his phone and, knowing that there would be no going back, resolutely tapped out a message.

Zoe has been taken. I know you know who it is. If they even so much as bruise her, our arrangement is terminated—along with your anonymity. Tell me where she is.

He knew that the message would decisively sever their arrangement. Amicus and Smith understood each other, knowing that neither would hesitate to follow through on any threat. Amicus was not in the habit of being dictated to or threatened, and if she did co-operate, he would pay a heavy price. Smith knew when he had taken the job that it could possibly be his last. A public assassination was not something that could be escaped from easily. Subconsciously, maybe he wanted this to be his last job; murdering people for a living was not what he had imagined for his future. Perhaps all the years of living alone with only old memories for company had finally taken its toll.

This was it. There was no coming back from here. The line had been crossed.

Chapter 12

Amicus had been anticipating the message from Smith, although it had come sooner than she had planned. Her clients had made contact with Smith, and the next part of her plan had started to advance. For a moment, Amicus felt a pang of regret. Smith had been a loyal and faithful comrade in their former lives during their postings in Afghanistan. They had shared traumatic experiences and dealt with impossible circumstances that neither would forget. Even so, whatever sentiment she briefly felt, she had settled her debt long ago.

Smith had served her well, but it was now time to move on from being a bagman for other people. Paradox was going to be her way out, it provided the secrets and intelligence she would need to ascend to a higher level of influence. Amicus envisaged herself as a master puppeteer, with the power to pull strings and influence outcomes. It was not the politicians and diplomats who ruled the world. She had fought hard during her career to receive the recognition of her talents and skill set but was denied continuously and passed over. After everything she had done and sacrificed for her country, she could not comprehend how dispensable she was. She was so quickly condemned and left in the cold.

Her arrangement with Smith was purely business; she would not let sentiment cloud her judgement. *Nobody* threatened her. Smith must have had a temporary loss of sanity if he supposed her to feel intimidated. Amicus would not allow Smith or anyone else to regard her as vulnerable because of her gender. Amicus was not weak.

Smith now had to be handled. The intelligence that he had amassed during their years together would have been vast, and its exposure would be catastrophic to her reputation. Amicus knew that this state of play would transpire at some point, and she had her ace card ready.

Smith's vendetta would undoubtedly lead him northbound to locate Zoe and he would then be hell-bent on exacting revenge on her captors. Amicus had no doubt, given the calibre of his hunters, that Smith would be taken care of. His connection to Zoe made him weak. Amicus was confident that the result would be in her favour; however, she needed confirmation that things were moving in the right direction.

"Come in here, would you?" she requested. Alice Butler, her right-hand woman, appeared to take direction.

Smith was not the only contractor in the employ of Amicus. Although she believed him to be the best working assassin, he was not the only one and was not irreplaceable. For Amicus, the most important person within her network was Alice Butler. A graduate of GCHQ, Butler had fast become one of the leading technicians in the service, working on high-profile cyber terrorism. Butler was a natural. Her synapses worked at a million miles an hour, calculating how to bypass systems and develop new pathways. It wasn't long before she had developed quite the reputation. Despite this, her employment came to an abrupt end when a senior male colleague made unrequited advances. Although devastated by her departure, Butler understood her talents and knew she had to select her new employer with care. She realised the value of her expertise but was also acutely aware of the motivation and calibre of potential employers she would attract.

Amicus had close contacts within the Boathouse, and Butler was suggested as a potential addition to her inner circle. Within hours of Butler's resignation, Amicus had made contact. It was also made clear that although Butler was fiercely patriotic, her experiences of GCHQ had left a bitter taste in her mouth. Butler was looking for a new position.

After hours of discussions at the prestigious 45 Park Lane, Amicus had dazzled Butler with her strength and composure. Amicus's elegance and demeanour appropriately communicated that she was measured and purposeful in her actions. Everything Amicus detailed made complete sense to Butler, so she was sure that she wanted to be a part of Amicus's operation. Butler understood the gravity of the situation and listened carefully to what was being asked of her, although she felt sure that even if she wanted to, Amicus would be an impossible person to refuse. For Butler, the opportunity to work with a woman was an exciting prospect. They had worked together ever since, and Butler was never far from Amicus's side. She provided all of the intel and technical support that was essential to Amicus's organisation.

Butler stood waiting in the broad doorway of the suite, ready for Amicus to deliver instructions. She had already furnished Amicus with the information she had requested about the exact location of Zoe Turner's house but was not informed why the data was required. Amicus often told Butler later on in the process how pieces of the jigsaw fitted together.

"We need to find out the exact location of Paradox. Taylor knew he had to return it or his family would face the consequences. I think the best bet is to follow his son; his wife is unlikely to have been dragged into this. I don't think Taylor was *that* stupid," Amicus commanded. "Find out everything about Taylor's son. If anyone will know where it is, it's likely to be him."

"Okay, I'll get on it," Butler affirmed, ready to begin her task.

"Oh, and close the doors behind you, would you? I need to take a nap."

Butler gripped the chrome handles of the separating doors and slid them together.

Chapter 13

After Nick died, Hunt had pushed away anyone who had tried to get close. Walker, however, was different. He was stronger, both mentally and physically. Although her first impressions of him irritated her, the consistency of his bluntness was refreshing. Hunt knew that her pursuit of Smith was deeply personal, but she now had to reconcile herself to the inevitable and realise that she couldn't work alone. Hunt had found herself telling Walker more than she wanted to, but her determination to locate Smith and find answers overruled her sensibility.

Walker led her to an industrial car park around the corner from the Old Bailey. The security guard at the entrance didn't bother to look up from his paper, clearly riveted by the *Daily Mirror*. It was eerily quiet because of the lockdown, and as they strode across the concrete, their footsteps echoed. The flash of Walker's key fob lit up a bleak corner, revealing the parked vehicle. Walker's car was not standard issue from the Met. The BMW E30 was immaculate, and from its condition, clearly cherished.

Through its window, Hunt saw the interior was as pristine as the ebony bodywork.

"Yes, sir, we're on it now. I'll report back with our progress in the next hour." Walker slipped his phone back into his pocket. "They're getting twitchy. No-one's managed to pick him up on CCTV yet. If he's as bloody good as you say he is, he's probably already disappeared. Shit." He sighed, shaking his head while opening the car door.

As he climbed into the driver's seat, she saw his prickly demeanour relax a little. Hunt watched the corners of Walker's mouth soften as he placed his hands gently on the steering wheel, ready to take command. He loved this car. For the first time, she saw a brief flash of joy. As she reached for her seat belt, Walker decreed the rules of carriage.

"As you will have undoubtedly noted, obviously due to the nature of your primal instincts as an intelligence officer, this is no ordinary vehicle. She is a classic and will be treated as such. Therefore, no eating, drinking, smoking, or bringing filth into my car, or you will bloody walk. Clear?" he announced, raising his eyebrows.

"Crystal. I wouldn't dream of it," she said.

"Right. We need to find Smith now before he goes completely subterranean. What did you want to show me?"

"His last movements must be important," Hunt replied. "We've got to find out where he went and what he was doing when he went off-grid for those three days. I think we should look at the intelligence Nick collected. There must be something in there. Maybe I've missed something."

"Agreed. If this job is completely out of character, there

must be a reason why Smith would risk exposure. He knows that he'll be hunted down until he's found. It's only a matter of time. There must have been a reason for him to say those words to you—he obviously wants you to find out what he means." Walker turned the key in the ignition; the engine emitted a velvety roar. The exit of the car park was like a backwards helter-skelter, circling upwards and sweeping round and round to reach the main road. Although the car provided a smooth ride, Walker was not a careful driver. His disregard for the 10 mph speed limit was evident as he swung around each corner.

"Where are we going? You haven't told me, and we're about to hit the main road."

"I've been logging everything that I've got so far in my flat. It's all written down with dates, times, and locations, both leading up to and following Nick's death. I recorded all the information and transferred it to my thinking wall. You need to see it." Hunt hesitated, looking for Walker's reaction. "If we're going to find him, the answer has got to be somewhere on that wall. We just need to work out what it is."

"Thinking wall, really? Is this just some sordid way of getting me back to your flat?" Walker murmured.

"Believe me, I'm not that smooth."

Walker flicked his indicator up with a wry smile and shifted into first gear. "So which direction are we headed in?"

"Back on to the main road and I'll direct you." As she gave Walker instructions, Hunt explained how she had located the information about Smith. She had visited Nick's wife, Ali, after his death. Ali trusted Hunt and had depended on her for support. Hunt had accessed most of the files on Nick's laptop but couldn't break all of the encryptions. She had no idea why he was collecting this data on Smith, nor could she make sense of it. Ali had allowed Hunt to borrow the laptop but needed to have it back because of the personal photographs on its hard drive. Ali had no idea what Nick was doing and had no reason to question him.

Within two days of Hunt returning the laptop, Ali had invited her for dinner. While they were eating, Ali had mentioned that a technician from the service had been to the house to examine the computer, explaining that it was standard procedure. Hunt checked the laptop afterwards and saw that files had been wiped.

"I didn't mention this to Ashford. I knew he'd tell me to let it go. Ashford said that Nick had been 'killed in action.' Something doesn't add up."

"Why didn't you take it to someone to get the files decrypted?"

"I honestly didn't know what I was dealing with or think I had a deadline. If I needed to retake the laptop, I knew it wouldn't be a problem. Don't worry, I've regretted not taking it every day since, and it's driven me bloody mad."

"Well, there's no point regretting it now. It's too late. Christ! I've got the chief superintendent breathing down my neck, asking me where the hell I'm up to, and we haven't got any solid leads. So far you've tried to disappear, you've withheld information, *and* I'm pretty sure you're still holding back."

"Look, I haven't worked closely with anyone since Nick died, and sharing is not something I find easy."

"No more secrets. If we want to find this guy, we have to work together."

Chapter 14

Waiting for Amicus to respond felt like torture. Smith had control over every element of his life; it was regimented, routine. Now everything was spinning out of control. Questions filled his head like a balloon full of air, building pressure. Who were they? How long had they known about Zoe? What did they want? Anyone who understood Smith would anticipate his retribution. This was obviously linked to one of his targets or to a previous operation. Images spun around his mind like a tornado, dates, locations, people. Presumably, it was a recent hit; otherwise, his movements would have been too difficult to track. There was no other logical reason why Zoe would have been abducted in that way.

It was Amicus who assisted them—she was the only one who knew everything. Had she been planning this all along, or had her hand been forced? If this was the case, why had she waited until now? Was he now the lamb to the slaughter? He agonised as he started to unpick the last two years, the faces of his victims flooding his mind as he tried to piece together a timeline of targets.

It was no use. Smith's head throbbed. It was then he realised it had been hours since he'd had a drink and dehydration was only going to fog his thinking. Scanning the street in front of him, he saw a small, independent cafe. After crossing the bustling road, weaving through bike messengers and taxis, he walked into the cafe, its background music soothing. He bought a bottle of water and a double shot of espresso, needing the stimulant of the caffeine. Shunning the window seats, Smith favoured a quiet table in the far corner. He always chose a position with the most comprehensive vantage point. People around him sat with open laptops and earphones plugged in. No-one noticed his arrival, as they were preoccupied with their screens.

Smith removed his backpack and took out a notepad he'd picked up from his hotel stay. He began scribbling, drawing arrows, boxes, writing names like Alexandrov, Nazari, creating a timeline of kills in the last eighteen months. To anyone watching, Smith would have looked like a man possessed, his notes resembling the ravings of a madman. They were not designed to be deciphered; to him, they made perfect sense. He had finished his bottle of water almost in one shot and was now administering his hit of espresso.

He sat silently, trying to forge links and analyse the impact of his victims' deaths. After careful and detailed analysis, he narrowed it down to four targets. He now needed to digest his thoughts before arriving at a definitive answer; looking at a list of names on a piece of paper was not working. A long car journey would provide the headspace he needed.

The long-stay car park at London City Airport delivered a plethora of potential vehicles suitable for the journey to Manchester. After surveying the CCTV, then selecting a car to commandeer, he pulled out a key fob–sized device from his backpack. Since the advent of the keyless car, anyone with a modicum of electronics training, mixed with ingenuity, could construct a simple tool to unlock keyless cars without tripping an alarm. The appearance of the vehicle he chose was irrelevant, but he needed something that would move with ease and transport him up north, fast. On his right, furthest away from the security cameras, was an Audi A4 in gunmetal grey. How apt, he thought. Without issue, he employed his device and slipped into the driver's seat. Getting out wasn't going to be a problem either, as he had a card with a specially programmed strip that lifted the barrier of any car park after inserting it into the machine—again, standard stuff if you knew the right IT geek. Within minutes, he was heading east towards the A1, which would eventually lead him to the M1 northbound.

Smith didn't want to listen to the radio; he didn't need entertainment. He had placed the piece of paper with his musings on the passenger seat. In the darkness, it was illuminated by the amber streetlamps, which, like a lighthouse, provided a brief flash of light before quickly fading into the shadows. This solitary confinement with his thoughts relaxed him a little. The monotony of the grey tarmac and its white stripes was hypnotic. Now calm and rational, he was able to contemplate his last four kills.

All of the targets were significant enough to be worthy of

retribution; none of them, except Taylor, had been on British soil. It was clear that the individuals or organisation tracking him were international. Smith had to determine whether this was personal or retribution for a political target. All of his targets had been men; they usually were. There had been one woman, but that was years ago, at the beginning of his new career. It had haunted him ever since.

Despite his ability to compartmentalise, Smith's slumber was often tormented by images of his victims. He regularly replayed the scenes in his dreams, often with different outcomes. His experiences of war questioned his faith in humanity. He believed that if hell did exist, he would be headed there without question. He provided a service to mankind, ridding the landscape of individuals who had caused the unnecessary deaths and suffering of innocent people. It was this justification that allowed him to close his eyes and sleep.

As he was cruising in the direction of the M6, his deliberations led him to two possible candidates. Both of whom were complex; both assassinations had created shockwaves in their respective countries. So which one was it? Then it came to him. Why had it taken him so long to work it out? He berated himself. Of course, it had to be.

Tarek Ahmadi.

Chapter 15

Amicus didn't take a nap in her suite after dismissing Alice Butler. However, she did lie-down. The firm pillows supported her head as she rested, and with her body relaxed, she could clear her head. Smith's communication had terminated their arrangement, but this was anticipated. With Smith out of the equation, Amicus needed to access the other resources at her disposal. She would use her connections within the Boathouse (MI6) to execute the next phase of her plan.

Amicus was ready to proceed.

She rolled over onto her side and lifted her phone from the bedside table. Shouting like a banshee was not her style; besides, she could not guarantee that Butler was still in the adjacent room.

"Come in, would you, we have work to do," Amicus instructed. Butler's delay in arrival indicated that she had left the suite entirely and probably headed back to her room. Amicus liked that Butler could anticipate her needs, but she also knew that in her absence, Butler would be working tirelessly on her previous task.

Less than five minutes passed before Amicus heard the

light click of the door unlocking. Butler let herself in with a keycard; Amicus trusted her.

Amicus had moved back to the sofa and was checking her emails while rehydrating with a glass of water.

"Have you found Taylor's son?" Amicus questioned.

"Yes. His name is Ryan Taylor, and he currently lives at home with his mother. He doesn't have a record, and he's not one of the Wheelers' lads. It looks like he's the brains of the family. He went to college and got himself a job. I've managed to triangulate his phone, and he's currently at the address listed as his parents' house."

"Good. Let me know when Ryan moves. We need to watch him; he might know where Paradox is."

"I'm on it," Butler replied before returning to her laptop on the other side of the suite.

Amicus's contacts in the Boathouse would provide the personnel to recover Paradox. However, Amicus wasn't prepared to reveal what they were recovering; they would be returning a laptop that contained sensitive information. That was all they needed to know. It was imperative no-one else was aware of Paradox's existence.

Smith was no longer a concern for Amicus. She knew enough of Zoe's captors to be confident that Smith would not be a problem, especially in the light of his clouded judgement regarding Zoe.

Amicus tapped a message into her phone: *Await instructions for recovery operation. Place operative on standby.*

It was no more than ten seconds before the reply *Understood* appeared on her screen.

Chapter 16

Walker's erratic driving seemed to be a perfect reflection of his mood. He grunted and sighed through gear changes and red lights and was not afraid to honk his horn in rage when he felt aggrieved. He couldn't seem to get to Hunt's flat fast enough. Hunt felt the opposite. She had never told anyone about her wall because no-one knew what she was doing. Letting Walker into her home was a risk, but there was no other choice.

As they drove, Hunt watched Walker tear in and out of the traffic. It was true, she had no interest in him physically, but his maverick attitude did amuse her. Personal relationships were not her strong point and never had been. She supposed it was because she had grown up in a house full of men. Any relationships she had were short-lived and physical. She didn't have the time or capacity for anything else. Her job was her life, a dedication very few understood.

The view of Peckham Rye Common signalled that Hunt was nearly home. She had always loved looking out at the vast open space from her window; it was calming. Walker seemed surprised by the location, uttering a small "Huh."

"Is that so you can make a quick getaway?" He smirked.

"Something like that." The road was quiet; however, cars lined every inch of the pavement like horizontal Jenga. Walker parked very carefully, taking care not to damage the alloys, amusing her greatly. Hunt's flat was the upper floor of a townhouse, with one neighbour beneath. Set back off the road, the neat lawn and ivy-covered fence greeted visitors as they headed towards the front door. Walker surveyed the road before following Hunt up the path. Hunt turned and looked at him in exasperation.

"Force of habit," he said.

Once through the forest-green front door, they headed up the stairs to her flat. Inside, the alabaster walls of her living room were clean and simple, complemented by stripped wooden floorboards. It was a functional and practical space, without a sense of softness. The small rug laid on the floor, along with a handful of small cushions on the grey sofa, were the only furnishings to absorb sound. In the kitchen, the unblemished chrome and steel next to the bright white splashback tiles evidenced their lack of use.

The open-plan space lent itself perfectly to entertaining, but it was clear that there was no such life in this space.

Walker had not uttered a word since they had walked through the door and seemed to be taking it all in. Hunt watched as his face changed. He had seen it. Adjacent to the kitchen and the living area was a large wall plastered with pictures, notes, and maps. Lines of string stretched like a spider's web, linked different parts together. It had taken her months to compile, and looking at it now from a different standpoint, she could see how hard she'd worked. This was her artwork. It was beautiful to her. Walker's eyes stared at her as if checking it was okay for him to approach. "Go ahead," she said, before joining him to analyse and admire its majesty. This road map made perfect sense to her, but Walker looked bewildered by the extent of information. "Jesus, you weren't kidding," Walker declared.

"I know it looks unorganised, but once I explain it to you, you'll be able to decipher it."

"Good God, I hope so! How long have you been doing this? How do you make sense of it all?"

"There were too many files on Nick's laptop to process. Until I started adding dates, locations, and details, I couldn't see a pattern or make a timeline. I wanted to be logical, so I coloured everything that happened before Nick was murdered in green, and everything after in red."

Walker moved closer to the wall and started to try to unpick some of the information.

"This guy was elusive for how many years? And nobody's put all of this together? This is a whole world of shit waiting to hit the fan. This guy is an enigma, way beyond anything I've ever seen." Walker paused. "And this is only the intel that was collected by Nick and then you? I'll bet there's a whole lot more."

"I'm sure there is. That's why I wanted to confront him. I wanted to get a read on him."

"Whoever he's working for has made him an executioner enforcing their justice."

He wandered along the wall, reading Hunt's notes and their parallel connections. Hunt began to explain some of the links, but he only appeared to be half listening, his eyes transfixed on the tangled web in front of him. Something or someone on the wall had caught his eye. He stopped in front of a section that was colour-coded green, which pertained to the period before Nick's death. Hunt watched him as he closed his eyes like he was trying to think through some of the links in his head.

"Coffee? I think it might help," Hunt offered, breaking their silent contemplation.

"Definitely, my brain needs to wake up."

Hunt went into the kitchen and returned with two mugs, handing one to Walker. Just as she was about to take a sip, she saw it. Scanning the data from a different angle ignited something in her brain. Her mug fell from her fingers, smashing and sending a wave of coffee like black lava across the floor.

"Jesus, Hunt, watch what you're doing!" Walker dashed into the kitchen and grabbed the kitchen roll to clean up the mess. Hunt stood motionless, lost in thought.

"I can't believe it. It's been staring at me the whole time."

"What has? What are you going on about?" he said impatiently, still trying to wipe up the coffee that seemed to have exploded everywhere.

"Here!" Hunt walked forward and pointed to a document on the wall with numerous names and dates.

Walker moved to her side. "I have no idea what you're looking at. You need to give me a clue."

"Pass me that piece of string from over there," she instructed, pointing to another part of the board. Walker obliged. Hunt went to a desk at the other side of the room, took out a piece of paper, and wrote furiously. She then stuck the paper to the board and connected the string to an image.

"Maybe this is why," Hunt announced finally, her face beaming in triumph.

Chapter 17

Hunt's heart was singing, ecstatic that she'd worked out one of the missing links that had eluded her for months. It was funny; it wasn't Walker who made the connection. Hunt had made the connection herself without help. Maybe working alongside him was giving her a fresh perspective. Having another person invade her personal space, albeit by invitation, made her feel strangely liberated. Yes, it was a risk, because she had reams and reams of classified information that if found in her position would land her in a whole other world of trouble, but his reaction to her work was more gratifying than she had imagined. To Hunt, this was now a piece of art, ever-evolving and changing. Hundreds of times, she had sat in front of the wall. It was absorbed and modified, with new connections and suppositions created and investigated.

Since their arrival, Walker's phone had been ringing nonstop, patching in with senior officials regularly and delivering progress updates. After a detailed comb of the area, unsurprisingly, they reported not a trace of Smith. Given the information that Hunt had shared with Walker, it was evident this was no terrorist rampage. Smith was controlled. With the chances of him striking again deemed slim, the evening news downgraded the story to a gangland revenge attack. London appeared to be calming and returning to normal; however, Walker and Hunt were still very much active.

It was getting late. It had been one hell of a day, and the peaks and troughs of the adrenaline were making Hunt's eyes flicker. Walker stretched out his back as he grimaced in discomfort; Hunt knew both of them needed sleep to clear their heads. The wall had become a blur of shapes and lines. They had been sitting in front of it for hours.

"Come on. It's late. Enough," Hunt said wearily. "We're not going to get any further without sleep." Walker lifted his head in agreement, his eyes red. She could see he was struggling to find the energy to move; she was also trying to summon the strength.

"You can stay if you want. I think the sofa's quite comfortable. We need to look at this again in the morning. I can't see it now. My brain's given up." The words spilt out before she realised what she'd said. Maybe he wasn't comfortable staying; perhaps he just wanted to go home, wherever that might be. Just as she was about to retract her offer, panicking that she had made things awkward, Walker rubbed his eyes with his hands before running his fingers through his hair.

"I knew you'd try to get me to stay," he teased. "Look, as long as you don't mind. I'm knackered. I haven't got the energy to drive home right now."

Hunt sighed in agreement, then went to a small storage cupboard to get out her winter duvet and spare sheets. "Night, then," she murmured as she yawned and walked into her bedroom. It wasn't long after she had turned off her lamp that she realised that Walker had also finally succumbed to sleep. The creak of the sofa eventually faded away as Walker settled into position. As she lay still with her eyes closed, Hunt once again replayed her interaction with Smith as she drifted off.

Chapter 18

Tarek Ahmadi was Smith's highest-profile assassination and one of his most complex. Ahmadi's murder sent shockwaves through the Arab world. Up until now, the identity of his executioner had remained secret. After his death, the remaining Ahmadi family declared they would stop at nothing to find his killer and exact their revenge. Smith was confident that the Ahmadis were not capable of tracking him down; however, the game had changed. He was now the hunted, not the hunter.

Ahmadi was a high-ranking officer within Colonel Gaddafi's government, with significant personal holdings in Libyan oil. He was identified by the British as a possible asset and offered a role within the national transitional government during Gaddafi's demise. This would preserve his future, providing continued asylum in Britain for members of his family. Ahmadi agreed. Before it was enacted, Ahmadi was arrested and tortured by Gaddafi's soldiers. Ahmadi divulged details about the rebel leadership in exchange for the lives of his family. The rebels were then ambushed and brutally slaughtered. Gaddafi planned to execute Ahmadi for treason, but before he had the opportunity, the rebels triumphed over Gaddafi when a surge of the Libyan people joined their ranks.

With Ahmadi's interests in the oil fields seized by the new government, the only bargaining chip he had left was a thumb drive that he had stolen from Gaddafi's compound. It was codenamed Paradox. It contained confidential files that held the passwords, account numbers, and locations of Gaddafi's secret accounts. These accounts held billions of dollars, money that had been syphoned by Gaddafi as his war chest to purchase nuclear weapons. Few knew of its existence, but in Gaddafi's inner circle, two knew of its location, one of whom was Ahmadi. The intel he revealed during torture had also led to the massacre of British field agents stationed in Tripoli. The British government immediately revoked the asylum agreement for Ahmadi's family in Britain, and his fate was sealed. After his death, Ahmadi's sons and daughter vowed not to rest until their father's killer had been brought to justice.

Smith had dealt with these types of people before during his career with the SAS. They had no fear and took risks because they had nothing to lose. The Ahmadis were going to impose their justice upon Zoe and eventually Smith. Zoe was not like him. She was an ordinary girl who had become involved with Smith when they were teenagers. He hated that he had now endangered her life.

Smith's only option was to call upon his long-standing military connections. Men with whom he shared a unique bond that could never be broken. He had never asked for help before, but now was the time. He was hours away from Zoe in Manchester and had no idea where she was being held captive. He was resigned to the fact that he could not do this alone, this was not a vendetta purely focused on him. Smith was not concerned for his own life—he had expected to die at some point and was ready for it. This was different. He loved her. He would not let Zoe suffer because of his mistakes.

Up ahead was a road sign for a small truck stop. Smith slowly pulled into a dark section of the car park, tucked away from the glaring lights. He picked up his phone, opened an email. A network had been established years ago, where contact could be made in a dire emergency and anyone with access could respond. As he awaited a response, he watched the passing traffic, the coloured blurs like shooting stars as they faded into the distance. His phone shattered his contemplation like a bullet piercing glass. A number. He tapped it into his phone and took a deep breath. He counted the number of rings. Five…six…seven.

"Hello." A calm voice answered.

"Hello. Assistance needed," Smith replied, relief flowing over him.

"Are you far?"

"Three hours." Their conversation purposeful, emotionless.

"Agreed place, twelve p.m."

Before he made his way to his final destination, Smith needed to leave bread crumbs. He had chosen a small truck stop where he would be easily noticed. Anyone present would be able to describe him clearly and recall his movements because he did not fit in with the regular clientele. It was there that he left his message for Hunt.

Chapter 19

Hunt slid her tartan-clad legs out from beneath the warm sheets, then scraped her hair into a messy ponytail. Bedtime was about comfort and warmth—women who wore satin nightdresses only existed on TV or in romantic novels. She gently opened the door of her room, trying not to wake Walker. Her face wrinkled as the aroma of sleeping man hit her like a wave, and she couldn't help but lift her hand to her mouth. This was something she was definitely not used to. Any interaction with men that was not on a professional level was usually short, physical, and never lasted until the next morning. She didn't have time for awkward small talk or false promises. She bit her lip in amusement as she caught sight of Walker's long legs hanging off the end of the sofa, his body scrunched up into what looked like an uncomfortable position. The greying stubble on his chin had emerged, a couple of days' growth, which perfectly matched the subtle strands that lightened his hair. Gazing at him while he was asleep, Hunt realised that she didn't really know anything about Walker. She had allowed him into her home, yet she had no idea where he lived or who he lived with. Was there a wife or girlfriend at home? she wondered.

"Couldn't resist me, eh. I've been told I'm beautiful when I'm sleeping," Walker uttered with his eyes still shut. Hunt could feel her cheeks blushing. He opened his steely grey eyes, increasing her unease.

"I was actually wondering if you were still alive. It certainly smells as if something's died in here," she retorted as she raised the blinds and thrust open the window. Walker shielded his eyes like a vampire damaged by the light.

"Thanks for that." He sat up slowly, running his fingers through his hair. He turned and examined her, seemingly enjoying her agitation. "Well, well, if you think you can seduce me in those pants, you've got another think coming. Wait—hold on to them, we might need to go undercover in Scotland."

"Wow, comedy genius. Peter Kay will be shitting himself," she scoffed. "Coffee?"

"God, yes, if you expect me to function."

Comfortable that she had shut him down, Hunt strolled into the kitchen and flicked on the kettle switch. As she returned with the coffee, Walker was parked on the sofa, the duvet pulled up to his chest. His eyes glued to the wall once again.

"You do realise that this is not normal, don't you?" Walker concluded.

"Of course it's not normal. Not everyone has a wall in their house with classified information stuck to it."

"No, I don't mean that." Clarifying his point, "I mean,

I'm just amazed that someone's mind can process information like this. This looks like a complete bloody mess to me, especially those scrappy bits of paper, but you can obviously make sense of it all." Hunt had never thought of it like that before; there was a backhanded compliment in there somewhere. She handed him his coffee, and he flattened the duvet so she could sit alongside him.

"I've never shown this to anyone. You are the only other person who's seen it. If Ashford knew I had all this..."

"Relax. You may think I look stupid, but I'm actually not. There's no reason for me to tell Ashford anything about this. I have to say, though, I'm not surprised you've never had anyone back here. Any poor guy would be terrified by this. Seriously, you need to get out more." Walker took a sip of his coffee, then winced as he swallowed. "You need to invest in a decent coffee machine. Come on, we've got work to do, and for the love of God, put something on that the Proclaimers aren't going to want back."

Hunt emerged from her bedroom in a crisp, light blue shirt tucked into her navy trousers and short brown hair swept back neatly, which was smart and functional. Makeup was not a priority; there was no-one to impress. The sleeping-man smell had finally dissipated, and Walker had obviously taken the hint and freshened up in the bathroom. He moved to the wall and was about to pull down one of the photographs, when Hunt grabbed his arm.

"Don't! If you move it, we'll lose a connection that might be important."

"Okay. I'm sorry, I just wanted a closer look," he

acknowledged sincerely, responding to her brief panic. "Why did you think Ahmadi was the link to Smith?"

It suddenly dawned on her that the assassination of Ahmadi, although high profile, wouldn't have come across the radar of a Met officer.

"When I was piecing together Nick's information, he'd written times and dates in 2011," she explained, pointing to a scrappy Post-it stuck on the wall. "I hadn't looked at that section for a while, but last night, it popped into my head. I remembered the dates of Ahmadi's assassination. Until I linked them together just now, I wouldn't have recognised the dates because there were no other details with them."

"Do you think Nick knew Smith was the assassin?"

"It's possible, but I'm not sure him knowing that would be enough for Smith to kill him."

"So there's got to be more to this, something we're missing or we don't know yet. Was there anything else that linked Nick and Smith together?"

"I've told you, I've looked at this over and over, I just can't see it." She dropped to the sofa, putting her head in her hands, willing her mind to remember something, anything, a detail. "It's like something's lurking in the shadows that connects everything." Hunt was heartened by her breakthrough, but it wasn't enough. They needed more. The chime of Walker's phone broke the silence.

"Walker. Yeah…yeah. Uh-huh. Yeah…you're certain it's him?" His eyes darted at Hunt. "Send it through now. Make sure you contact our friends in the north, they might be able to get eyes on him first." He tapped his phone to end the call. As he spoke, he started to collect his things. "He's been picked up on the CCTV at a service station on the M6 heading north. Where the bloody hell is he going?"

"This isn't like him to be so reckless. He wants us to know where he's heading. This is not a mistake. We've got to move fast."

She went back to her wall and stood in front of his photograph. Her fingers traced the lines of string like a musician tuning an instrument.

"Jesus, it's like watching *Rain Man*."

"Before he was a hired hit man, he was part of an elite SAS regiment. Again, I only found out about this from Nick's files. This information was way beyond Nick's level of clearance, so I'm not even sure how he got hold of it. The answer has got to be somewhere on this wall."

"Let's try and be logical about this and go back to the beginning. What connects Smith to the north?"

"His family does, and an old girlfriend from years ago, before he joined up."

Walker thought for a minute. "Has he been back to the north in the last two years?"

"No, there's nothing on here to suggest he has, but I can't be sure, because he was back in the country when he killed Nick. This guy is a ghost. It's entirely possible that he's returned another time and I've missed it."

"What's the story with the old girlfriend?"

"Apparently from his file, she was the reason he joined up. There was some sort of fallout with her parents."

"Sounds like unfinished business."

"Smith obviously wants us to track him to wherever he's going, so there must be something that he knows he can't do on his own. He's an expert at travelling undetected."

"Agreed. I'll call it in and find out where the girlfriend is. Smith wants us to make a link to the north. The image was captured hours ago, though. He'll be there now. I need her name." Walker reached for his phone.

Hunt furiously scanned the board, holding her breath as she reabsorbed the information. Walker's twitching fingers betrayed his impatience.

"Just hang on, I've nearly got it...erm...Zoe Turner!" she blurted.

Walker pressed redial. "This is Walker. Find out everything about Zoe Turner, Manchester, about thirty-four. Get on it. This is urgent. Call me as soon as you've got anything."

Hunt continued to scan and lift scraps of paper and Post-its on the wall. "Turner, Turner, Turner," she repeated aloud, trying to help her brain remember where she had heard the name before.

"What's wrong? We've got to get going if we're heading to Manchester."

"I've seen the name Turner somewhere else on this wall. I just can't remember where."

"Slow down, just think." Walker placed his hands on her upper arms to calm her, turning her to face him. "Close your eyes."

She glared at him.

"Just do it and stop being an arse."

"All right, all right."

"Visualise where you saw it. Was it on the right or left side?"

She took a deep breath before responding, picturing the wall in her mind. "It was on the left, near the bottom."

"Okay, was the piece of paper big or small?"

"I'm not sure."

"Just try and think. Was it written or typed?"

She pressed her lips together firmly, willing her brain to remember. "It was typed, a list." She opened her eyes and launched herself at the wall. Within seconds she shouted, "Here, got it! I knew I'd seen it somewhere before."

Walker held out his hands and smiled as if proclaiming his brilliance. "Well, go on. Don't keep an idiot in suspense. Who is it?"

"It's someone from Smith's SAS team. Sean Turner."

"He could be…it's possible?"

"It would be one hell of a coincidence."

Walker grabbed his phone once more. "It's Walker again. Find out whether Zoe Turner's got a brother called Sean. Send me everything you can dig up."

He hung up, then turned his phone to the side.

"What are you doing?" she questioned.

"I'm taking photos of the rogues' gallery. You don't think I'm going all the way to Manchester for you to turn around and say, 'Oh, that info might have been on my wall,' do you? I'm getting photographic records, so if we need to, we can look at it again. I'm not just a pretty face, you know."

"Let's just go, shall we?"

Chapter 20

Eve awoke in her clothes, light streaming in through her blinds, surrounded by papers from the Taylor prosecution files. The chaos that encircled her was unnerving; she hated disorganisation. Fee was right. Last night, she had been in no fit state to find anything. Despite having had some sleep, Eve did not feel rested. If anything, she was more dejected now than she was the day before. This case had been a catastrophe. She understood its significance, not only in sending down one of the Wheeler's lynchpins but because her future rested upon it. Whenever she had lost a case before, she'd understood why. Earlier in her career, she learned tough lessons about being thorough. Eve had become a control freak, although she preferred to think of herself as organised and fastidious, checking and double-checking everything.

Now a sniper was on the loose in London. Something she had no control over. Her safety was not her main concern—she was more perturbed about losing the case. Eve came to the conclusion that whatever the reason was for Taylor's murder, his assassins knew that Eve had no idea what it was.

If it was something incriminating, she would have used it as extra leverage in her case.

Her phone buzzed next to her. It was Fee.

"How are you this morning? Did you get any sleep?"

"I woke up surrounded by all my files, with my clothes on, drooling. So I think we can safely say I passed out."

"Well, don't worry about today. I've told the partners you're taking some time out after yesterday."

"Oh God—they're all going to think I'm hiding. I'll be in later. I've got to show my face eventually."

"All right, but sort yourself out. A drooling mess is not attractive."

"Thanks for that. Love you too."

Fee could always make her smile, but Eve loathed the prospect of facing her colleagues at Chambers. The senior partners would be exasperated, to say the least, and she hated disappointing them. There would also be a large contingent of her fellow associates who would be revelling in her failure. She imagined their smug faces as they heard the news, her dreams of Silk in tatters.

Eve looked at her phone and there were four missed calls from her father. Her heart throbbed. She knew how panic-stricken he would be, thinking the worst. It was unfair of her not to have called him, to tell him that she was safe. She hoped it hadn't stirred up the memories of the night her mother died, she owed him everything. He had brought her up virtually single-handed after her mother had been killed in a hit-and-run when she was six. Her death had devastated her father because the driver was never found. Eve was spurred on to become a barrister, fighting for innocent victims, prosecuting those who should face justice for their actions. This was a responsibility that she took very seriously.

The forest of papers encircling Eve made her twitchy, but she knew her priority was to call her dad. The plush velvet of her headboard provided comfort as she leaned against it, waiting for her dad to pick up. Her eyes scanned an open file as the rings continued. Before she realised, a minute had gone by, and he had not answered. Her engrossment of the data from the file had made her temporarily lose track of time. She decided to give up and ended the call. Perhaps he had left his phone in another room and he couldn't hear it; this was not unusual. His landline would probably be the safest bet. This time she was more aware of the number of rings as well as the passing time. There was still no answer.

Biting her lip, she stared blankly at the phone in her hand, willing it to give her an explanation. This was not her dad. This was not like him at all. Why would he call her so many times, then not pick up the phone himself? She agonised. Eve checked the time stamps of his missed calls and all had been from the night before, 8:10 p.m., 8:40 p.m., 9:15 p.m., and 10:00 p.m. He'd desperately tried to get hold of her; maybe he called Fee and she had told him that she was safe. Whatever had happened last night, he was not answering now.

Eve decided to call Fee back. Maybe Fee had forgotten to mention that she had spoken to her dad. Just as Eve picked up her mobile for the third time, it vibrated in her hand.

"Dad?"

"Thank God you're okay. I called you over and over last

night, and you didn't answer. I've been so anxious! I called Fee in the end, and she said you'd gone home, so I assumed you'd fallen asleep."

"Dad, I am so, so sorry. I'd never want to worry you like that. I must've passed out." Eve turned to her bedside table and saw the empty bottle of red wine she had drained. "I'm fine. Honestly, you don't need to worry."

"Okay, but please, just keep sending me little messages to let me know you're all right. You don't have to keep phoning me, as long as you keep in touch."

"I promise. I'll message you later to let you know how this hangover is panning out."

"Love you, Eve. Please take care, you're very precious to me."

"I will. Love you too, Dad."

Now she understood why she was so groggy. Eve was starving and hoped that some stodgy carbs with a strong cup of coffee would sort out her head. She swung her legs off the bed and managed to knock half of her files onto the floor. As she knelt on the floor trying to gather the files, her phone pinged. A message from an unknown number appeared on her screen: *12pm Cafe des Amis, Covent Garden. Information about Taylor.* She looked at the number closely but didn't recognise it. A wave of nausea hit. She never gave out her number. A Google search also did nothing to confirm its identity. Taking unnecessary risks was not in her nature, but there was no other option.

Who is this? she replied, her fingers shaking.

12pm. If you want the truth about Taylor. Come alone.

Chapter 21

Smith knew Hunt and the police would be tracking him like a bloodhound and his timed truck stop would lead them to his message. Months ago, Amicus's contacts in the Boathouse confirmed he was being pursued by Hunt, a female MI6 agent.

Amicus had been assured that Hunt had been dealt with and was no longer a threat. Clearly, Amicus was mistaken. Hunt would have accessed his personal file and discovered his connections to Manchester as well as his SAS disciplinary action involving Sean Turner, which was the result of an argument over Turner's sister, Zoe.

Smith used the CCTV to mobilise the police, which he hoped would prevent Zoe from being moved. An APW, All Ports Warning, would guarantee she couldn't be taken through border control. Smith had seen Zoe days before the assassination but hadn't envisaged returning to Manchester so soon. Driving up the M6 regurgitated painful memories that he had chosen to forget.

Smith was accustomed to going headfirst into the fray,

but endangering the life of someone he loved was disconcerting. His blood ran cold at the thought of what Zoe was being subjected to. He had taken a risk in contacting his former associate, but he had no other option. Smith didn't have friends or acquaintances. Amicus was the only person he'd worked with for years, but this hadn't always been the case.

Smith had been altered by his experiences during conflicts. His unit had disbanded with the understanding assistance would be given if required. None had ever made the call.

Smith now resolved to enact his contingency plan. His instincts were never wrong, and arrangements needed to be made. He knew too much; he was vulnerable.

Smith's shoulders relaxed as he reached the end of the M62 with its calming familiarity. The car crept alongside the railway line, bolstered by row upon row of LEGO-stacked flats. The traffic moaned gently as the car headed into the City Centre. His vehicle had served its purpose but had to be abandoned before it provided intelligence for the police. Manchester had been his home and it was one of the only places he felt connected to. He remembered a car park which lay under an old railway bridge, the perfect place to conceal a vehicle. Its prime advantage was the absence of CCTV. Because he'd arrived early, Smith chose his spot, then left.

He checked his watch as he began his ascent into the city, conscious of the schedule he needed to keep. The emptiness in his stomach reminded him it had been over twelve hours since his last meal. Although mentally focused, hunger and exhaustion would only cloud his judgement. Smith needed to be mentally and physically strong enough to withstand whatever was coming.

Years ago, he had purchased an apartment in Manchester, mostly out of sentimentality, and rented it out while living abroad. The apartment was a shrewd investment, one that had generated passive income for years. Fortuitously, his last tenants had not renewed their contract, and the property was vacant. It was the perfect place to recuperate and regroup.

The apartment on Little John Street was around the corner from one of his favourite places. When Smith was a young boy, his grandad had taken him to the Museum of Science and Industry, a place that ignited and indulged his curiosity. He was very close to his grandad and was devastated when he died. Smith loved the apartment, not only because of its location but because of its exposed bricks and walls of glass which unveiled the urban skyline. The street-corner supermarket provided the supplies he needed. As his key turned in the door, he was engulfed with relief as his exhaustion took hold.

Leaning against the wall of his rooftop balcony, Smith sipped a glass of water as he looked out over the city skyline, deliberating his next move. After he had eaten, he clambered beneath the fresh sheets of his bed, then set the alarm for two hours. Power napping would give him the necessary recharge.

The shrill beeping of the alarm jolted him awake after what felt like a minute. Unlike most ordinary people who would hit snooze, Smith headed straight into the shower, its flowing hot water soothed his aching skin. He dressed and packed what he needed, then wiped everything down. Not necessary in his own property, but it was his routine. He stepped out onto the balcony one last time as if wishing it goodbye, not expecting to ever return. Before he left, he made a phone call. His plan was initiated. He knew that events now in motion would be resolved one way or another. As he closed the door, he did not look back.

Chapter 22

Walker and Hunt navigated their way out of London before the sting of rush hour, making good time towards the M1. Greater Manchester Police had found an address for Zoe Turner and were sending a team to investigate. They were making progress; however, Walker infuriated Hunt by making a pit stop at a greasy spoon for a bacon sandwich. Her stomach turned as Walker opened his mouth while chewing, revealing its mushed contents.

"You can't expect me to get all the way to Manchester without anything? Jesus, woman," he carried on, steering with one hand, shoving the bread, oozing with ketchup, into his mouth. "What? It's the breakfast of champions—that'll keep me going for hours."

"Wow! I didn't realise your body was such a well-oiled machine. I must record the details of these nutritional tidbits. Maybe one day, I too can have a physique like yours. Anyway, I thought eating was banned."

"This is an emergency," he replied.

Although not averse to the odd bacon butty, the smell of

fat blended with cheap tomato ketchup was making her gag. Opening the window provided some much-needed fresh air.

"Where about was he picked up at the service station? How far north was it?" she questioned.

"He was walking into a truck stop in Crewe. I expect he chose it because it's quiet. He'd be noticed by the staff and customers. It's also near the exit for Manchester."

"Did they get the car plate?"

"Yes, but he'll have ditched it by now. I've got a team scrutinising the CCTV to see if they can pick it up, but that could take hours."

"So after Crewe, we've got no clue where he went, but it was probably Manchester?"

"Yep, so we'd best hope our boys come up with something about Sean Turner. Let's pray GMP are on their way round to Zoe's house now to find out if she's there," Walker replied, not sounding particularly hopeful.

When his last mouthful was finished, he turned to Hunt with a sated expression akin to a lion after a kill, wiping the corners of his stubbled mouth with his fingertips. Hunt imagined that Walker liked to behave in a brutish manner, but she couldn't help think that beneath his sandpaper exterior, there might be something softer hiding.

"So, is there anyone you need to call to let them know that you won't be home tonight?"

"Prying, are we? Well, well. Didn't think you would be that interested."

"It just strikes me that you have been into my flat, where, believe me, few have ever ventured before, slept on my sofa, insulted my PJs, and I actually don't know anything about you. The only things I know are that you love your little car, are naturally abrasive, and have terrible taste in takeaways. The rest is a mystery."

"Abrasive. Well, I thought I was assertive. Listen, you don't get anywhere in the Met by being soft-spoken or sitting on the sidelines. And as for my 'little car,' *this* is a piece of art, an incredible example of human ingenuity at its very best, and if you call it a 'little car' once more, you'll be riding on a little train back to London."

"Okay, but seriously, why did you become a copper? You don't choose this job on a whim."

"Believe it or not, I grew up in a not-so-nice neighbourhood, and I was surrounded by scumbags and lowlifes who wanted to damage and corrupt everyone and everything. My mum and dad tried their best to get us out of there, but we couldn't afford to move away, so we were trapped."

As she listened, Hunt could hear the sincerity in his voice. Perhaps his caustic demeanour was the result of a hard childhood; attacking was his first line of defence. Walker then fell silent. Hunt imagined he had peaked with his honesty.

With Walker focused on the road, Hunt took out her laptop and searched for British connections to Tarek Ahmadi. She logged in to the MI6 interface to access their servers. The correlation that she had made on the wall had thrown other significant players into the equation, and this created divergent lines of possibility. Nick's laptop clearly held sensitive content that, if divulged, would be catastrophic to specific individuals. Hunt hadn't entirely unravelled their identity but was resolute that ultimately they would be located—hopefully sooner rather than later, as it had consumed her for far too long.

"What are you looking for?"

"Any links to Ahmadi in the UK." Hunt didn't even look up, she was so engrossed in the data. "If Smith is the assassin, the family may be seeking revenge. They were well connected in Libya with numerous contacts through their oil conglomerate. They had millions in assets. Money that could easily buy them influence and access to information."

As she tapped away, a message flashed up on her screen. It was from Peter Ashford, her supervising officer at MI6. Hunt had been so single-minded, she had not paused to consider the ramifications of what she was doing. Ashford had initially agreed that Hunt could work with Walker to recover Smith, but she knew that chasing Smith around the country was perhaps pushing the limits of acceptable collaboration. Ashford would expect timely progress reports, as well as debriefing at the Boathouse.

Just then, Walker's phone buzzed.

"Walker. Yeah, yeah. Blood? Enough to indicate death? Okay, right. We'll be there in a few hours." He said exchanging looks with Hunt. "Well, there's not enough blood to suggest that she's dead, but she definitely put up a fight. They're sending me images of the scene."

His phone beeped again. Hunt held it up so they could both see the screen. The house was ransacked, with chairs knocked over and photos smashed on the ground.

"Pull over so we can look at these properly."

Walker pulled into the hard shoulder, his tyres crunching over the loose gravel.

"Send these to me so we can see them on the big screen."

"How the hell do I do that?"

"Give it here." Hunt took the phone from Walker and airdropped herself the photographs, opening them on her screen. Both were transfixed by the images, searching for any shreds of evidence that would indicate Zoe Turner's whereabouts or the identity of her captors. The blood that GMP mentioned was a long, crimson smear against the wall, not a pool on the floor. Zooming in tightly, they could make out strands of blond hair stuck within the clotted spray. A cordless phone lay flung on its side, its screen shattered, likely due to a blunt force.

"Well, she's alive. I can't see anything helpful. Photos, cushions, usual stuff." Suddenly, she noticed something lying on the carpet. "Oh shit!" Hunt pointed to the screen, swiping her trackpad to enlarge the image. Walker regarded her gravely, then picked up his phone.

"It's Walker. Have you found the child?"

Chapter 23

Eve locked her front door, turned, and climbed into the waiting black cab. "Covent Garden, please," she instructed, and the driver nodded and pulled away. Her black blazer and dark jeans were both smart and casual; Eve wanted to feel comfortable in her clothes, if nothing else.

It was 11:30. She was following instructions and making the journey to Cafe des Amis. She was not in the habit of being late. Deep breaths calmed her a little, but Eve couldn't help the tiny flicker of adventure hiding beneath the anxiety. She couldn't bear to miss the chance to get closer to the truth. But something bothered her. How had this person obtained her mobile number? Data protection at Chambers was secure. Just then her phone rang.

"How's your head? Feeling better now?" Fee asked.

"Just about. The coffee and paracetamol are starting to kick in."

"Where are you, by the way? You keep breaking up."

Eve hated lying to Fee, but she didn't want to worry her. "I'm meeting a friend for a coffee."

"You don't have any other friends. Eve, what's going on?"

She knew she would have to tell her something, but she couldn't risk Fee's safety. "I'm meeting the Arosio family on neutral ground. Yesterday was such a crazy day, no-one could make sense of it. Now they've had a night to digest, they want to discuss their options." Not bad, she thought to herself. She hated that her lies had come so readily.

"Okay, but call me later. Let's get a takeaway."

As Eve disconnected, she could see Covent Garden approaching, and her heart quickened. The taxi pulled up alongside the tube station, then she opened its door with a deep breath. Covent Garden was a short walk from Chambers and was one of her favourite places. Every time she wandered along the cobbles, she felt invigorated by the cacophony of sound, her senses ignited by the creativity on every corner. But not this time. As she advanced toward her destination, she felt very aware of those around her. Her eyes surveyed the crowd, searching for anyone out of place. Eve had always been oblivious to the sheer number of congregated people but now appreciated the difficulty of escaping with speed or efficiency. Finally, she saw it: Cafe des Amis. Ironic. The message she'd received was far from friendly. Eve would never jeopardise her safety, but the lure of the truth was enough to take a risk. After all, they were meeting in a public place. What was the worst that could happen? Eve could feel her heart beating out of her chest as she grasped the metal door handle.

The ambient lighting in the cafe created a cosiness, which under different circumstances would have been relaxing; yet to Eve, it was eerie. Beams of light from chandeliers reflected off the marble floor, guiding her to the bar like an aeroplane coming in to land. With each footstep, she examined the other patrons. All were indifferent to her existence. She took a seat with a clear view of the door and waited.

"Do you have a table booked, miss?"

"No, I'm just waiting for someone."

"Can I get you a drink?"

"Just a coffee, please."

The barman was friendly, but Eve paid him no attention, her gaze fixed on the door.

After sitting anxiously for some time, she glanced down at her half-full cup. Her coffee was cold, its foam dissipated. Her phone hadn't chimed or vibrated since her arrival; there was no waiting message. It had been a complete waste of time. Someone had obviously enjoyed messing her around. She was on a wild goose chase; she felt foolish.

"Thanks," she uttered, settling her bill, before she wandered out of the cafe, exhaling in annoyance. Covent Garden was in full swing with the crowds swelling. Today was not going to be a write-off. Eve was determined to move forward and find out about Taylor and strode purposefully towards the station to grab a waiting taxi. Suddenly, a hand grasped her upper arm.

"I hoped you would come."

Chapter 24

Smith's rendezvous point was not in an abandoned warehouse or a safe house. It was public, though not covered in CCTV. Located in the Northern Quarter of Manchester City Centre, Afflecks Palace was where Smith misspent most of his youth. To him, the eclectic mix of coffee bars and vintage shops was more interesting than wasting hours on the main drag. His favourite shop was Zeffa, a vintage-clothing emporium—the word *shop* was not quite eloquent enough. Nothing could beat the musty aroma of clothes from classic decades, the texture of man-made fabrics and silhouettes that undoubtedly blazed a trail. The owner, Kenny, who was ageless, had offered Smith a job after he spent so much time hanging around.

Smith knew the cross-section of the building, having trudged stock and empty boxes in and out for years. In the basement was a stock room where he had spent countless hours. He often sneaked down for a ciggy away from adults who would give him a clip round the ear.

Smith's route to Afflecks Palace involved side streets and

alleys; it was one he could navigate with his eyes closed. He checked his watch, making sure he was early. Being back in the area ignited old memories, but he could not jeopardise his freedom because of nostalgia; the possibility of being recognised by Kenny was too dangerous. Forgoing a quick tour through his old haunts, he slipped down to the basement unnoticed.

The room was vast, with numerous dark corners. Hearing the clatter of approaching footsteps, Smith concealed himself. A young man entered, wearing an apron and T-shirt emblazoned with the logo of a juice bar. His hair hung limply around his narrow shoulders as he lumped bulging bin bags down the stairs, which he hurled onto the floor. He then took an e-cigarette out of the front of his apron and took two puffs, the smoke filling the air like a dense fog. Finally, he trudged back up the stairs, letting the door bang behind him.

"I'm impressed that you've still got it. I almost didn't notice you," Smith whispered. A stranger slowly emerged from the shadows. Smith's stomach dropped.

"Not who you were expecting? Well, I am sorry to disappoint."

Chapter 25

The hand that had grabbed Eve firmly guided her into the White Lion, a pub opposite the station where she was heading to catch a cab. A sudden rush of adrenaline through her veins rendered her incapable of fighting the person moving her. She couldn't think clearly.

Their final destination was a table to one side, which was slightly more secluded than the others. It wasn't until Eve sat across from him that she saw his face.

"I wanted to make sure you weren't being followed before I spoke to you. I didn't come into the other place—it would have been too risky. I waited outside for half an hour to be certain. I knew you'd come," he explained nervously.

Eve narrowed her eyes, her legs still trembling under the table, determined to work out who she was staring at. Then it hit her.

"Oh, my God! You're Ryan Taylor."

"Shhh! Keep your voice down," he whispered, his eyes bulging.

Eve subtly scanned the room and realised that if she

wasn't careful, she could draw attention to herself.

"I saw you with your mum in the gallery when your dad was released. What the hell are you playing at? Why have you brought me here? If this is some sort of vendetta, then there are plenty of witnesses—"

"Will you calm down. I'm not interested in revenge. Whether Dad went down or not, they were going to get to him at some point. He knew too much."

"What on earth are you talking about? Who are *they*? And how the hell was he found not guilty? He was clearly there that night."

"Andy Wheeler promised me that he'd get him off, said he protected his own and that he'd sorted it, whatever that meant. We didn't actually believe it until it happened. In some ways, I wanted him to get banged up, because it would be more difficult to get to him on the inside."

Eve leaned back on her seat. How could she believe this man sitting in front of her—why should she trust him? After all, his father was a lying scumbag, why would his offspring be any different? Then Eve realised she hadn't told anyone where she was going; no-one would know if she went missing. She thought quickly.

"Look, if we're going to talk about this, you'd better buy me a drink. Otherwise, it really will look suspicious."

Ryan hesitated for a second, looked over his shoulder, then said, "Okay, I'll be right back."

Ryan approached the bar and ordered two drinks. Eve seized her moment and tapped a text message to Fee: *Meeting in Covent Garden, no text before 6pm, track me.* Eve clicked her phone onto silent, then slipped it back into her pocket before Ryan returned from the bar. Fee had used the Find My Friends app several times, as Eve was notorious for not answering her phone. Ryan returned and carefully placed the drinks on the table with shaky hands.

Eve looked at his face. She hadn't realised until now that Ryan was similar to her in age. But he looked tired. The large circles under his eyes were emphasised by his pale skin and dark hair. He was taller than Tony, with broad shoulders. He clearly did not follow the same diet regimen as his father; he seemed to have looked after himself, very different from his family. Ryan took a sip from his glass as if to steady his nerves.

"Look, why have you asked me to come here? What can I *possibly* do to help *you*?" Eve demanded, her confidence beginning to return.

"You probably won't believe this, but my dad told me to contact you. When Dad knew he was in trouble, he said you were one of the most honest and relentless people he had ever com across, and if anyone could set things right, it was you." Eve narrowed her eyes, clearly communicating her sentiments, as Ryan continued to explain, "You were right at the trial. Dad was there that night, but he was in the wrong place at the wrong time. But that's not why he was shot. That was just a coincidence."

"What do you mean?"

"Before he got caught up with the Arosios, Dad was involved in something else. He was a bloody idiot. He'd been doing a job for Andy Wheeler in one of the hotels, dropping off an envelope. He didn't ask questions, he never did, that's why Andy liked him—Dad just did as he was told. When he was walking back through the hotel, he stole a laptop. My dad was never the brightest spark in the box. Dad told me he saw it sitting there, so he thought he could make a few quid selling it on. It was in a nice case, so he thought it would be an expensive one. One thing you could say about my dad—what a thief! He lifted it unnoticed, then quickly headed to the car. The person he stole it from discovered it was missing minutes after Dad had taken it and must have clocked him getting in the car. They probably got the number plate before he drove off."

"That still doesn't explain why he was killed. A laptop can be replaced easily."

"It was what was on it that got him killed. Now I've got to protect Mum because they're not done."

"Why?" Eve was so confused as to why his mum was in danger.

"I can't tell you here. I need to show you. It's safe, but we need to move it before my dad's killers work out where it is."

"Okay, but don't try anything funny. There are many senior police officers I know very well."

Ryan downed the rest of his drink, wincing as he swallowed, before pulling his hat down to mask his face. Eve left her drink untouched, then collected her handbag and followed him out the door. They bundled into a cab, not making eye contact until Ryan spoke.

"Whitechapel, please, mate."

Chapter 26

Smith's eyes had quickly adjusted to the darkness of the basement; the pungent stench of rotting food from the burst bin bags had almost dissipated. Smith glowered at the figure before him. They stood eyeballing each other like gunfighters about to draw, neither making any movement to break the deadlock. It was true, he had been expecting someone else, but he was more annoyed than afraid. Where the hell was his contact? Why hadn't he shown up? Had he betrayed him after all these years? He was mindful not to reveal his inner dialogue and remained stone-faced and static. Smith's adversary was also unflinching. Aside from her face, every inch of the lean, athletic body was covered in black clothing, which provided the camouflage for darkness.

"Who are you?" Smith demanded.

"Who I am is not important, but the message I have is of most value to you. We have obtained something precious of yours, and no doubt you would like it back unharmed. In return, you have something of equal value to us. If it is not returned, we will dispose of your property."

Smith advanced towards her but was interrupted by her words.

"Please, Mr Smith—if that is your chosen moniker these days—do not imagine for a second that because I am a woman, I am not perfectly capable of handling myself, despite your extensive military experience." Her condescending tone demonstrated contempt for her opponent. "I am not daunted by your presence or threatened by your physique. If I do not return to my colleagues in my present state, your property will automatically be destroyed without mercy. It is in your best interests to remain calm and follow the instructions that I am about to give you."

Her sleek, raven hair was wound efficiently into a tight bun, with not a single hair out of place. There was no softness in her manner, nor in her flawless skin. Her brown eyes were emotionless as she delivered the carefully crafted message. She demonstrated no signs of fear or doubt, and Smith believed her claim that she could handle herself.

"I have no idea what you want from me," Smith said.

"What we seek is information. Information that you stole from Tarek Ahmadi after you assassinated him. You took something that did not belong to you, Mr Smith, and now you must return it."

Once again, she was dispassionate—until she mentioned Tarek Ahmadi. Smith noticed a slight flicker in her gaze, as though the words she spoke were more poignant than she was willing to reveal.

"I don't have it—I didn't keep it for myself. It was just another contract. You need to take it up with my former employer. This has nothing to do with me." He felt the tension in the room rising.

"On the contrary, Mr Smith, it has everything to do with you. Deliver the information, by whichever means you deem necessary, or your friend will perish." As her threat left her lips, she placed her hand in her pocket and withdrew a phone. "Take this. We will be in contact."

"How do I know she's still alive? I need assurances that she won't be harmed!"

"Check the lock screen," she responded. "That was taken two hours ago. You can check the time stamp." He pressed the phone, and there was an image of a very dishevelled-looking Zoe. She appeared tired and scared, but she was okay. She was holding a child.

Smith's stomach lurched. Zoe was holding Hannah, his daughter. Anger raged inside of him. He felt like a volcano about to erupt. He was about to attack, but his SAS training reminded him otherwise.

"If you even bruise my girls, I'm going to kill you and all of your associates slowly, without mercy. You'll be begging me to end it quickly," he seethed.

"Now, now, Mr Smith, follow our instructions, and neither of us will have to engage in such brutality. You have twenty-four hours. We will be in touch." Her eyebrows raised as if she were enjoying the moment. She turned on her heel and quietly trod up the stairs. As she pulled the heavy door towards her, she delivered her parting shot.

"Just in case it had crossed your mind, Mr Smith, please refrain from following me. My colleagues have eyes on me at all times, and any attempt on my life will be regarded as an act of defiance, and therefore your precious little girl will certainly obtain those bruises that you are so keen for her to avoid." With that, the door closed.

Smith would deal with them later. They would not escape his justice. The woman was not someone he recognised, but he presumed she was linked to Ahmadi's family. Smith knew some of Ahmadi's sons had fled persecution and were living in Europe with members of his extended family.

Smith's only emotional attachment had been to Zoe, and over the years, he'd learnt to bury his feelings. His whole world had turned upside down. He refocused quickly, realising the need to leave before he was identified. Finally, he left the building and headed towards the City Centre.

The fresh air helped clear his head, and as he strode along the pavements full of shoppers, he accepted that he couldn't do this alone. It was Sean whom he had contacted for help. Why the hell hadn't he shown up? Smith had no alternative. He took out his phone from his pocket and pressed the number.

The phone rang for ten seconds. Smith knew he was being ignored. He would persist until he was answered. It took another five rounds of ringing. Inside he was shouting, "For God's sake, pick up the bloody phone!" Just as he had finished his mental rant, the call was answered.

"*What do you want?* Why are you calling?" Butler bellowed.

"I need your help. You know I wouldn't be calling unless

I absolutely had to," he replied earnestly.

"I shouldn't be talking to you. If she finds out, we're both screwed."

"They've taken Zoe and my daughter, Hannah, and I know you know who they are. I have never, ever asked you for anything, so you know how desperate I am."

She didn't reply. Smith closed his eyes, willing her to agree. "Please."

"I can't believe what I'm about to say." Butler hesitated. "What do you need?"

Chapter 27

Walker needed no encouragement to press the pedal to the floor as they sped towards Manchester. They glided along the motorway, the trees and fields on either side passing in a blur. Walker was right; it was a good car. His earlier bravado was now replaced with solemnity. The image of the child's doll abandoned on the floor, its eyes staring and limbs disjointed, disturbed Hunt. It had struck a chord with Walker too. Perhaps he had a child of his own or a sister or niece. He'd previously diverted conversations about himself, reluctant to reveal any personal details. Hunt was not in the habit of prying; she understood his need for privacy and in many ways, it mirrored her own.

"Remind me again why we've stopped here and not just sent the local coppers in?" Walker challenged, his brow furrowed as he pulled into the truck stop where Smith was earlier captured on CCTV.

"Because he's bloody calculating, and there's a reason why he stopped here. If you didn't know what to look for, you'd miss it," Hunt retorted, 100 percent secure in her decision.

"Miss what?"

"That's what we're going to find out. There." Hunt pointed to a parking space in front of a brown brick building with the word *Welcome* in black plastic lettering. Despite the modest size of the facilities, the surrounding car park was generous enough to accommodate a large number of trucks and lorries. Couriers for Bartlett's, Stobart, and Farrall's parked in lines, promoting their services from the sides of their tarps. As they came to a final stop, Walker's brakes squealed, as if amplifying his annoyance. Hunt's door was halfway open before Walker had lifted the handbrake. "Watch it!" Walker cried. Hunt didn't wait to see if he was behind her, already striding her way past the tables. The smell of deep fat fryers filled the air as she approached the counter. The reek turned her stomach. All around, knives and forks gently clattered like applause for the chef's fried eggs and bacon. Hunt turned to Walker, acknowledging that his taste buds would be in seventh heaven. He peered over her shoulder to see the chef cooking sausages; she could almost hear him salivating.

"What can I get you, my love?" The waitress smiled, holding an order pad and pen. Her kind eyes framed by the checked hat and wisps of white hair that escaped from its edges.

"Doreen, is it?" Hunt read her name badge. The woman nodded. "I'm Agent Hunt, and this is DCI Walker," Hunt said as they held up their credentials. "We need some information about a male customer that was here earlier this morning. I believe our local colleagues have already been in contact and looked through your CCTV?"

"Oh yes, a very nice young officer. Glover, I think his name was. I gave him everything we had this morning."

Walker pulled up the CCTV stills sent to him earlier and showed Doreen to jog her memory.

"Yes, I remember him. I've worked here for twenty-five years, and I know all the usuals that come in. We're a bit out of the way, you see, on our little plot, and most people go to the big service stations. The people that come here are our truckers; they don't want to be bothered with all those busy folks. They just want to have some good food and a friendly place to stop." She paused for a moment and looked at Smith's image again. "That's why I can remember him, you see, we don't get too many strangers around here. And he was a bit odd, really, not the usual type. Very serious. He didn't crack a smile once."

"Can you remember what he did while he was here? What he ordered, where he sat? Was there anything unusual?"

"Uh-huh. He had a cup of coffee but didn't have anything to eat. That's why I thought it was strange. Alan makes the best bacon-and-egg butties for miles around, and no-one can resist the smell of his cooking." A rotund man with a baseball cap and moustache stood at the hot plate and waved his spatula in agreement.

"Of course," Hunt said and smiled as she felt a gentle nudge from Walker in her back. "Where did he sit?"

"He sat over there by the window." Doreen pointed, wrinkling her nose. "Seemed odd, really, to sit by the window but not look out of it."

"Why was that? Did he drink his coffee and then leave?" Walker asked.

"No, he had a piece of paper that he was writing or drawing on that he kept to himself. He didn't sit there on his phone like some, and he didn't watch the TV either. We were quiet at that time, that's why I think I noticed him more. After a quarter of an hour, I went over with the coffeepot, you know, to see if he wanted a refill. He said no thanks. Then I think he went to the bathroom. Yes, that's right. He finished his coffee, then left a fiver as a tip. Quite nice, really, considering he only had one cup. I didn't see him again after that."

"Thank you, Doreen, that was very helpful. We're just going to have a quick look around. Where are the men's toilets?"

"The toilets are just at the back to the right, where you came in." Doreen leaned forward over the counter and used her arm as a signpost. "If there is anything else you need, just let me know. I might be able to get you a little discount," she added with a wink.

Walker and Hunt approached where Smith had been sitting. It was a square wooden table; its exposure to the sunlight had faded it on one side. Little packets of sugar and salt stood back-to-back in a white china dish which flanked half-used bottles of ketchup and brown sauce. Nothing seemed to be out of place. Hunt sat in Smith's chair for a moment, as if sitting in his former position would help to understand his motives. She then slid her fingers under the table, searching for anything concealed. Unsatisfied, she dropped to the floor and looked under the table as Walker searched the opposite side.

"Anything?" Hunt asked Walker from under the table.

"Nothing. What exactly are we looking for?" he replied.

"If he was writing, maybe he's left something for us. You know what this means." She sighed and rolled her eyes in anticipation of the innuendo she was going to be subjected to.

"If you want to go into the gents', you go ahead. You don't need my permission," Walker teased.

Hunt rose to her feet and glared at him. "Right then, let's get this over with."

Hunt and Walker stood outside the toilets for a moment. Hunt took a deep breath. "Hello?" she called as she slowly pushed open the door, checking she wasn't about to come face-to-face with an angry trucker in mid-flow. Getting no response, she proceeded. She was surprised at the cleanliness of small toilets; considering the truck stop was heavily frequented by men, the odour could have been substantially worse. The intermittent splash of water flushing the urinals echoed around the beige tiled walls as Hunt and Walker scrutinised the room. Hunt handed a pair of latex gloves to Walker, inviting him to join her in the search. Once her gloves were on, Hunt took out a pen and carefully began to search the contents of the metal bin on the floor. Crisp wrappers and old tissues composed the majority of its contents, mixed with screwed-up receipts and paper towels. Although she knew Smith wouldn't have been so obvious, Hunt had to ensure no stone was unturned. Opposite the urinals was a cubicle. The mottled MDF door creaked as Walker pushed it open.

"Whoever this Tracy is, I think she's up for anything," Walker mused from behind the door as he read the comments left by its patrons. "They need to follow a decent team, though. Nobody supports this lot anymore." Suddenly the door jerked forward and hit Walker on the shoulder. "Ow! That hurt, you know."

"I'm sure it did," Hunt said. "Just move out of the way, will you, I need to have a proper look."

Walker edged out of the way without protest. "Be my guest."

Until now, the smell hadn't bothered her; however, remnants of brown sludge glued to the pan made her gag.

Once again, there was nothing out of place. The narrow windowsill above the seat was clear, and there was nothing written on the door that looked like a deliberate message. Hunt moved back so she could analyse the entire space. She stood biting her lip, perplexed by the puzzle. "So you think he's left a note or something?" Walker questioned.

"He's not going to leave it somewhere wet for obvious reasons, so where the hell else is he going to hide it for us to find?"

Walker moved past her towards the cistern and began to remove it.

"It's not going to be there."

"Well, you haven't got any better ideas." Walker grunted as he tried to slide the heavy porcelain lid of the tank. "Nope, nothing here."

"Damn it!" she huffed. Hunt hated feeling defeated. Walker laid the lid against the back wall, then proceeded to shake droplets of water from his gloved hands. "Here," Hunt said as she grabbed a handful of tissues. As Walker wiped his hands, Hunt stood and stared at the plastic dispenser on the wall. It was only seconds before Walker caught up. Hunt once again scoured the room for something to break the container; she couldn't wait for the key. She picked up the small metal bin she had earlier searched and launched it at the plastic. Walker darted out of the way, assured of an injury if he remained still.

The plastic was cheap, and after two blows, Hunt knocked it cleanly off the wall. The tissues created a white blanket across the tiled floor. Walker checked the inside of the container—it was clear. Just to be sure, Hunt examined it herself. She crouched by the edge of the mess and delicately sifted through the tissue. Out of the corner of her eye, she saw a grey line poking out from within one of the folds of fabric. She could feel the blood rushing to her cheeks; her heart was hammering. Hunt leaned forward, steadied herself with one hand, and delicately picked up the paper.

"This is what we're looking for!" she announced triumphantly. Walker's expression was sincere; she could almost feel his relief. He moved to her side as she stood so they could both see the paper. "What the hell is that?" Walker blurted.

"I have absolutely no idea, but we're going to find out."

Chapter 28

As soon as Ryan Taylor left his mother's house, Butler picked up his phone signal and relayed the information to Amicus. Now that Smith was no longer available, Amicus used resources that were made accessible at the Boathouse. Amicus always dealt with the Boathouse directly; Butler had no idea who *they* were. Amicus informed Butler that Paradox would be located and returned, and she would have to prepare the data for an important meeting in Geneva. This part of the operation kept Amicus busy; Butler could assist Smith from the comfort of her room, undetected, for now.

Butler didn't know the exact details of Smith's and Amicus's association, but she knew Amicus well enough not to ask. Helping Smith against Amicus's wishes was not going to end well. Her stomach twisted as she answered his call.

"They want the information I took from Ahmadi. I've got to retrieve it, or Zoe and Hannah are dead. Where is it?" Smith demanded.

"We haven't found it yet. Amicus thinks Taylor's son's got it. We're waiting for him to make a move."

Smith explained that he had contacted Zoe's brother, Sean, and that Sean hadn't shown up to their meeting. He now presumed that Sean was dead. Smith said that Sean would never let him down, and death would be the only reason for his absence.

"I know it's Ahmadi's family. I had the pleasure of meeting his daughter."

Butler hesitated before replying, knowing she couldn't retract her next words. "It wasn't his daughter. It was his niece Haya. They've done a deal with Amicus. I don't know what it was, by the way, before you ask, in exchange for you." She closed her eyes, the wave of regret building inside, regrets that her actions had led to this moment.

"Alice." He had never called her Alice before, which unnerved her. "I need to know where they are. I haven't got much time."

She thought for a moment. "You know they're not going to have phones I can trace. Besides looking at CCTV from where you met, or from streets around Zoe's house, I don't know what else I can do." Despite earlier saying she didn't want to help him, Butler now wasn't sure if she could. People like the Ahmadis were adept at being ghosts, revealing themselves only when necessary. She closed her eyes tight; her mind focused on a solution.

"Wait—they gave me a phone and said they'd contact me with instructions," Smith said.

"As soon as they send you a message or call, I can triangulate the signal and work out where they are," she replied with relief. "What's the number?"

"I don't know. It's a cheap smartphone."

"Turn on your Bluetooth and hold your phone next to it. Open the other phone's settings and turn on Bluetooth. I've picked up yours already. Go to the Bluetooth settings, and it should pick up the device." Butler held her breath as she waited for Smith to follow her instructions.

"I've got it. You are a genius!" he cried.

There was no goodbye; there wasn't time. All Butler could do was wait. Wait for Ryan Taylor to make his move and for the Ahmadis to make theirs.

Chapter 29

Despite her eagerness to examine the piece of paper left by Smith, Hunt decided that the floor of the gents' toilets was not the place. Her gag reflex had reached saturation point. They swiftly moved back to Walker's car to take a closer look. Still wearing her latex gloves, Hunt held the note so they could both examine it. On the scrap of paper was a sixteen-digit number with a symbol drawn below. It was a rectangle merged with a triangle with a curve at the back.

"What the hell is that supposed to be?" Walker exclaimed. "I've never seen that before."

"Me either, I've got no idea. This must be a phone or account number or password," she replied, pointing to the digits. "Whatever it is, I think we should keep it to ourselves for now. He clearly wanted only us to find it. I'll Google it and see what comes up."

"Okay, but we need to get to Zoe's. If we can find her, we'll find him."

"I'll keep looking for links to the Ahmadis, and I'll check out Sean Turner's file too." One of the numerous phone calls that Walker had received had confirmed that Sean Turner was Zoe's brother. Walker turned his keys in the ignition and sped towards the truck stop exit. As he merged onto the motorway, his phone rang.

"Walker…Yeah, okay, call me back when you're in. Proceed with extreme caution. Turner is highly dangerous." He replaced his phone in the cup holder. "They're at Sean Turner's flat. There's no answer, so they're going in."

"He's not going to be there. He's long gone," Hunt said, not looking up from her laptop.

"Well, we're about to find out."

"He's got to be the person Smith contacted. Smith hasn't got friends—believe me, I know this guy. He works alone."

"Okay, explain this to me. How does Smith operate? How does he get his jobs?"

"Have you ever heard of Tor?"

"Nope, what the hell is that?"

"But you've heard of the dark web?"

"Obviously." He raised an eyebrow. "I'm not in the cybercrime unit, so I don't know exactly how it works. Please enlighten me."

"Well, whenever you use the internet for anything, without knowing it, your device sends out information about you, which includes your IP address. This tells the website you're on what your device number is and where you are in the world. Following?"

Walker didn't speak but glanced at her.

"Okay, so if your IP address is being stored, then your device and location can be traced. That's why when you've been looking at fluffy slippers on Amazon, they come up again when you go back online. Because your details are stored," she explained.

"Actually, when I'm online, it's pink fluffy slippers." His humour made her smile; there needed to be something to lighten the mood.

"So if you're planning to do something illegal or you want anonymity, you can use a network called Tor, which is part of the dark web. It's run by volunteers with questionable motives who route your internet traffic through their encrypted personal servers. It means that someone who's based in Macclesfield trying to buy drugs online looks like they're in Brazil."

"Clever bastards, aren't they."

"It was created by the US Navy for covert communication, but it wasn't managed securely and got into the wrong hands. There was a site called Alphabay, which the FBI shut down because it was selling weapons, drugs, and child porn—terrifying stuff."

"So how did Smith use it?" Walker asked.

"Well, you can download the Tor browser from the app stores. It's not that difficult if you know what you're looking for. All he'd need to do is access Tor and log in with a username and password. He could then access websites to leave messages and purchase weapons or 'specialist items,' ones that he couldn't nip into B&Q for."

"So that's how he was communicating with his handler and, I presume, with Sean to arrange contact."

"Exactly," Hunt confirmed.

Hunt was accustomed to dealing with individuals using the dark web. MI5's and MI6's specialist technicians scanned Tor's traffic daily for useful intel.

Walker's phone rang again, and Hunt turned to him with an "I told you so" expression plastered on her face.

"Walker…What? You've got to be…Okay, we're nearly there." Walker flung his phone forward towards the passenger footwell. Hunt reacted quickly and moved her legs to one side, pulling her laptop against her chest. "Shit!" Walker shouted, furiously running his fingers through his hair.

"What was that for?" she implored, trying to make eye contact with him. "What?"

"They've found Sean. He's dead," he snapped.

It wasn't long before they had reached the Manchester exit. Once again, both were silent. Hunt was glad of it—she was not in the mood to pander to his tantrums. Losing Sean Turner was a setback, but they had to move on. The smallest, most insignificant scrap of intel could lead them to Smith. During her search for links to the Ahmadis, Hunt completed a sweep of Sean's profile. Sean was unemployed and struggling to assimilate into society. His employment was unstable; he was rarely with a company for longer than a couple of months.

Following Walker's satnav, they reached Sean's flat, which, they were informed, was a short distance from Zoe Turner's house. A police cordon had closed the street, but after showing the duty PC his ID, Walker was allowed to drive to the property.

It was a quiet street, with cars parked on pavements and trees lining the road. Wheelie bins, full to the brim, waited for collection. The slightest breath of wind would have created pandemonium, with papers and packaging ready to fly around like confetti. Residents peered from behind their curtains, trying their hardest to fathom what was going on. Forensic units were setting up; the whole scene was a circus.

Hunt was the first to step out of the car, and she examined the surrounding area, keen to absorb as much as she could. Sean's flat was on the first floor, with another directly underneath. The GMP detective, DI Woodside, stood at the doorway awaiting their arrival. She was tall with dark hair; her smart clothes and confident stance gave her an air of authority. She introduced herself, smiling formally as she explained her credentials. Walker and Hunt did the same, to quickly dispense with the formalities.

"We've been asked to assist you in this, part of a wider investigation," Woodside stated.

"Thank you," Hunt replied.

"We wouldn't usually encroach on someone else's turf, but needs must," Walker added. "I believe his sister's place is close?"

"It's about ten minutes away. We've already been there. I'll take you through the scene later. But you need to see upstairs first." Woodside turned and led them up the stairs.

The door of the flat was open. Scenes-of-crime officers moved busily, taking photographs and collecting evidence. The flat was "bijou" in estate agent terms, with a kitchen behind the door upon entry. A range of cheap wall units encompassed a cooker, sink, and under-counter fridge, all spotlessly clean and relatively untouched. Natural light streamed in from two square windows at the opposite end of the room, reflecting off the pale laminate floor. Blank walls and the absence of personal effects emphasised its sterility. This was not a home; it was a base. Walker and Hunt studied the room carefully. It was unlikely that they would find evidence of his killers. It looked pristine.

"So far, the only prints we've found are the victim's. There aren't any prints or evidence identifying any other party. This wasn't random—it was a professional job," Woodside explained. "He's in here."

Woodside led them into another small room, adjacent to the kitchen. There was a single bed pushed against one wall and a small desk and swivel chair against the other. Sean was slumped in the chair. His head hung back on his neck, his eyes wide open. He was shot at point-blank range in the forehead with a single bullet. It was an execution. His green eyes penetrated those whom they met. Hunt knew it was not a look of fear. It was stoicism.

"He's been dead a couple of hours. This was clean, a get-in-and-out job. They took what they wanted and left," Woodside stated. Hunt noticed that there was a laptop charging cable disconnected under the desk.

"Have you found his laptop yet?" Hunt questioned. "What about a phone?"

"Not yet, although I think that's what they were looking for."

"Gov," cried a SOCO from the kitchen. "You need to come and see this!"

Chapter 30

As they arrived in Whitechapel, Eve leaned forward and handed the taxi driver a £20 note. "Thanks, keep the change."

Ryan had not spoken during the journey at all. Eve gazed out the window, convincing herself that she was handling the situation. They walked towards a row of paint-flaked lockups. Ryan stopped outside a green door; its heavy chain and padlock secured it like a guard dog growling at passers-by. Around them, the streets were bustling. There was nothing out of the ordinary, so Eve relaxed a little. How could they be in danger with so many people around?

Ryan's hands trembled as he retrieved a key from his pocket. His head flicked from left to right, checking that no-one was approaching, before he inserted the key into the lock. Just as he was about to turn it, both jumped as Eve's pocket vibrated. She placed her hand on her chest and exhaled with relief. It was Fee. She signalled to Ryan that it was okay, then answered.

"Where the hell are you? I've been trying to call you for

the past half an hour!" Fee demanded.

"I'm fine. I'm on Gibb Street in Whitechapel. I'm about to go into a lockup to find something. It's okay, I'm with someone I know."

"Eve, what the hell are you doing? First you lied to me, then you sent cryptic messages. I don't want you to go anywhere near a bloody lockup with 'someone' you know. Get in a cab and get out of there now!"

"Stop panicking, it's fine. I'm not going to be long. Look, I promise I'll call you as soon as I'm done. I know what I'm doing. Trust me."

"I am not happy about this. It's dangerous. If I don't get a call in fifteen minutes, I'm coming to find you."

"Okay, okay. I'll call you in fifteen. I'll tell you everything later, I promise."

"Make sure you call me or I'll be jumping in a cab to drag you out."

Eve replaced the phone in her pocket and faced Ryan.

"Sorry," she said softly. "I think we need to calm down. No-one is following us. Let's just get in and out quickly. You need to show me what this thing is."

Ryan didn't respond; his pale face and wide eyes said everything. He removed the padlock, then used his body to slide the unyielding deadbolt to one side. Once again, he peered over his shoulder before opening the door. Eve stepped over the bottom plank of the door and followed him in. Ryan pressed a light switch attached to the grey wall. A row of single bulbs hung from wires which lit the dingy garage space, its outside appearance mirrored by its internal state. This was a place used to forget and discard. The absence of natural light, combined with the enclosing concrete walls, began to put Eve on edge.

Nothing was organised, all was a mess. Boxes, tools, and materials were strewn everywhere, dumped with no concern for their preservation. Eve wondered how they would find anything, let alone something important. Ryan frantically riffled through boxes and bin bags, dispensing with them without care or attention. The hairs on the back of her neck began to stand, her apprehension growing. Ryan seemed oblivious to Eve veering towards the door. He was focused on shifting a substantial wooden cupboard out of the way.

"You're going to have to help me with this. I can't do it by myself." He laboured, trying to use his shoulders.

"What is it? Have you found it?"

"Dad said he had hidden it in here and I'd need help to get to it. Grab that side, and when I say, slide it forward. One, two, three, go!"

The unit was hard to manoeuvre. Eve was not accustomed to using her upper-body strength. She pressed her lips together firmly, using her shoulders to push the cupboard forward.

"Oh God, this thing is really bloody heavy!" She grunted, her body temperature rising.

"Just slide it, it's nearly there."

The screech of the unit against the floor reverberated around the room, and they both stopped. Stuffed behind it was a laptop bag. Ryan grabbed it from against the wall, then quickly moved to a grit-covered table, where he unzipped the sides. He took a deep breath, but as he reached out to open the lid, Eve felt a dull blow to the back of her head. Her legs crumbled beneath her, then her forehead struck the table.

*

Eve had no idea how long she had been unconscious for, but as she came round on the cold floor, she reached to the back of her head. Her fingertips were wet; she knew it was her blood. Ryan was in a similar state next to her, although he was still unconscious. She put her palms on the floor to steady her body, then tried to lever herself upright to check on Ryan.

"Ryan! Ryan, can you hear me?"

No response. Eve touched his face, careful not to move his head. She leaned over his mouth to see if he was breathing; she was relieved when his breath warmed her cheek. Eve tried to rouse him again, this time grabbing his hand to get a physical reaction—still nothing. She panicked and reached for her phone to call an ambulance. As she was beginning to dial, his eyes flickered, his mouth opening to communicate his agony.

"Oh, thank God! Are you okay?" Eve fretted.

"Yeah, I think so. My head feels like it's been hit with a sledgehammer. What happened?" he said, his face wincing in pain.

"Well, apparently we weren't alone." Eve moved so she could see the table. "No surprises there, the laptop's gone."

"Shit, I thought we were in the clear. We must have been followed. This was a mistake."

Ryan and Eve slowly rose to their feet, grabbing the table to steady themselves.

"At least we're still alive—that's something to be thankful for. What was on the laptop, anyway? You never got the chance to tell me before we arrived here." Eve's head throbbed as she spoke.

"Dad said he asked one of his techie friends to unlock it and have a go at wiping it before he could sell it on. The techie didn't usually look through the files, but for some reason he did, and he found something terrifying. Dad only told me about it when he came out of court. He told me where it was and that I needed to see what was on it."

"Well, he was obviously right. We need to find out what was on that machine. Who was his techie contact? Do you know where to find him?"

"I'm not sure where he is. We'll have to ask around—one of Andy Wheeler's lads will know. But they won't bloody talk to me if I'm with you."

"We can discuss that later. And now all we're left with is this empty case."

Eve pulled the bag towards her, desperately looking for answers. As she dropped it back on the table, they heard something shift. Something small inside the case had slid from one side to the other.

"Did you hear that?" Eve said, glancing at Ryan.

"Yes, what the hell was it? I thought you said it was empty."

"I thought it was!"

Ryan held the case and ran his finger over the seams. All

seemed as it should, until he found a tiny opening at one of the edges. Using a screwdriver that he'd carelessly tossed to the floor during the earlier search, he ripped the stitching.

"What is it?" she whispered.

"You little bugger!"

Ryan pulled his hand from the back of the lining and held the small object between his fingers. It was a flash drive, no longer than a 50p piece. He held it up to the light.

"Now, I wonder what nasty little secrets this is hiding," he mused.

Eve felt a rush, unsure whether it was excitement or hysteria. "Shit! We'd better go," she urged. "It won't be long before whoever took the laptop realises that they're missing the drive. Next time they'll kill us."

Chapter 31

With her head pounding from the injury, Eve realised she was vulnerable. Thankfully both she and Ryan were alive with minor injuries, but it was clear they had been attacked by a professional who could have easily killed them both. As terrifying yet thrilling as it had been to meet an anonymous informant and locate the laptop, Eve had to admit that Fee was right. She wasn't a detective, and this wasn't a game. Whatever the content of the flash drive, it had unfathomable value, and someone was willing to recover it at any cost. There was now a tiny window of opportunity to disappear before they were hunted down.

"We've got to get out of here before they come back to finish what they started," Eve said. "I just need to get a few things from my flat before we can head somewhere safe."

"Are you joking? That's the first place they're going to go if they haven't been there already," Ryan replied. They stepped through the door of the lockup, then Ryan attached the padlock to secure it once again. Eve clutched the wound on the back of her skull in an attempt to soothe the throbbing. Suddenly a hand grabbed her shoulder.

"Aaaah!" she shrieked as she whipped round to see Fee standing there disconcertedly. Eve gripped her, pulling her close. "You frightened the life out of me."

"That's rich, coming from you! I've been beside myself."

"How did you find us?"

"There aren't that many lockups on this road, plus I used the Find My Friends app—it usually works when you're hammered."

"Well, I'm fine, really," Eve replied, trying to reassure her friend. Fee moved Eve sideways to examine her head. "Honestly, it's nothing, it's just a scratch," Eve said, trying not to worry Fee.

"You're bleeding! What the hell have you got yourself into? We need to get you to a doctor so we can get it checked out."

"Ladies, I hate to ruin your little reunion, but we've got to get out of here, and fast," Ryan interrupted. "And you need to turn your phone off, because if she can find us, they can too."

"Oh God, you're right!" Eve replied, switching her phone off.

"Hold on a minute. Who the hell are you?" Before Ryan had the chance to respond, flickers of realisation, followed by horror and disbelief, flashed across Fee's face. "Are you out of your mind?" Fee screeched at Eve. "His father has just been gunned down in broad daylight, and you're traipsing around London with this reprobate. He's probably next on the hit list!"

"I can hear you, you know," Ryan muttered.

"Great—not completely stupid, then! I'm glad I won't have to repeat myself." Unmoved by his retort, Fee turned Eve by her shoulders like a petulant child and marched in the opposite direction.

"Stop, stop! Look, I know you're trying to protect me, but I'm too involved now, and I need to get to the bottom of this. You know that I'm not going to let it go. I have to see this through."

"You've only been with this guy for a few hours, and you're already bleeding! I seriously believe you're in danger. I couldn't live with myself if I didn't try to stop you from getting yourself hurt—or killed."

"I know, and I love you for it, but right now we have to move, all of us." Eve's eyes pleading with them both. Ryan raised his hands in submission, and Fee turned to face the road, hailing a taxi. "Now that's the Fee I love!"

"Whatever. Just get in, the pair of you. But I think it's time we called the police."

Eve turned to Ryan. "Where do we need to go?"

Before he could utter a word, Fee leaned forward and gave the taxi driver her address. "There is no point going back to your place, as they could well be lying in wait. Hopefully, they don't know anything about me. You need to lie low for a while until it's safe to move."

"She's right. Rude *and* clever—who would have thought it!" Ryan said, narrowing his eyes with a forced smile.

"As obnoxious as I may be, *she* is the best woman I have ever known, and I will do everything in my power to keep her safe. For some reason, Eve seems to trust you, and I trust her judgement, so I expect you to do likewise. Because failure to do so would be catastrophic for you and your family," Fee whispered, trying not to draw the driver's attention to their conversation, glaring at Ryan. His silence offered no rebuttal.

"Marvellous. We have an accord."

Chapter 32

Part one of Amicus's operation was complete. Tony Taylor was dead, and Smith had been handled. It was true, she and Smith had had a mutually beneficial relationship, but he knew too much; he was a liability. For Amicus, trust was fundamental and once broken was almost never repaired. Betrayal, especially that inflicted by her former comrades and country, could neither be forgiven nor forgotten.

Butler had provided Amicus with the information to track Ryan Taylor, and then an operative from the Boathouse had been dispatched to recover the laptop. As Amicus awaited confirmation of its acquisition, her mind focused on the Geneva meeting. Paradox was a game changer, but Amicus needed a specialist to unleash its potential. Geneva provided this individual.

The message *Laptop acquired* appeared on her screen with an image of the laptop in good condition.

"Excellent." She tapped, *Go into the case. Flash drive stitched into the inner lining. Send image of drive when found.*

Shortly after, a reply arrived. When Amicus saw it, her

blood boiled. It was not the case that she saw—it was the sleeve that the laptop had been kept in. It had been sliced open like a loaf of bread and laid flat. The caption read, *Flash drive missing.*

Where the hell was Paradox? There was no point messaging the bagman; she would speak to her contact. Her future depended upon the recovery of Paradox. She took a different phone from her bag and made the call. She paced, waiting for him to answer.

"What the hell is going on?" she demanded. "You had a straightforward job, and you've completely screwed it up."

"Hold on. My agent did precisely as you asked. It's not his fault the flash drive was missing. You only asked for the laptop—which we collected. Maybe Taylor's son and his friend have it."

"What do you mean 'friend'? Who the hell was with him?"

"Lucky for you, my man took a photo when he knocked them both unconscious."

"Send it through now. This is not finished. You know what's at stake here."

"I am very well aware. Careful with your tone, or my patience will wear thin."

She was not going to let him intimidate her. "Then you'd better get this sorted quickly before it destroys us all." She hung up, ensuring she had the last word.

Vulnerable was not a feeling that Amicus had experienced for a while, neither was it one she enjoyed. To say that this was a monumental blunder was an understatement. She needed Butler. Within minutes of being summoned, Butler arrived in Amicus's suite. Amicus explained what had happened; they needed to determine the identity of Ryan Taylor's friend. The image came through quickly.

"I know who that is," Butler agonised, her fingers tapping her forehead. "I've definitely seen her before. Where, where, where?" she said. Amicus watched as Butler closed her eyes, trying to place her. "It's the barrister, the one who was prosecuting Taylor. Ah, what's her name?" Butler huffed. "Blake, it's Blake—Eve Blake!"

"Are you sure?" Amicus enlarged the image on her screen. "What the hell are they doing together? Is there something we don't know?"

"I have no idea, but that is definitely Blake. I am one hundred percent sure."

"We need to deal with this. Now."

If Blake and Taylor hadn't found Paradox before the laptop had been retrieved, surely they would have discovered it now. But Amicus was not prepared to assume anything. If they were able to decrypt Paradox, her entire operation would be over. This was not going to happen. She would not let anyone tear down her empire of associations and networks or expose the secrets she had amassed. This was going to be resolved, and quickly. As she responded with her final message, she could feel her rage building.

Go back and get the case and flash drive now. Terminate Blake and Taylor. Find them, and clean up this mess. No more mistakes.

Chapter 33

The rattle of the slowing taxi signalled their arrival at Fee's place. Fee brandished a crisp note from her LV monogrammed purse and gestured to Eve and Ryan to get out. The house in Wimbledon was on a quiet street which radiated charm. Hanging baskets complemented the red bricks; the glossy front doors smiled in the fading sunlight. Inside were clean wooden floors and monochrome walls embellished with expensive-looking artwork. There were also books everywhere, a stark contrast to Ryan's mother's house.

To Ryan, everything around him looked expensive, but he felt no envy. This was a consequence of enduring his father's inherent lust for money. Tony wanted to provide for his family in a way that was superior to his own upbringing and Tony was determined never to let his son suffer the misery and pain he had experienced. Ryan believed the ultimate cost of his father's desire for wealth was his life. He was not interested in making the same mistake. He wanted to break the cycle.

Being around Fee, who looked down on him with disdain and snobbery, riled him. However, he was an expert at hiding his feelings. He'd had years of practise wearing a brave face for his mother, pretending Tony's trips to prison didn't bother him. Eve, on the other hand, was more bearable. At least she was willing to give him a chance and listen, but now they were at a crossroads.

"So what the hell do we do now?" Ryan directed his question at Eve.

Fee jumped in before Eve could respond. "It's obvious, isn't it? We go straight to the authorities. You two are in way over your heads!" Fee thrust paracetamol into both their palms and began cleaning Eve's head wound.

"You're right, we can't do this on our own." Eve winced as the antiseptic Fee was dabbing stung the cut on her head. "We were nearly killed."

"No," Ryan argued before throwing his head back to swallow the paracetamol. He then shook his head, trying to get rid of the disgusting taste of the tablets. "If we go to the police, we might never find out what's on this." Ryan held up the flash drive. All three stood, staring at the enigma. "Whatever is on this drive is powerful enough to get my dad murdered. There are people on the inside, bent coppers, who will make this disappear."

"Now you really have lost it. Have you forgotten what we do for a living? We have both dealt with enough coppers over the years to know that if there is any wrongdoing, it's lower down the food chain. It is never high-ranking officials. It doesn't happen. You've clearly been watching too much crap television." Fee turned her gaze to Eve. "And besides that fact, it's far too bloody dangerous. You've already been knocked out once today. Enough is enough!" Fee protested.

"Eve. Please." Ryan saw a glimpse of doubt in Eve's face. "How do you think my dad got released? There had to be someone powerful on the inside." He had to deliver his last shot: "My dad can't have died for nothing." He searched Eve's eyes, willing her to agree. He hoped tugging her heartstrings would persuade her.

Despite Fee's earlier sneering, she too fell silent.

As his own words sank into his subconscious, Ryan realised he hadn't yet processed his father's death. His mind flooded with the devastation he had seen etched on his mother's face. His first thoughts were of her pain and grief.

The tension was broken by Eve, who moved to sit next to Fee. "I know this is hard for you to understand, and I know you want to protect me, but we've got to find out what is on this drive. I need to understand what this is all about."

Ryan looked on as Eve and Fee fixed eyes on each other, imploring the other to concede. Although no longer than a few seconds, the moment felt like hours. Ryan watched Eve as she seemed to wrestle with her decision. Then finally, she uttered, "So either you can help us, or we can leave."

Fee leaned forward and embraced her friend, her face flushed.

Ryan silently exhaled; his body welcomed the release.

"Can you think of anyone your dad knew who could have done this?" Eve asked.

"No. I honestly can't. I never got involved in any of Dad's

business—he kept me well out of it. He didn't want me to make the same mistakes. The Wheelers don't have a sideline in espionage. They're in the protection game with theft as a sideline."

"Why are you asking him?" Fee said. "He hasn't got a clue, because if he did, he wouldn't be sitting here with us." Fee's caustic remarks were now angering him; she was crossing a line. "Like he said, his father worked for a firm that used violence and intimidation to extort money. They're not master criminals, just scumbags."

Ryan's body changed from being awkward to confrontational. Before he could act on his instincts, Eve stepped in.

"This is getting us nowhere. I need to think. You sit over there," Eve scolded, directing orders to Ryan. "And you, get that coffee machine on. I need caffeine."

Ryan could see Fee was annoyed; even Eve's appeasing smile couldn't alter her soured expression. Ryan sat quietly, trying to replay conversations he'd had with his dad to recall any detail that might link to someone or something.

Eve stood and walked into an adjacent room, then returned carrying a laptop. She sunk to the plush white sofa, the laptop balanced on her knees.

If Eve was able to access the drive, Ryan was not going to miss it. He positioned himself next to her to see the screen. Fee returned from the kitchen. "Password, please," Eve asked. Fee obliged and tapped it in. "Drive, please." Eve turned to Ryan, who'd forgotten he was still holding it.

Eve inserted the drive into the USB port, but no matter

how many different ways she tried, she failed to access it. "It was worth a try," Eve conceded.

"It was never going to be that easy," Fee said.

"We need someone who can break the encryption," Eve replied.

Ryan looked on as Eve leaned forward with her head in her hands. Fee went back into the kitchen to pour the coffee. Just as Fee returned and passed her the china cup, Eve jumped to her feet, almost knocking the cup out of her hand.

"Jesus, Eve, what are you doing?"

"Oh God! Why didn't I think of this before!" Her words spilling from her lips.

"Think of what?" Ryan asked, bewildered.

"Not *what*, Ryan. Who."

Chapter 34

Smith decided to get out of plain sight and commandeer another vehicle to continue his journey. It wasn't long before he felt a vibration in his pocket followed by ominous ringing from the burner he was given at Afflecks Palace. He knew Butler would be waiting and monitoring traffic to the number. He let it ring twice to allow Butler to set up without arousing suspicion.

"Smith," he said coldly.

"As promised, Mr Smith. Once you have obtained the information, you are to bring it to the Manchester and Salford Junction Canal twenty-four hours from now. I do not doubt with your experience that you will be able to locate it. We will be waiting for you. Remember, failure to deliver the information will result in your property being irreversibly destroyed." She paused as if allowing him to take in the instructions. "Further to our earlier conversation, Mr Smith, this is a matter that is between you and us; therefore, the involvement of other parties will also be considered a display of defiance. Twenty-four hours." The line went dead.

The voice on the other end had been transactional and emotionless, the same woman he had met earlier.

Moments later, his own phone rang.

"Just give me a little time. I'll let you know where they are," Butler uttered.

There was nothing he could do but wait. In his line of work, patience was a skill he had refined. As a trained sniper for the SAS, there were times where he lay in wait for his target for hours on end, unable to move, eat, or rest. Smith also had to undertake many days, often weeks, of surveillance. His experiences in Iraq had changed him irreversibly; there were parts of him, parts of his soul, he considered lost forever. Smith believed this void of emotion and empathy allowed him to see his kills as a job, nothing more. He and Amicus had seen and experienced things no living person should ever have to witness. Ending another human life was not something to be taken lightly or wantonly, but it was necessary.

*

Butler worked furiously to pinpoint the exact location of the phone from which Smith had received the call. She wanted to help and get the job done as swiftly as possible to ensure Amicus did not discover her involvement. It wasn't long before she had tracked the coordinates of the phone and fixed a location.

The Ahmadis were on the outskirts of the City Centre, in Salford, in an abandoned property called the Adelphi Building. A former manufacturing site, the building and its adjacent plot of land were up for sale. From its brochure, the building appeared to be dilapidating rapidly, billed as perfect for demolition and redevelopment.

Butler dialled Smith. "I've sent you everything you need. The rest is up to you," she said.

"Thank you."

She sensed he was trying to think of a closing sentiment but spared him the trouble. "I hope that Zoe and Hannah are all right. I was just doing my job."

"I know." And with that, he hung up.

*

Smith knew his way out of the City Centre towards his location. As he approached, there were several side streets where he could conceal his vehicle. The building occupied a large corner plot and dominated the surrounding streets. At one point, it was a thriving factory, but it now looked tired and dishevelled. He scanned the site and found a concealed side entrance. The doors were not appropriately secured, enabling Smith to slip inside easily. The corridors were vast, with fragments of debris and dust coating the windows. There were three levels: a basement, ground floor, and first floor. The path upwards was congested with old furniture and boxes. Any astute captors would utilise a room that had viable access—up was not an option. He moved carefully around the ground-floor level, observing that a path had been cleared. He paused, listening intently for the slightest sound that would reveal their location, but he could only hear a dull hum that sounded like a TV in the distance. He stealthily moved along the corridor, checking each room he passed. Smith froze outside a doorway, then saw a figure on the far side of the room. It was Zoe.

He verified there was no-one else in the room before he made his move.

Zoe was lying on the floor, her hands bound behind her back with cable ties. As she rolled onto her back, Smith saw Hannah snuggled up against her chest. He quickly crept towards them, then knelt on the floor beside her. She was delirious and shaken, but alive. Hannah was still facing the wall, apparently sedated as she slept. He was just about to speak when he noticed something on Hannah's shoulders. It looked like a jacket from the back, but as he moved her gently, he saw the real horror of what it was.

She was wearing a suicide vest.

Chapter 35

Hunt and Walker looked on as the SOCO lifted a tray out of the oven. A layer of tin foil covered its metal grill with the remnants of what appeared to be melted cheese and breadcrumbs welded to it.

"Not a candidate for *MasterChef*, then," Walker remarked sarcastically. Both Woodside and the SOCO seemed immune to his humour and focused on the task in hand. Hunt, however, rolled her eyes, anticipating his comment like the punchline of a Christmas cracker joke. The SOCO raised the foil to reveal the object concealed underneath. He then used a pair of tweezers to gently grasp what appeared to be a passport. Walker reached into the box of latex gloves, taking one for himself before handing another to Hunt. He looked to Woodside for permission to touch the passport, which she gave with a conciliatory nod. The passport was intact, but upon closer examination, its owner was not Sean Turner. It was Steven Shepard.

"Right, who the hell is Steven Shepard? Are we sure that this is definitely Sean Turner?" Walker asked.

Hunt took hold of the passport and checked the photograph. "I've seen his file and photo. It's definitely him."

"Why would Sean need a false passport? From what you've told me," Walker turned to Hunt, "he had PTSD. He was in no fit state as a gun for hire, surely?" As he flicked through its pages, a thin white card slid out. Walker held it up so all could examine it. It was the size of a business card, with a symbol on the front and an extended number printed on the back. Walker and Hunt looked at each other.

"That's the same symbol that Smith drew." Hunt took Smith's message from the truck stop out of her pocket and placed the two symbols side by side.

"We've got to find out what this is. Your boys at the Met need to track it down, and fast."

Walker photographed the symbol before he made the call. He was not a quiet man; it was likely the whole building heard him dishing out orders. "Find out where Steven Shepard has travelled to in the last twelve months and what the hell this bloody symbol is. I'll send it through now. Find it and get back to me ASAP. There's no time for pissing about on this." He turned to Hunt and Woodside. "Nothing like a motivational pep talk, eh?'

Walker and Hunt said their professional goodbyes and left the building. They were heading to Zoe's house next to look for any scrap of evidence that could lead to Smith or Zoe's captors. Hunt's head throbbed. She was angry that they were always one step behind. If this was to do with Ahmadi's family, was this only revenge, or was there more to it? Was Nick's death linked to it at all?

She noticed Walker watching her as they moved towards the car. It was like he was waiting for her to share her inner ramblings. As he was about to speak, she blurted out, "I just can't see the connection with Nick. His remit wasn't to hunt assassins. I don't understand why he was so obsessed with Smith."

Walker looked at her, bemused. "Just give me a minute to catch up. Unfortunately, I didn't hear the first part of the conversation you just had with yourself."

Hunt took out her phone and saw numerous missed calls from Ashford with a message to contact him urgently.

"I'd better call in. Ashford is trying to contact me. Either he has something for us, or he's pissed."

"Wow, Hunt, that might have been the first time I've heard you properly swear. I didn't know you had it in you!"

"I have an edge, Walker, you just haven't seen it yet."

"I look forward to it."

Dreading Ashford's reaction, Hunt dialed his number. Ashford picked up the phone before it had the chance to ring for the third time. "Where the hell are you? What's going on?" He growled.

"I'm in Manchester. This is all linked to Ahmadi. Smith carried out the contract on him in Libya, and we think his family are getting their revenge," she stated, without apology. She respected Ashford, but he had no idea of the extent of her investigation into Nick's killer, and if he did, she would face severe consequences. He'd told her to let it go, and her acceptance of the facts was a condition of her return to active duty.

"If the Ahmadis are making a move on British soil, we need to be on them. This might be the start of something bigger. They're very well connected. Keep me updated, and I'll start prepping a team. Now listen. Check in every two hours, or I will have you back behind a desk buried in paperwork until your hair turns grey."

"Understood," she replied.

While Hunt was on the phone, Walker had returned to his car. He leaned against the edge of its bonnet, his brow furrowed as she strode towards him.

"I get that Nick was your partner, and obviously—because I've seen your flat—you do not have many friends—no offence—so you were close." He paused for a moment. "So why do you think, based on the fact that this guy is so deadly and no-one has even come close to catching him, that you can get any sort of justice or resolution? You're not going to win in any of this, you do know that, don't you?"

Hunt detected genuine feeling in his voice but quickly dismissed him. "I just need to understand why. I can't get past this. I have to know what happened." Her shoulders began to tense.

"I appreciate that you were close, but the chances of Smith spilling his guts and telling you everything are nonexistent."

She could feel her fingernails digging into her palms as Walker's comments riled her. "I know that. I'm not bloody stupid!" She wasn't naive. She knew that this was her last chance.

"Then why can't you let this go?"

"He was my friend! We relied on each other. Clearly something you wouldn't understand, seeing as no-one wants to work with you." She could feel her temperature rising.

"You think I don't understand what it's like to lose a colleague? Of course I do, it's part of the job. You think I haven't lost people too? Well, I have. You've just got to suck it up and get on with it."

"But he wasn't just a colleague. I loved him!" she shouted before realising she'd lost control.

The tension between them had reached fever pitch. Both had steadily moved towards each other. Now they were eye to eye, glaring at each other. Hunt was the first to break. She melted onto a wall opposite his car. Her head in her hands. Walker looked at her, then perched next to her on the wall. He exhaled with a loud sigh, his arms folded against his chest.

"Well, you've made a right cock-up of this, haven't you," he said, puncturing the silence.

She slowly lifted her head from her hands, exposing her flushed face. All she could manage was, "Huh." She smiled ironically, then exhaled with an enormous breath, releasing pressure.

"Come on, let's go. I think you've got some explaining to do." He nudged her gently as they moved from the wall.

Back in Walker's car, Hunt disclosed how her relationship with Nick had evolved. They had worked together for years before anything changed. It was after an operation in close quarters that Hunt felt a deeper connection between them. She had initiated, and at first, he'd rebuffed her. Nick loved his wife. Hunt respected his decision and withdrew her sentiments. Despite being rejected by him, he was still her closest friend, the only one who had ever understood her. She was in love with him based on their connection rather than the need to be physical. A few months later, they were ensconced in an assignment where Hunt had endangered herself to protect him. It was then that Nick couldn't deny his feelings towards her, igniting their affair. Hunt saw nothing sordid in their actions. They were kindred spirits, finding solace after intense experiences. Their affair was not about holding hands or a stolen kiss. It was an unbreakable bond. Their physical relationship was about release; their desire for closeness was to soothe and decompress.

It was not Hunt's goal to replace his wife. Ali provided Nick with a sense of humanity, a life that could be normal. Hunt had resigned herself to the fact that her job was her life. She was not going to grow old and grey, and certainly not with a soul mate; her days were finite.

"Okay, I get it," Walker said. "It happens all the time. Christ, if you've got a stable marriage and you're a copper in the Met, you'd get a medal. People who don't do this job don't get it. They don't have to deal with this shit every day and have to pretend that they haven't just seen the contents of someone's head plastered all over the floor. It doesn't make for polite conversation over the dinner table." His sincerity suggested he was speaking from personal experience.

"So is that why you don't talk about your family?" She

paused for his response, but he remained quiet. "Is there one?" she pressed.

"Once. But that was a long time ago. An all-too-familiar story. Got involved with someone I shouldn't have, and it cost me." Walker shut the conversation down quickly, unwilling to divulge more. He pushed the keys into his ignition and was about to turn them when his phone buzzed.

"Walker... Yeah, right, send me the details now," he said, then ended the call. "They've found the symbol."

Chapter 36

Amicus did not *wait* for anyone and was certainly not being held to ransom by the ineffectual actions of others. Blake and Taylor's involvement was now putting her entire operation in jeopardy. There was too much at stake; they had to be dealt with. Their deaths would be linked to Tony Taylor's assassination and passed off as part of the gangland killing. It was not a part of her original plan, but she was accustomed to adapting.

Amicus had worked all across Europe for MI6, in numerous guises, with increasing authority. She was pragmatic, helping to lead the way for many women in the Service, continually pushing the ceiling. She was recommended for a position within a cadre called the Reserve, where her skills and talents were fully utilised. This was where she'd met Smith.

Smith was Special Forces, selected for his exceptional marksmanship. The Reserve was a black-ops unit established to undertake clandestine missions involving the reconnaissance of vital intel, covert military assistance to foreign governments, and the insertion and extraction of assets and field agents. All of their missions were deniable by the British government should they be exposed. Maximum discretion was imperative.

One such operation involving both Amicus and Smith ended in catastrophe. Plausible deniability was enacted by the British government, and Amicus was dishonourably discharged. She was the scapegoat, singly held accountable for its failure. She was fed to the lions, who ripped and tore her reputation to shreds. Amicus understood the risks of the unit, but after decades of service and fierce loyalty to her country, she found her expulsion incredulous. How quick they were to condemn her and leave her in the cold. The world had changed. When she first joined the Service, they protected their own and valued loyalty and devotion. The clear lines that previously existed, separating their adversaries and allies, had blurred. Now no-one was indispensable; everyone had a target on their back.

It was then that Amicus resolved to never be made a fool of again. She had always abided by the rules and manipulated them when it was required. To what end? To be lied to and discarded by the organisation to which she had devoted her entire life. No, she would not let it be so. If she was to be successful in her own right, she needed to operate independently, on *her* terms. Her unwavering grit and determination had been rigidly instilled in her throughout her childhood. Her mother's stoicism was inherent in Amicus; her strength of character would now be tested to its limit. Leaving the Service was the ultimate betrayal, and something changed in her that would never be the same.

After what seemed like an eternity, a message pinged on her screen with an image attached. Its accompanying caption stated, *Part 1 complete, part 2 soon to be concluded.* The image was a body sprawled on the wooden floor of someone's living room. A scarlet puddle oozed from the victim's head. At first glance, she assumed that the task of terminating Ryan and the lawyer was complete; however, after closer scrutiny, her initial relief was replaced by horror. She pinched her screen to enlarge the image, and her gut instinct was confirmed. This was not the body of either Ryan Taylor or Eve Blake. Who the hell had been killed?

Corpses were part and parcel of her business; nevertheless, unwarranted deaths served only to confuse and complicate matters. From her analysis of the position of the body, it was evident this was not an operation undertaken with any element of finesse. It was impulsive and dangerous. In the background were clear indications of a struggle: an upturned table, papers and books lay strewn across the floor, and a wine glass and picture frame shattered as if ravaged by a tornado. The entire scene felt sloppy and incompetent. Whoever had been sent to handle the situation was obviously a fledgeling, unprofessional and inexperienced. As she studied the face of the victim, she saw his eyes glaring, like he was stunned by his unexpected demise. This was not Ryan Taylor. This man was clearly ambushed, his termination unfortunate.

Amicus needed to hastily establish his identity. This mess had to be managed; otherwise, unwanted attention would divert in her direction. The victim was smartly dressed—she could see the crimson-stained collar of his crisp shirt inside the charcoal grey of his suit. This was not someone who worked in retail or in a call centre. He was clearly on his way home; the neck of his shirt was unbuttoned, far too casual to attend meetings. The shine from his black brogues reflected his pride in his appearance, which added further irony to the scene. There lay a well-presented young man with his whole life ahead of him, sprawled on the floor, surrounded by chaos in a pool of his own blood. The smooth contours of his face and absence of facial hair betrayed his youth. He was more of a boy than a man, in his early twenties, in the prime of his life. Amicus was not without feeling, the tragedy of the scene did not leave her unmoved; however, sentimentality would be costly, and time was already of the essence.

Amicus picked up her phone. "I'm sending you an image. The location is Blake's flat. I need to know who the hell this is, and I need to know now."

"Of course, right on it." Butler knew better than to argue.

How could her contact have been so reckless! He had unlimited resources at his disposal yet still made monumental mistakes. Her trust in him was waning by the minute, but with Smith gone, she had little choice. It wasn't long before her phone buzzed.

"His name is Thomas Bailey. He's a trainee barrister, Blake's junior," Butler reported.

Damn it! she thought as she launched the phone at the sofa.

Amicus seized her burner phone from the table, ready to communicate her instructions concisely; there was no room for ambiguity. "You need to send in a cleaner to sort out this shit! It's not Ryan Taylor you murdered, it's Eve Blake's junior at Chambers," Amicus roared, her face red with rage as she paced the room. "Clean up your mess, and do the fucking job I asked you to do in the first place!"

Chapter 37

Smith was stunned. The sight of his daughter wearing a suicide vest paralysed him. His whole world was ripped from underneath him. He struggled to breathe as his chest tightened. Zoe started to come round; her eyes filled with tears upon recognising him. He placed his finger to his lips, signalling for her to remain quiet. Smith lifted Zoe towards him, her warm tears brushed against his face.

"Thank God you're here," she sobbed quietly.

"I'm here. You're going to be okay, I promise," he said with conviction, holding her face in his hands. He meant it. Smith knew he might not get out of this unscathed, but he was going to make damn sure that Zoe and Hannah were safe.

Smith took his backpack from his shoulders and retrieved a knife and a bottle of water. He severed the restraints binding Zoe's hands and feet before he held her against his chest. She trembled in his arms. He held her tightly for a moment, then looked at her to signal his release so he could move to Hannah.

He positioned himself so that he faced the entrance of the room, facilitating a clear vantage point. His senses on high alert, every sound was analysed. His Glock 17 lay on the ground beside him. Hannah was still sleeping and relatively still. He needed to examine her without touching the vest.

Smith had developed his expertise in suicide vests during his Middle Eastern tours in Iraq and Afghanistan. This device was comparable to those he had seen before. He was sure it was not yet armed, but he wasn't going to leave it wrapped around his daughter's body for a second longer than necessary.

The signal sent from the burner phone emanated from their present location. The Ahmadis were either still in the vicinity or had recently left. Their hostages would not be left alone; however, if they were certain their location was secure, they could leave only one or two men on site.

"Do you know where they are?" he whispered.

"No," Zoe managed to say. "We were just left here."

Smith handed Zoe the bottle of water. He could see she was dehydrated, her heavy eyes showing her exhaustion.

Smith had two options: find their captors and kill them, or remove the vest from Hannah, then kill them. Either one could result in the vest being detonated. Smith picked up his Glock and crept towards the door. He stood motionless against the wall, listening intently for any indication of movement. He had already checked the adjacent rooms before he'd found Zoe. They were not on this floor. His heart was racing. Every second that Hannah was wearing the vest was a second too long.

Decision made. The vest had to come off. Smith heard nothing from below; he would deal with the Ahmadis later.

Removing the vest would not be simple. He had to remove it from Hannah without killing them all in the process.

He had seen a range of these devices, from very simple to highly sophisticated. Upon first inspection, this one fell into the former category. Although deadly, its construction was rudimentary. It would undoubtedly cause the death of the wearer and anyone standing in close proximity, but it was not going to take down a building or crater the earth. Because it was unarmed, it could be carefully removed. This was not going to be a problem. Being patient and methodical was Smith's second nature.

The vest was black with pouches on each side. Inside the pouches were vials, all with a wire emerging from the top and silver tape holding them together. The wires from each side were wound together, linking both sides of the jacket. Smith did not touch the vials but saw they were packed with nails and broken glass. The colour quickly drained from his face. Its detonation would kill his daughter and seriously maim anyone within a five-metre radius.

All of its components were simple. They could be easily picked up at any hardware shop without M15 being alerted. The old cliché of "cut the blue wire" did not apply. Time was running out; it had to be removed. The weapon would still be intact—and viable if required for another purpose, or another person.

He gently lifted Hannah away from the wall and placed

her flat on her back, his hand supporting her head as she was lowered. The sedative they had given her was clearly strong; there was no danger of her regaining consciousness anytime soon. Smith blocked out everything and focused on the task before him. Zoe watched silently, barely breathing. He slid his fingers slowly underneath one side of the vest. It was heavier than he'd anticipated. Calmly, he began to gently lift one side, keeping it flat to avoid bending the wires. Eventually, the side was raised so high, it bent upwards. All remained intact. He turned to Zoe, his expression serious and composed.

"I need you to do something for me," he whispered. "I need you to come over to this side and slowly lift her arm out of the jacket."

There was no hesitation. Zoe carefully shuffled to his side and reached for Hannah's hand. Smith could see her eyes filling again. "It's okay," he reassured her. "You can do this."

His words had the desired effect, and she took a deep breath before gently removing Hannah's arm from the vest. Smith then continued his motion and lay the open side carefully on the ground, exhaling slowly.

Zoe was still holding Hannah's arm gently as the child continued her slumber. Smith expertly manoeuvred himself over to the opposite side to repeat the operation. Once again, he placed his fingers slowly underneath the side of the vest, lifting it carefully. He had moved it less than an inch before he saw the shards of metal and glass sliding in the vials. Zoe inhaled sharply, her eyes bulged. Smith paused, examining the wiring to ensure it had not dislodged. Beads of sweat trickled down his forehead; this was a different pressure, one that felt alien to him. He gently lifted one of his hands from the vest and brushed his forehead. Zoe was silent. He replaced his hands underneath the flap of the vest and once again began to lift it. Suddenly Hannah moved her legs and turned her head to one side.

"Mummy!" she uttered breathlessly as her eyes slowly opened. Her expression turned to terror as she saw Smith and her mother kneeling over her.

Shit! Smith thought as he looked at Zoe in panic. Zoe leaned forward and stroked Hannah's head, whispering in her ear to calm her down. This did not work, and Hannah began to writhe. Smith had to work fast. A flailing arm or leg could easily disconnect one of the wires or crush a package, detonating the device. He grabbed the little girl's arm through the vest hole and lifted her free from the vest. Smith carried her to the other side of the room, the child still crying, was distressed by Smith's tight grip on her slight frame. Zoe had also found the fortitude to move and followed him to the other side of the room, before taking Hannah into her arms. Smith knew the commotion would alert their captors, so he hid Zoe and Hannah, along with his backpack, in a dark corner behind a stack of dusty office chairs. Zoe had managed to console Hannah, calming her to a whimper. Smith concealed himself behind heavy, pitch-black drapes, ready to ambush.

It was a matter of seconds before a young man flew through the doorway. He was in his late twenties with a muscular build. Smith remained motionless behind the curtains, watching his opponent. His movements were quick, but his awareness of his surroundings was not sharp. The man stood deliberately still in the centre of the room. Within seconds, he spotted the discarded vest on the floor. He turned swiftly, his eyes searching for his captives.

Smith seized his moment and lunged forward, using the hilt of his Glock to strike the back of the man's skull. Disoriented, his victim fell to the ground, then rolled onto his back, grasping his head. Unmoved by his cries, Smith reached forward and grabbed him by the hair, lifting him to his knees. Smith swung his fist at the man's face. Its blunt force knocked him back towards the floor, and blood sprayed from his nose. His defeated opponent lay still. His eye and nose were rapidly swelling; his head swayed as if drifting in and out of consciousness.

Confident he had disabled his adversary, Smith retrieved his backpack and ushered a terrified Zoe and Hannah toward the doorway. As they hurried to leave, the man on the floor, his face soaked with blood, reached into his pocket and took out a small device. Smith knew exactly what it was.

"*Move!*" Smith shouted to Zoe, flinging himself on top of them, dragging them to the floor. But it was too late. The man moved his thumb into the centre of the device and pressed. The blast vibrated around the room, which shuddered from the impact. Smoke and dust filled the air.

All was still.

Chapter 38

The ringing in Smith's ears from the explosion was deafening. He coughed and spluttered as the dust filled his lungs. He tried to wipe his stinging eyes, but the grit coating his skin made it worse. His whole body throbbed. He could feel wet patches on his skin where his wounds were seeping. But all this was nothing—all thoughts of himself evaporated quickly as he looked for Zoe and Hannah.

When the vest had detonated, Zoe had thrown herself on top of Hannah to protect her from the blast. Smith spotted Zoe only six feet away from him. She was still. He scrambled across the chaos to reach her. She was covered in blood, surrounded by nails and glass. He knelt at her side and held his cheek against her mouth. She was not breathing. It was almost futile checking her pulse, he had seen enough bodies to know that Zoe was dead. He gently kissed her on the forehead and moved her hair from her face. The nails and glass had pierced her body, but it was the wound on her head from hitting the ground that looked to be the probable cause of her death. Smith had let her down. He'd sworn to protect her, and he had failed. As Smith stared at Zoe's broken frame, a searing pain entered his chest like a thousand knives twisting and stabbing. He struggled to breathe, almost like he had forgotten how. His body was frozen. His only focus was Zoe. Her skin was sullied with blood and dust, but she was still beautiful, she would always be beautiful.

Despite his torment, he knew he had to get to Hannah. Smith gently rolled Zoe's wounded body onto its side to release Hannah from underneath her. His arms trembled as he moved her, his own injuries impeding him. Smith closed his eyes momentarily to muster his strength, then prised Hannah from within Zoe's arms. Hannah's chest was rising. She was still alive. His eyes filled as he pressed her close to his chest. He was not going to let her go. He then leaned forward and grabbed his bag. Hannah's frail body was deceptively weighty in her unconsciousness, but Smith's adrenaline rush pushed him to lift her from the ground. He gazed at Zoe's face in the rubble, the pain in his chest taking his breath away, his knees beginning to buckle. Zoe looked at peace.

He would never be at peace again. It was not only Zoe that had died, but there was also a part of him that was now lost forever.

Smith looked down at Hannah. He had to move. He used his sleeve to wipe away the warm trickle of blood from his forehead that threatened his vision. Every fibre of his body was screaming in agony as he struggled to carry Hannah to the car. Hannah needed medical attention, but he could not stay with her. He would finish this. Hannah's captors would face retribution.

Although his hearing was muffled, he could make out the sound of sirens in the distance, knowing they would soon arrive. He hesitated for a moment while he racked his brain to remember where he had parked his car. Despite his eyes stinging and weeping, the metallic paintwork of his vehicle glinted in the sunlight. He placed Hannah in the back gently, quickly checking she was still breathing. He then eased himself into the driver's seat, smarting as he sat upright. As he looked down at his ripped, bloodstained clothing, he noticed a fragment of glass protruding from his leg. He grasped it tightly with his fingers, easing it out to prevent more damage, gritting his teeth as if removing a red-hot poker. He grabbed a spare shirt from his backpack, tore off a strip of material, and tied it tightly around his thigh to apply pressure.

The high-pitch screech of his tyres barely registered with his ears as he accelerated, desperate to get Hannah to the hospital. Confident that he was far enough away from the scene without being detected, he pulled into a side street and retrieved his phone from his pocket. He dialled a number he had never forgotten, a number that he associated with anger and suffering. As the phone began to ring, he closed his eyes, his silent prayers willing it to be answered.

"Hello?"

"It's me. Don't hang up." Smith could hear the sharp intake of breath from the person at the other end. "I found them, but Hannah's hurt. I'm on my way to the hospital. You need to meet me at the side of Salford Royal, and you need to come now." He could hear Zoe's mother crying as she learned the fate of her family, but then she pulled herself together to be able to answer his request.

"Okay, okay. We'll be there in ten minutes. Do the police know?"

"No, not yet, but we've got to move fast. I'm going to get the bastards that did this, Lynn."

She paused as a small sob left her body. "Okay, we're leaving now."

He knew what was coming. The utter devastation upon realising that Zoe was not with them was going to be horrific. But Smith couldn't think about that now. He had to focus on getting Hannah to the hospital in one piece. He peered behind him to check on Hannah. She was so peaceful, but her body was ravaged and weary. She was still breathing, but that was not proof that she was unharmed. Smith had experienced enough conflicts to understand that internal injuries could quickly be fatal if undetected. Every car he followed crawled along; his pulse raced as every red traffic light stacked his anxiety. He weaved through the traffic, and the car jerked as it mounted the pavement at the side of the hospital. There were CCTV cameras, but by the time the authorities could identify him, he would be long gone.

It was a matter of minutes before the sturdy family car raced towards him. Zoe's parents had arrived. Smith recognised Zoe's father Steve, driving her mother Lynn, next to him in the passenger seat. They hadn't changed much since the last time he'd seen them; they were just a little greyer. Their eyes still held the same misery he had remembered from their previous meeting. Lynn released her seat belt and jumped from the car before it came to a complete stop. She ran to his car and looked in the back. There was a brief moment of solace at having recognised Hannah, but it was quickly replaced by terror when she realised the second part of the story.

"Where is she?" she roared, tears raining from her eyes. "Where is she?" She launched at him, grabbing the lapels of his jacket, pushing him against the car. "Not my girl too. Not my babies."

Smith was numb. Lynn's fists were beating him, and rather than stop her, he remained motionless until she struck a shrapnel wound. Smith cried out and stumbled forwards as Steve grabbed Lynn by the shoulders, pulling her to his chest. She wailed uncontrollably into Steve's chest, her legs collapsing beneath her. "She didn't make it," Smith strained to say. "She was protecting Hannah. I…I…" He stammered, fighting through his heartbreak to utter his words. "It was fast. She wouldn't have felt anything."

"We need to get Hannah to a doctor," Steve insisted, taking Lynn's face into his hands. He then turned to Smith. "Go. Get the bastards that did this!" His eyes were full of hatred, his face pale. Smith nodded, acknowledging his demand. Steve then carefully lifted Hannah from the car. Smith stepped forward and kissed her forehead tenderly before Steve carried her swiftly into A&E. Lynn followed behind, unable to control her grief.

As he watched them disappear, Smith knew that this was the last time he would ever see Hannah. She would never be safe if his enemies knew she existed. He would not be responsible for causing the Turner family any more grief. They had now lost both of their children within twenty-four hours. They would not lose their grandchild as well. Smith vehemently climbed back into the car. It was time to finish this.

He reversed quickly and manoeuvred himself back onto the main road. He needed to regroup and determine his next move. Focus and strategic thinking were his forte. His injuries had undoubtedly weakened him, therefore having a physical fight with someone who was at full strength was not an option. He had to lure the Ahmadis into an ambush. It had to be meticulously planned to place him in control, at a location where he could manipulate the variables.

His first instinct was to contact Butler again. Amicus would now be well aware that Butler had assisted him because the Ahmadis would have communicated details of the explosion to her. He would be direct—he had nothing to lose—and send Butler a message to deliver to the Ahmadis.

But first, Smith had to plan his attack. He needed to choose a location he knew well, somewhere he could make noise without being disturbed. Smith thought back to his childhood. Where did he escape to? Where did he go when he didn't want to be found? Like a light bulb, the solution illuminated in his brain. Mayfield Station.

As teenagers, Smith and Zoe would head into Manchester at the weekends with their friends. They would spend hours hanging around the derelict station because it was quiet and they felt free. It was one of Manchester's best-kept secrets. No-one really knew it was there, and they were guaranteed to be left alone. Mayfield had been closed in the 1960s and never used again as a station. Most of the original roof had been removed after a fire, but there was still enough left to provide the cover he needed.

Amicus would want all loose ends taken care of—he knew her well enough to predict her compulsion to eradicate anyone or anything that could jeopardise the end game. It was time to send the message:

Mayfield Station, behind Piccadilly. Three hours.

Within a moment, the message disappeared. The countdown to his last stand had begun.

Chapter 39

Butler's stomach cramped as she pushed the keycard into the door of Amicus's suite, her laptop under her arm. As she entered the room, Amicus stood waiting, glaring at her. The knuckles on Amicus's hands were white as she gripped her phone. Her cold eyes and tight mouth only made Butler's stomach churn faster; she could feel her face flushing. "What the bloody hell is going on?" Amicus growled.

"What do you mean?" Butler replied tentatively; she knew what was coming.

"I *mean*, why the hell have I had a phone call from the Ahmadis claiming an explosion has just killed one of their operatives in Salford?" Amicus threw her phone on the floor, her rage crystal clear.

"I don't know anything about an explosion," Butler said in earnest. She paused, then realised she had to come clean. "He was desperate. He called me because they took Zoe and his daughter. Did you know they had a daughter?"

Amicus hesitated, her expression slightly softening. "No, I didn't." She stopped for a moment; this was new information.

Amicus sighed as she sat down. "Regardless of whom they've taken, it still doesn't solve our problem. You know better than to get emotionally involved. What were you thinking?"

"It was just one last time. I felt like I owed it to him."

"That was not your decision to make!" Amicus barked, her eyes bulging.

Her words hung in the air like a chandelier falling to the ground in slow motion, ready to shatter into tiny shards. Butler knew this mood only too well. She had seen it many times but had never been on the receiving end. Assisting Smith was always going to position her on dangerous ground, the consequences of which Butler was fully aware. Throughout her life, she had been true to herself without compromise, and if she had to do it all again, she would. Amicus's next move would be decisive, and it was inevitable that Butler would have to pay the penalty for her actions. Amicus was a methodical thinker and strategist, and Butler did not expect Amicus to be rash in her punishment. She would play her team to their greatest strengths, reserving her reprimand for a more appropriate moment.

Butler remained standing, like a schoolgirl scolded by the headteacher. Amicus returned to her table and drained her espresso in one. Butler knew she had crossed the line when Amicus took a cigarette from her bag; she only smoked when under severe pressure. She inhaled deeply before the smoke spiralled from her lips like a volcano ready to erupt.

Butler was uncomfortable making eye contact with Amicus at that moment, not because she was lying, but because she had broken their trust. Amicus had always trusted Butler and been loyal and unwavering in her support. Amicus had to understand that for Butler, the choice to defy orders must have been an agonising decision to make.

"Be under no illusion that your actions are forgiven. We will address this later. Right now we need to straighten out this holy mess that you have helped to create," Amicus hissed. Butler knew this light chastisement was not the end of the matter. She nodded, trying to demonstrate her repentance. "We need to get that drive," Amicus continued. "This lawyer is more astute than I thought. We need leverage if we want to get it back. Find out everything about her. If we apply pressure, she will come to us."

Butler complied without a moment's hesitation. She seated herself in front of her laptop like a virtuoso, commanding her instrument to perform with precision.

*

Amicus picked up her mobile and walked into the adjoining room.

"There's been a change of plan. I will be sending you instructions. This time, use someone you can trust. I will not accept any more fuckups!" she snapped.

"Do you realise who you are talking to?" replied the man on the other end of the phone. "I would be careful with your tone."

"I know exactly who I am talking to and *exactly* what's at stake. Don't ever speak to me like that again."

Chapter 40

Hunt glared at Walker, desperate for him to enlighten her about the symbol after his cryptic call. Although they had elected to keep Smith's note secret, the fact that the symbol was also left at Turner's flat meant that the police would now be investigating what it represented. They didn't need to know Smith's involvement.

"Well?" she questioned.

"It's not local. It's a bank, a French bank, La Banque Postale," he replied, in a mock French accent.

"Those digits could be an account number. But why would he leave us that? He's not going to lead us to money. He must have a safety deposit box there—wherever it is."

"London. That's the obvious place, surely?" Walker suggested.

"Nothing about this guy is straightforward or obvious."

They both sat in Walker's car and furiously dialled numbers. La Banque Postale's London branch's safety deposit boxes did not correspond with the digits Smith had given them. After numerous phone calls and much cajoling, they discovered that the box was in Paris. Hunt opened her laptop and went back through the records of Smith's alias's passport movements. He had indeed been in France within the last four weeks. She likewise checked the files for Sean Turner's additional passport. He had also been to Paris, although their visits did not coincide.

"If Smith has left us information, he thinks it's game over," Hunt mused. "Why else would he want to lead us to his box? There's got to be something important in it. How are we going to explain this one away? We've got to do this on the quiet—we need to access the box without anyone else knowing."

"So what do you suggest?" Walker asked. "If we're going to disappear for a couple of days, we'll have to leave now. Although how that's going to be possible with you having to check in with Ashford, I've got no bloody idea."

"That's what I'm afraid of. We need to work out our priority. Do we find Smith and ensure Zoe is safe, or do we get into that deposit box? So far we have no idea of his location, and we've only made it this far because he left bread crumbs. If he goes underground again, it's over. The next time we see him, he'll probably be dead." Hunt knew Walker's remit was to apprehend Smith, but this wasn't a straightforward murder case. There were more complex elements at play here. Surely Walker couldn't simply ignore the other pieces of the puzzle. Opening the box could be the key.

Ashford was the issue. He was focused on the Ahmadis and their UK network. He had no interest in whether they were after an assassin, but he was concerned with their growing influence. If Hunt could steer Ashford towards the Ahmadis and *their* movements and motives, he would be less focused on hers.

As Hunt looked out the window, Woodside was pacing towards their car. Hunt gestured to Walker to turn the ignition, then quickly lowered her window.

"I'm glad I caught you," Woodside said, bending towards the window and grabbing the frame of the car. "We've had a call in. There's been a suspected explosion reported in an abandoned building in Salford. It could be nothing, probably just kids messing around, but we're sending officers and an ambulance there now."

"It could be a coincidence, but I've got a feeling about this. Shit—if it is Zoe, she could be dead by now. Let's get over there. We need to be sure."

Hunt turned to Woodside, who was still leaning against the car. "Thanks for the heads-up. We'll get over there now." Woodside then proceeded to give Hunt the postcode for the building.

Looking at the Google map, it was very close to the City Centre. As they studied the images of the building, it appeared to be set back in its plot, slightly away from surrounding houses, with plenty of space to hold someone captive. Walker shifted into first gear, and the car roared away.

The traffic in Manchester was congested, and much to Hunt's annoyance, driving to the location took longer than anticipated. Unsurprisingly, Walker's road rage reached new heights, effing and blinding at every driver who dared to slow his passage. With every passing minute, Hunt knew the chances of locating either Zoe or her captors were deteriorating; her teeth gnawed her thumbnail as Walker weaved in and out. Finally, Walker turned into Silk Street and followed the road as it ascended past redbrick houses with wooden fences and satellite dishes. The bland, concrete blocks of flats that towered above were like any other inner-city area, nothing out of the ordinary. As they approached the junction into Adelphi Street, their final destination, Hunt noticed the side door had been forced open with an attempt made to reseal it.

"Look!" She pointed. "Someone's been in. Not sure kids would've put it back so neatly."

"How the hell do we get in here? Shit!" Walker slammed on the brakes as he drove past the rear car park. Hunt shot her hand forward to break the force. He then twisted his body to check the traffic behind him before he shifted into reverse and accelerated, swinging round into the car park. Hunt was quiet. Her bemused expression communicated everything. The Manchester Met coppers were already there, as well as the fire brigade, who were likely assessing the building's integrity. An ambulance with paramedics was waiting to be directed. Their doors were closed, protecting themselves from opportunists. Walker and Hunt were getting out of the BMW when the paramedics appeared to receive intelligence, grabbing their bags before dashing towards the building. Hunt shot a look at Walker. "Follow them," she commanded. Both darted behind them, their credentials ready to show.

Additional fire engines and patrol vehicles were starting to fill up the car park, each ready to perform their respective duties. The paramedics approached the building slowly, followed by Walker and Hunt who showed their IDs to the patrolling police officers manning the exit. They both looked young and enthusiastic, clearly taking their jobs very seriously.

"There's internal damage, sir. We're waiting for the go-ahead from the fire service. Sorry, sir, I can't let you in." He directed his words at Walker, ignoring Hunt.

"You've just let the paramedics in!" Hunt was aghast. She squared up to the officer, "I know you're following orders, but this is a matter of national security, and I will be entering the premises," she asserted before barging past him. Walker followed, and the other constable held up his hand to Walker's chest to try to stop him.

"Sir, I—" pleaded the other officer, his face flushing.

"Stand aside, constable, and remove your hand." Walker eyeballed him now. The duty constable removed his hand from Walker's chest and stepped to the side. Walker and Hunt then started along the corridor, the red-faced PC on the door using his radio to alert the control room.

Having searched every room in their path, Walker and Hunt stumbled through dust and grit. Both lifted their clothing over their mouths as they coughed and spluttered, their lungs battling the conditions. Under their feet crunched fragments of glass and splintered wood from the internal windows.

All the rooms they had inspected were abandoned, with

no evidence of recent human activity. Ahead was a black wall stretching along the corridor, part of it collapsed with firemen working to remove the debris. This was the place. They carefully manoeuvred themselves closer to the entrance of the room. After showing his ID to the fireman in charge and receiving a nod of recognition, Walker moved towards the doorway. Inside the room was carnage. The remains of an office space demolished beyond recognition. Charred remnants of chairs and desks lay intertwined with twisted metal and broken glass. The scene was utter devastation. Hunt moved to take a step forward but was thwarted by Walker.

"Wait," he said calmly.

On the floor amidst the anarchy was the body of a man. Walker gingerly edged into the room, careful not to disturb anything. Hunt was about to follow but was halted once again by Walker's outstretched arm. Unfortunately, Walker did not see Hunt's blazing eyes boring into his skull—she did not need to be protected. Walker picked his way through the rubble to reach the body, which was face down. Hunt followed close behind as Walker forged a path to the body, then stooped beside him.

"Ready?" Walker asked, hooking the shoulder of the corpse to lift him to see his face.

Hunt took out her phone to photograph his face. "Ready."

"One, two, three!" Walker strained as he held the body up for Hunt to take a photo. Then, his arms shaking from the weight, Walker gently lowered the corpse back into position.

Hunt shot a look at Walker. "It's not Smith, but it could be his work."

Walker took a latex glove from his pocket and patted the body. He removed a phone from the man's pocket, whose screen was destroyed, but there was no ID. The room was chaotic. It was impossible to determine whether Zoe had been held there. Hunt photographed the scene as best she could but knew that its value as a crime scene was lost. It was a dead end.

"We're not going to find what we're looking for. If this is Smith, he's long gone. I think we're done here," Hunt conceded, her brow furrowed in her exacerbation. She turned and trudged towards the doorway, and then something caught her eye. A shiver ran down her spine.

"Walker!"

He turned and stepped up beside her.

"Is that what I think it is?" Hunt pointed to something that had been concealed by the murky atmosphere. A light breeze from the windows was beginning to clear the air.

"What? Where are you looking?"

"There!" she exclaimed, her hand on his shoulder, pushing him forward.

Walker leaned forward, narrowing his eyes and screwing up his nose. Then his face dropped.

"Oh, God. I think we've found Zoe."

Chapter 41

Their exit into the clean, fresh air was greatly welcomed. Both had faced a long day, and neither had stopped to take care of their own basic needs. They needed sustenance. With Smith missing without a trace, Zoe dead, and Sean executed, they had reached a fork in the road.

Although not Hunt's cuisine of choice, the convenience of a drive-through provided nourishment and tolerable coffee. Walker was less particular and was content to satisfy his stomach with whatever he could lay his hands on. Hunt was surprised his arteries were still performing, given the amount of grease and salt he had consumed since they had first met. After selecting from the "gourmet" menu, they pulled into a car park space, the heat from the paper bag warming Hunt's legs. Just as she lifted the cup to her lips, Walker stopped her vehemently.

"Are you joking? What is the first rule in my car?"

Hunt glared at him.

"No food! She is a pristine machine. There's a picnic bench out there. You look pale, Hunt. You could do with the fresh air."

Hunt tilted her head backwards with an enormous sigh. "Really, after the day we've had, are you actually going to make me get out and eat at a crappy picnic bench?"

"Absolutely!" He grinned. "After you."

She turned to him before grabbing the bag, which rustled between her fingers, and swung the door open. He followed her over to the graffiti-covered wooden bench and deposited the food in the middle. As soon as she was seated, she pressed her lips to the steaming cup. As the hot liquid trickled down her throat, it was as if she could feel the magic of the caffeine beginning to relieve her senses. Walker positioned himself opposite, muttering under his breath in annoyance as he tried to nudge his legs underneath. After a moment he conceded and sat sidesaddle, as if riding a horse.

"That had to be Zoe. The fact that part of the building was a collapsed wreck is a surefire sign that Smith was there," Hunt said as she reached into the bag and distributed their food accordingly.

"He must have taken the child. She won't be in a fit state if that's what happened to her mother. He would have had to take her to a hospital. No father would let his own flesh and blood suffer." Walker paused slightly, and Hunt saw a flash of sincerity. She had no idea if he had a family of his own, but the involvement of a child had undoubtedly struck a nerve. He took his phone out and called HQ. With his usual directness, Walker ordered them to contact all hospitals in the Manchester area to check if the girl had been admitted.

"Smith obviously couldn't move Zoe and had to leave

her. If he's been looking for her all this time, he must be in love with her. I know Smith. He's not going to let this go. His next move is to take out the Ahmadis, so there'll be no mercy," Hunt continued.

"Well, we're not going to find him now. Even if he was in the blast, he would have sustained injuries too."

"It's simple, then. We need to access the deposit box and find out what Smith was storing and why."

"There is not a chance in hell that we are going to get a warrant to open that deposit box with any type of speed. If we want to see what's in it, we're going to have to bloody go ourselves."

"Got your passport?" she asked wryly. Before they could even think about getting to Paris, they had to return to London.

Feeling less than satisfied with her meal, Hunt collected their rubbish and dropped it into the plastic bin before heading back to Walker's car. "I'm going to the ladies' before we hit the road again," she said before heading into the building.

As she came out of the cubicle to wash her hands, she examined herself in the mirror. Walker was right, she was pale, and the fast pace of the day was wearing on her skin. She leaned forward and saw tiny pieces of grit and dust tangled in her hairline. She tried to loosen it with her fingers, which then created a grey snowstorm that fell into the sink. Walker must have seen it; he'd probably secretly been laughing at her. She doused her face in cold water, eager to feel clean. Hunt tried to tidy herself up, but why was she bothered? She was not trying to impress anyone, and certainly not Walker. He was abrasive and coarse. Yet he amused her, and at times, she appreciated his directness. Perhaps he wasn't quite so bad after all; she had worked out how to tolerate him.

Clean and straightened up, she was about to leave when her phone buzzed. It was Ashford, requesting a progress update about the Ahmadis. She quickly messaged him, explaining about the explosion and confirming she would provide a more detailed report after they had finished pursuing the current line of enquiry linked to Smith. Without waiting for a response, she replaced her phone in her pocket and left. Walker was hanging up when she opened the heavy door of the car.

"Any news?" she asked.

"Hannah Turner has been admitted into a hospital in Salford with shrapnel wounds and a concussion. They said she was lucky to survive. They couldn't trace Smith."

"It's getting late. If we stay here tonight, there's no way we can get to Paris tomorrow. I suggest we drive back down tonight and go tomorrow morning. It means we're in for a long drive," she proposed.

"Belt up, then, time's a-wasting."

Hunt worked out that if they left immediately, they could probably get back to London early in the morning and grab a couple of hours' sleep before catching the Eurostar to Paris. Smith always had a calculated escape plan; his military experiences had hardwired his brain differently. Leaving a note detailing his safety deposit box meant that he was sure that he was not going to need it again. Hunt could only assume that the recently renewed contact from Zoe and the resurgence of their relationship had unlocked a buried part of him. Perhaps, deep down, he had craved the love and bond that he once had with her. Hunt could relate to this. Her job was her life, and many of her relationships had dissolved. Close ties were formed as a result of intense periods of proximity and shared traumatic experiences—and usually physical. As Walker drove, his eyes fixed on the road as if hypnotised, Hunt regarded him surreptitiously. There was so much more under his prickly exterior. The sketchy details he had revealed about his family seemed to come from a place of regret and almost bitterness. From his behaviour, it was unlikely that he had any sort of long-suffering wife at home waiting for him to return from work late at night.

Hunt was confident she was as close as she had ever been to uncovering the truth about Nick's murder. She would finally be able to move on and perhaps provide Ali with some closure. It was good to work with someone else again, but in some ways, it reminded her of how much she missed Nick. He was the only person who had ever truly understood her. They had a connection, one that she had never had before with anyone else. She imagined other women would call her a marriage wrecker or fail to understand why she would not want more from him, but she didn't. Nick was her best friend, and he was always there when she needed him. Words could not describe the loss she felt when he died. She doubted Walker could understand this, as he seemed to have two methods of judgement. Black and white. There appeared to be no grey areas, and definitely no colour.

*

As they sped down the motorway, the rhythmic pulsing of the car had an anodyne effect. Unable to fight the exhaustion, Hunt gently rocked to sleep. Walker peered over at her, a wry smile crossing his face as her hair gently fell across her cheek. His quiet moment was interrupted by the single vibration of a message. Careful not to career into the central reservation, he cast his eyes on the message. After replacing his phone in the car door, he glanced into his rearview mirror. The road was quiet, but within the ensuing traffic, he had picked up a tail as they made their way south.

Chapter 42

The last time Smith went to Mayfield Station was over fifteen years ago. He knew from examining aerial images of the site that the roof had been dismantled; however, he remembered an old waiting room at the bottom of a flight of stairs that would provide the seclusion he needed. Smith had no idea who or how many would be sent to deal with him, but it would not be an army, he felt sure of that. This was his last stand. There was nothing left to live for. Hannah was much better off and safer without him. His injuries now weakened him. Blood poisoning, from the rusty nails that punctured his skin, was certain. Death was inevitable, but it would be on his terms.

Smith arrived at his destination quickly. Amicus would communicate the time to the Ahmadis; it would be in her best interest to resolve the situation expeditiously to minimise her exposure. His plan was uncomplicated but astute. He had neither the time nor the resources for a complex assault, and the last thing he wanted was a bloodbath. The only arsenal at his disposal was the equipment inside his backpack, which did not contain any sophisticated devices or technology. His two biggest weapons were a revolver and his intellect; he needed nothing else.

Mayfield looked very much as it had all those years ago; very little had changed. Its walls were plastered in colourful graffiti alongside the immense garden of weeds and brambles. The metal pillars once supporting the roof, formerly white and pristine, were now yellow and brown like an unbrushed set of teeth that had been left to rot. The carpet of moss that lined sections of its platforms sat alongside delicate ferns breaking through the concrete to create a calm wilderness. Although human life had stopped existing on the site, nature had claimed it. Dilapidated it may have been, but many of the redbrick structures on the site still held fast, with no sign of collapse. This was clearly indicative of how buildings used to be constructed; they were built to ensure longevity. Mayfield Station was an excellent example of well-crafted British engineering.

Smith had so many fond memories of Mayfield from his childhood, and as he walked back in, it still held the same charm. For him, this was the perfect place to take his last breaths. He would be at peace here. There was one particular building where Smith and Zoe used to sit, to talk about life, to plan their escape from their parents. Descending the familiar concrete stairs, he found it. It was still standing as sturdy as ever, tucked away in the corner. The glass in its windows was long shattered, but this left open vantage points in every exterior wall—perfect for detecting his enemy. Smith had to work fast; there was only one opportunity to get this right, and he was not going to let the Ahmadis escape unscathed.

As Smith advanced into his bunker, he calculated different scenarios and outcomes. His ability to rapidly scrutinise and take swift and pragmatic action was the key to his longevity and success. His objective was to inflict as much pain and suffering as possible so they could die knowing this was revenge for their treatment of Zoe. Smith was no saint; he knew that. Throughout his career, he had assassinated individuals who posed a definite threat to national security in the United Kingdom and their respective countries. Tarek Ahmadi was a perfect example.

It only took minutes for Smith to position himself for the ambush. The small sips from his water bottle were his final refreshment. It was the sweetest water he had ever tasted. The scarlet blood from his wounds steadily seeped into his clothes, like an hourglass, dripping slow and steady as time expired. There was nothing left now but to wait. His thoughts were of his girls, how he had failed them and destroyed their happiness. His death, and what followed, would secure Hannah's future. He took out his phone and quickly tapped one last message.

Tell her I died doing my duty, never the truth. I will always love her. Tell her I'm sorry.

His last moment of genuine sentiment. As the message sent, he realigned his focus. Smith was now in sniper mode, ready to finish the job.

Chapter 43

Haya Ahmadi had not planned to become embroiled in violence. She wanted to be a diplomat. She had earned a first-class degree in international relations while in the UK and aspired to return to her country to contribute her ideas and experience to effect change. Her family meant everything. Smith had to be stopped. Death was unfortunate, but Haya was a pragmatist, not an idealist. She was willing to do what needed to be done.

Her cousin Saif, the eldest son of Tarek Ahmadi, was the man killed in the explosion. The information from Amicus facilitated her plan to exact revenge for her uncle's murder, and now her cousin's. Smith was her target to eliminate. The information on the drive could wait a couple of hours.

Haya and her brothers, Ibrahim and Khaled, and her remaining cousin Tarek Junior, approached Mayfield in a blacked-out SUV. The street was quiet apart from one other car parked fifty yards ahead. Empty beer cans and takeaway boxes lay idle in the gutter, the din of the surrounding traffic a low hum. Before they stepped out of the vehicle and onto the road, they armed themselves, ready for Smith. They moved carefully towards the car ahead. Haya signalled to Khaled to proceed first; she was not about to endanger all their lives in one fell swoop. He cautiously approached the passenger side with his firearm ready, but with a wave of his arm, Haya knew it was clear. The rest of the group swiftly ran towards the vehicle and examined its exterior for evidence of Smith.

"There!" Khaled exclaimed. "On the driver's seat."

Haya moved to the window. "Blood. He's been bleeding heavily. He will be weakened, but we must not underestimate him."

Mayfield was like no other place she had been before. It was quiet, almost peaceful, an abandoned oasis with unrealised potential. It was the perfect location to leave a dead body and avoid immediate detection. Haya and her men stood silently surveying the area before them, hunters searching for their prey. They moved off the road and followed the concrete path to the entrance. The yellow brick road it was not.

The extended platform stretched in front of them, its rusty rails revealing the busy route once taken by its trains. It was open, exposed. Smith was not merely going to present himself; he would be lying in wait somewhere. The men turned to Haya, who signalled for them to head towards the stairs. Apart from Haya, they had all been in the Libyan army, following in the footsteps of their fathers. They had received combat training, but they were not quite in the same league as Smith. Haya was the strategist.

As they crossed the platform, they were vigilant not to let the pad of their footsteps alert Smith. The men ascended first, with Haya close behind. As they reached the bottom of the stairs, the stillness was unnerving. Her breathing quickened. The long grass gently whispered in the breeze: *Leave, leave.*

Dispersed, with their backs against the wall, they stood ready, listening. Nothing. The site was huge; however, Haya knew that Smith couldn't have travelled far. He was not playing hide-and-seek. Quick and clean were his methods, and she had no reason to assume Smith would change now. He would get down to business with urgency; this was the calm before the storm. The Ahmadis stood motionless, scanning and analysing their landscape.

Then she saw it. Moisture on the ground. A light spattering, easily missed. She stooped, with eyes still focused on her surroundings, then touched the fluid. The crimson liquid outlined the loops and swirls of her fingerprints. Smith was close.

Thirty yards along the platform was a former waiting room, its glass long since shattered. An eerie shadow fell from its walls, like a prison cell waiting for its inmate. This was the place. Haya signalled to her team. Each of the men clicked off their safety catches, readying themselves for battle. Haya remained in position, but this time she retrieved her firearm. She was not taking any chances. Khaled was the first to enter, with Ibrahim and Tarek following close behind to flank him. She held her breath, waiting for gunshots, but nothing came.

"Clear," Khaled whispered.

"What do you mean?" Haya hissed.

"He's not in here!"

Haya carefully proceeded forward, her body alert. She knew they were mistaken. They had to be. She edged along the outside wall of the waiting room, then tilted her head in through the empty hole of the doorway, desperately searching for evidence of Smith.

Suddenly, a dull thud came from behind.

*

Smith seized Haya. His arm tightly gripped her head and neck securely. She couldn't move, her windpipe crushed by force. Within seconds he lifted his other arm and, with his Glock, dispatched each member of her family, bullets cleanly piercing their heads. One by one their bodies dropped to the ground like toy soldiers, the silencer on his gun muffling his deadly aim. Smith had watched them from the roof of the waiting room, laying still. A tiger ready to attack. With the others dealt with, he disarmed Haya before pushing her to the ground, her hands clutching her throat as she wheezed and gasped for air.

"There is no need to kill me, Mr Smith, you have made your point." She struggled to speak.

"On the contrary, I'm just getting started," he replied dryly, before shooting her in the leg.

She cried out in pain as the bullet entered the soft tissue of her thigh.

"You took away the only thing in my life that was good,

the only thing that I hadn't ruined. This is for Zoe and Hannah." His words were followed by another bullet to her abdomen. This time she wailed, the high pitch of her voice denoting the torture. Smith grabbed her phone from her pocket and threw it down the track. It clattered against the rails before it came to a final stop.

*

Haya had no way of seeking help. She was alone.

Smith's eyes were full of hatred. Haya knew her demise would not be swift. With each hand clutching a wound, she lay on the floor, her blood steadily oozing from her body. One gunshot would have been manageable, but two was unbearable. Her mind felt foggy, and it would not be long before she lost consciousness. She would not die instantly; her injuries would ensure they took their time to ravage her before she finally gave in.

Haya's eyelids fluttered as she fell in and out of consciousness. She was anticipating a final revulsion, but there was only silence. She could only watch as Smith took himself to one side, turned his back to her, and fell to his knees. He lifted the gun to the side of his head, then squeezed the trigger. She shuddered as he hit the ground, her whole body cold and heavy. Haya could feel her strength draining away. Her eyes finally closed as she faded.

Chapter 44

Eve was wired. She knew she had devised the perfect solution to accessing the drive. Her eyes were wide as she stared at Fee's and Ryan's confused expressions. She paced around as she processed the thoughts running through her head, rifling through a mental filing cabinet, selecting and discarding information by its relevance. Her inner dialogue spilt from her lips as she connected ideas. Her two allies looked on in bewilderment as if watching her mental collapse.

"Seriously, can you stop moving? You're giving me a headache! God, it's like watching a wasp stuck in a glass. Are you going to enlighten us?" Fee demanded.

"A couple of years ago, Fee, you remember"—Eve turned to Fee, her expression even more perplexed than before—"I prosecuted Jamie Dawson for hacking and identity fraud. He hacked into the security filters of GCHQ and did some low-level stuff. He wasn't a bad lad, just bored and misguided. I'm sure he was put away for two years because he co-operated. Decoding this would be a piece of cake for him!"

"Are you serious?" Ryan was aghast, almost laughing.

"This is your brilliant plan? What the hell makes you think that even if we knew where he was, which I'm sure you don't, that he'd help the bitch who put him away?"

Eve looked at him, open-mouthed.

Fee was less offended by his comment. "Although it pains me to say this, I agree with him. Are you joking? I thought you had an idea that was going to keep you alive! Besides, it's completely illegal, and you could get yourself disbarred. Do you want to throw your career away because you think you're Nancy Drew? You need to put a stop to this right now and go straight to the police. We both know enough people on the inside that we can trust."

"I know you're right. That is the logical thing to do, and I would say exactly the same thing to you." Eve could see Fee was becoming exasperated, and she hated upsetting her best friend. "We've been through so much in the last forty-eight hours. Someone has died, and we almost ended up the same way. But we didn't, and I have to find out why. There's something not right here, and I can't just sit back and wait. I don't expect you to get involved, but I do need some help. I can't go anywhere near Chambers because it's too dangerous, so I need you to find the information that I need. Will you help us?"

What Eve really wanted to say to Fee was that she felt guilty, that she had played some part in Tony's death. By helping Ryan, she could make amends. Ryan had dragged her into something she couldn't walk away from. Eve understood the pain of a parent dying with no-one brought to justice; she couldn't knowingly subject anyone to the same suffering. But Eve knew her emotional response would be negated.

"All right, all right," Fee conceded, "but I'm not going until tomorrow morning. You two had better get some sleep. You're going to need it."

Eve took her friend's hand and squeezed. Fee responded with an exasperated sigh before she hugged her friend.

*

Despite the elegance of her room and the comfortable bed, Eve didn't fall asleep with ease. She had stayed in that room on numerous occasions, usually after having imbibed a liver-damaging volume of wine. Eve had never noticed the decor before, but tonight, its soft hues created a much-needed tranquillity. Eve lifted her hand to her head wound, which throbbed as her fingertips skimmed its surface. This was the first time in twenty-four hours she had stopped. As her head hit the pillow, her eyes closed, her body yearned for rest. There were a million questions that needed to be answered, but Eve knew there was nothing that could be done at that moment. Sleep was vital to function with any clarity.

*

Ryan shifted uneasily on the sofa, more concerned with marking it and receiving a savaging from Fee than anything else. He had not envisaged this turn of events; granted, he had approached Eve for her help, but he hadn't anticipated the gorgon to be in tow. Eve was a snob, but Fee was a piece of work. Ryan had stayed away from his father's work, never getting involved despite the Wheelers trying to initiate him into the business. Fee had assumed him guilty by association.

Under Eve's door, Ryan saw the yellow beam suddenly shift to black. At least one of them was getting some sleep. He pulled the soft duvet over himself, enveloping his body in a warm cocoon. Although she was a complete bitch, Fee had good taste in bedding. He then switched off the lamp, rolled his body towards the back of the sofa, and lowered his head onto the pillow. Just as his eyelids were closing, the squeak of a door opening forced his eyes wide open. The soft pad of footsteps then moved towards him. As much as he thought Eve was attractive, he was not interested in being seduced as someone's bit of rough. He turned his body around and could make out her silhouette, her hair brushing her shoulders. As he sat up, she sat close to him, forcing him to move back.

"Look, I'm tired. I just want to—" Before he could finish, he was interrupted.

"Shut up and listen, and *listen* well," Fee hissed. She had clearly not finished her warning; even in the dark, he could see her steely eyes.

"I have no idea why you dragged her into this, or what you think you can possibly gain. But if you think for one second that getting her involved will even the score for prosecuting your father, you have chosen the wrong person. Eve might trust you, but I certainly don't. I'm going to be watching every move you make, and I will hold you personally responsible if anything happens to her. You can wave goodbye to any future you might have had. I will finish you."

Ryan stayed silent and remained straight-faced; laughing at this moment would not be a wise decision. He refrained from replying as she rose from the sofa and walked back into her room.

Did Fee really think that he was intimidated by her stern face and pitiful threats? In her world, a wealthy cheating husband might have been scared by her words. But he had grown up in a different world, and although his dad had protected him from being involved, the people he had met were far more intimidating and terrifying than some posh lawyer.

Ryan returned to his previous position and closed his eyes. He finally started to drift off, but his slumber was once again interrupted by a scratching sound. Although reluctant, Ryan moved out from under his duvet to investigate the noise. He surveyed the whole room and found nothing, then crept towards the front door. Then he saw it. An envelope had been slid under the door. There was no sign of life from the bedrooms, so he tiptoed back to the sofa. He carefully opened the envelope and emptied its contents into his hands. It was a collection of photographs. Ryan strained to see the images in the dark but couldn't, so he crept into the kitchen, where the moonlight poured through a window. It took him a moment to decipher the content of the photographs—then he realised who and what they were. Ryan's stomach dropped to the floor.

Chapter 45

Hunt had not realised just how tired she was until she awoke by the M6/M1 interchange. She had been asleep nearly two hours, and as she moved her stiff limbs, she tried to stretch without poking Walker in the face.

"Don't ever try and be a stowaway on a ship. That snoring will get you thrown off straight away," Walker teased.

"I do not snore, thank you very much!"

"How would you know? When was the last time you 'slept' next to anyone for longer than twenty minutes before making excuses?" His response was met with a sarcastic smile. She was not a snorer; at least she hoped she wasn't. Despite having a short nap, she felt a little better, but her body craved more rest. The banging headache was not helped by the brightness of the streetlights guiding them along the motorway.

"Now that you're in the land of the living, look what we've picked up."

She looked in her wing mirror and saw a dark Audi

saloon further back in the slower lane.

"When did he appear?" Hunt asked.

"Just after we left Manchester."

"Any idea who it is?"

"I was hoping you could help me out with that one."

"Well, it's not going to be the Ahmadis. I think they'll be otherwise engaged." She pondered for a moment. "Unless Ashford has decided he doesn't trust me, which is a distinct possibility."

"Let's just let him follow for now. We're only going back to your flat to collect your passport."

"What about you?"

Walker reached forward and opened the glove compartment by her knees. "Always. Be. Prepared." He offered Hunt a triumphant wink.

Their journey back to London took another two hours, although this time, Hunt did not fall back asleep. She did suggest that they share the driving, which received a look of disdain, and Walker did not dignify her comment with a response. The first train left St Pancras at 5:40 a.m. At the rate Walker was driving with his lead foot, they would have more than enough time. The conversation between them during that final part of the journey had been on a lighter note. They shared their CV histories, more comfortable to discuss their experience than reveal information that was too personal. Walker talked about his transfer to the Met from the north, after being recognised as a rising star. He had been the senior investigating officer in a string of high-profile cases. Colleagues did not always appreciate his bedside manner, but Walker got results, and that was the name of the game. Policing had changed since he had joined the force; it was now all about targets and figures, doing things by the book, something that had burnt him earlier in his career that he had learnt from. Although well respected in his current position, he did not possess the finesse that those higher up required to be one of the Met's public faces, nor did he aspire to be one of the top brass. He was not willing to bullshit. She admired that about him.

Travelling through London, the black Audi was still in close proximity, although at a comfortable distance. He was not attempting to make contact. As they approached Hunt's flat, the vehicle slowed and parked further down the road. Its inhabitant stayed in the car. Walker and Hunt then entered her flat, leaving their watcher alone in the dark. Hunt quickly changed her clothes and gathered a small bag of essentials, including her passport. As she packed, she found an old jacket that belonged to Nick. Hunt took it from the hanger and lifted it to her nose. Nick's smell had dissipated; she was relieved. The last thing Hunt needed was to be distracted by his scent. She took a deep breath and passed it to Walker. "You might as well use this. It's no good to him now."

"Are you sure?" he said quietly.

"Please."

Walker discarded his signature overcoat and put on the jacket. It wasn't a perfect fit, but it was close enough. With the curtains closed and the lights on, they carefully climbed out of the kitchen window onto the fire escape and through the back garden.

At that time of night, all was quiet; the witching hour had begun. At the rear of the property was an alley that linked the houses with adjacent gardens. The end of the alley linked to the road where the car was parked. They needed to stay as far away from the vehicle as possible to avoid detection. Hunt had never walked there at that time of night; she'd never had to. Although most houses lay dormant, there were the occasional lights illuminated. There was a calmness. Windows were open everywhere. The heat from the air was not decreasing in the early hours, making it difficult for some to sleep. They expertly navigated their way through the jungle of foul-smelling bins, discarded takeaway wrappers, and broken glass to finally reach the end. But they had only just started. They needed to repeat this and head over to the next alley. Only the occasional car was now passing, headlights beaming like searchlights in their direction as they traversed the connecting road to make it through to the other side. Hunt's flat was directly opposite Peckham Rye Common, part of which was exposed. There were areas of shrubbery that would give them cover, but it was a risk.

The alley on the opposite side seemed to be a lot more congested; dog muck and rubbish had been dumped, without a care for its residents. The houses lining the alley had higher walls at the ends of their back gardens, making the area more concealed and dimly lit, perfect for someone who did not want to be watched. There were bottles and cans and cigarette ends, suggesting a group of teenagers had gathered to drink. A little further along were used syringes and condoms, another stark reminder of the daily struggles of others. Hunt felt a tinge of sadness. She had never realised that there was a microcosm of life beyond the high walls, individuals trying to exist; their only choice was concealment. It echoed her own life. She had survived in a world where she had to be a spectre, not making her mark or building relationships. Hunt was invisible—she had spent most of her adult life standing in the shadows.

Eventually, reaching the other end and rounding the corner, they crouched to remain hidden. They paused, searching for the car—then spotted it.

It was empty.

"Shit!" whispered Walker. "It's not going to be long until he works out we're not in there." His eyes darted around, searching for a solution.

"Look, there's a mini forest area over there. We can get cover under there. I've had an escape route planned through here for years. It was one of the reasons I bought the house. There are lots of areas we can disappear into and get through to the other side. I know it like the back of my hand."

"All right. I'll follow you."

They picked their way through parked cars and vehicles. Hunt was sure the pounding of her heart would wake the entire street. Her heightened state had been brought on by the resurfacing memories of Nick. She could feel the anxiety rising in her chest. With each small step closer to their destination, Walker and Hunt surveyed their surroundings for traces of their adversary. It was as if he had vanished. Neither was keen to hang around any longer than necessary.

There was something in the air, Hunt could feel it. The

midsummer heat remained humid in the darkness. The streets were still, the atmosphere charged. She couldn't put her finger on it, but something felt different. Within minutes, they had reached the trees and small forest area, Hunt guiding Walker to a secluded spot. The adrenaline pumped through her veins as they both panted from their exertion. They sat opposite each other, cosseted by an orb of bushes, trying to catch their breath. Moonlight peeled through gaps in the leaves, illuminating their hideaway. As each looked to the other for reassurance, their eyes locked.

Before she knew what was happening, they drew together. Their hands desperately searched their clothes for the warm skin which lay underneath. Their eager lips pressed together firmly as the electricity between them sparked and fed. She could feel the comforting prickle of Walker's stubble on her neck as burning kisses rained down. His strong hands supporting her tilting head as her breathing deepened. She arched her back, opening her body, inviting him to explore. His fingers expertly unbuttoned her clothes before moving to his own. She felt vulnerable and exposed, but Hunt's body ached to be satiated. As their feverish skin made contact for the first time, she could feel the exquisite connection between them, their bodies moving in perfect rhythm as their fervour began to build. Walker gazed deep into her eyes; she had never seen him more alive. With each passing moment, their ardour elevated before their bodies finally yielded. Walker rested his forehead on her chest as he sighed deeply, his final release. He then lifted his head, and catching Hunt off guard, kissed her tenderly.

Chapter 46

Hunt and Walker lay still for a moment next to each other after pulling up their clothes, their eyes to the moonlight, catching their breaths. Each taken aback by the unexpected spontaneity of what had transpired.

"Sorry," Walker apologised. "I'm not quite sure what just happened."

"There's no need, I was here too," she soothed, having seen his perturbed expression after his kiss. She was definitely not expecting that. After the rawness of their intimacy, he had been so tender, which completely threw her. It had never happened before. At no point had Walker even slightly alluded to any regard towards her since they had met. His words were always straightforward with constant sarcasm, not admiration.

Although she had developed a burgeoning interest in him, Hunt had never expected their relationship to take such a turn. Her comfort was that it had been mutual initiation; she could not be accused of seducing him, as he had also played his role. Her usual encounters were functional and fast. Although only lasting a few minutes, this was more reminiscent of her relationship with Nick. However, she was not prepared to expose herself to anguish like that again; it would only end in disaster, and they had to focus on their purpose. Hunt knew they were so close to finding out what had happened, she had no intention of taking her eyes off the ball.

"We need to get going if we're going to catch that train," she said, sitting up, completely changing the subject and refocusing their energies.

Walker looked at his watch. "Shit! We haven't got long. Have you got everything?"

"Yeah. Follow me, I know where I'm going."

"That's what happened last time, and look where we ended up," he teased.

Hunt edged slowly into the gap in between their leafy hideaway and scanned the open space before her.

"All clear. Let's go," she commanded, not waiting for his reply before cautiously moving out into the open.

Hunt had forgotten the sheer vastness of the park, seemingly stretching forever. The stillness of the night demanded that their movements were deliberate and calculated, avoiding exposure. As they quietly moved along the treelined path, it was not long before they were able to disappear underneath the covered areas, eventually reaching the main road on the other side.

What they hadn't observed was their tail, watching them vanish into the darkness.

The traffic on the main road was quiet. The vehicles that

passed transported single passengers, probably travelling to and from work in unsociable hours. As a street sweeper passed by, its brushes swirled like tornadoes against the pavement, searching for the debris created by the previous day. Taxis were unusually absent; however, it wasn't long before one appeared to provide a safe passage to St Pancras to catch the Eurostar. Timely, perhaps, but not unnoticed. The man who had been following them had managed to draw near, remaining in the background.

Hunt hailed the taxi, then collapsed on its back seat, breathless and full of adrenaline. The journey to St Pancras lasted approximately twenty minutes. Despite the lack of heavy traffic, the driver weaved skilfully through a fabric of peaceful streets. Hunt was sure this was a deliberate ploy to maximise his fare, perhaps after a slow evening. Hunt didn't mind the extended journey. It gave her time to recoup and catch her breath. The muted tones of Johnnie Walker's Sounds of the 70s filled their heads, Chicago and Elton providing their soundtrack.

Eventually, they were delivered to the drop-off point at the side of the station, the steadfast redbrick arches standing majestically alongside the modern glass structure. A perfect marriage of tradition and progress, each with its own unique beauty and charm.

Hunt purchased their tickets to Paris before they deposited themselves in a coffee shop where the baristas looked half-asleep. Their hunger was satisfied by fresh Danishes and piping hot coffee with extra shots. It had been days since they'd both had decent coffee, and Hunt could feel the buzz of the caffeine kick in quickly. Although it had only been a couple of hours, the nap she had taken earlier in the car had refreshed her. She was used to grabbing sleep in small pockets; regularly getting a full night's sleep was a rarity, and her body had adjusted. Walker was not faring quite so well. There was no five o'clock shadow; the dark hairs of his whiskers were more like a total eclipse. The dark circles under his eyes evidenced his weariness. Fortuitously, they were able to board the train well in advance of the departure time and located their seats quickly.

"You look like shit. Sorry, but you need to have your head in the game," Hunt told him. "Get your head down till we arrive, or you'll be no use to anyone. Trust me, we need to be sharp when we get there, or we won't be opening any box."

"All right, boss. Wake me up when you see the Eiffel Tower." And with that, he moved his arm to support his head and closed his eyes with a deep sigh. It wasn't long before he was asleep, the heaviness of his shoulder slunk against the seat. His phone seemed to be vibrating constantly, but he was undisturbed. Her first instinct was to reach for it and turn it off, but she did not want to wake him.

As Walker lay virtually comatose next to Hunt, her mind meandered back to their encounter. It had come out of nowhere, their hands all over each other, entangled within the moment. The intensity between them electrifying. It was raw, carnal. Then his kiss afterwards, so tender. He was not a gentle man; this was clearly out of character for him too. They had developed a mutual trust and respect, that was clear, but embarking on anything else, given the ramifications, would be senseless. Indeed, she had to remain focused. She had waited too long and sacrificed too much to falter now. The hypnotic rhythm of the train relaxed her, and before she realised, she had also succumbed to its rhythm.

It had been nearly an hour since her eyes had closed, but she awoke with a jolt knowing that they were rapidly approaching their destination. She had fallen to the side and rested her head on his shoulder. Carefully, trying to not disturb Walker, who was still out, Hunt lifted her head and rolled her shoulders so she was upright and on her own chair. Her stinging eyes and tight neck reminding her of the joys of rail travel. Her movement must have jostled him, because Walker then awoke with the same pained expression, tilting his head slowly from side to side in an attempt to loosen it.

"Jesus, I'm knackered! That felt like five minutes. I think I actually feel worse," he proclaimed.

"Nothing that a quick wash and a strong coffee won't sort."

"Are you okay?" he asked with genuine concern.

"I'm fine. I just want to get that box opened."

"All in good time. How's your French?"

"*Je suis plutôt bien en fait!*"

"Right then, you're doing the talking."

After stepping off the train at the Gare Du Nord, Walker stood, his mouth agape, clearly in awe. Hunt had been to the station on numerous occasions, but Walker's fascination clearly indicated this was his first time. They paused on the platform, taking in the enormity of its structure, with its high-reaching roof and row upon row of windows flooding light in. Its painstakingly maintained brickwork and immaculate platforms perfectly exhibited its architectural magnificence. Standing in the middle of it all, one could feel tiny and insignificant.

"I've never been here before. The French don't mess about, do they? No crappy concrete and cracked tiles here."

"Wait till you see outside." She smiled.

After they had passed through the guards and completed the necessary passport checks, they exited the main thoroughfare and headed to the other side of the road. From the outside, the main entrance was exquisite. Standing firm for over 150 years since its construction, the twenty-three beautiful faces of the female statues gracing its facade represented the citizens for whom it was built and designed to serve. Walker was transfixed by the spectacle before him, and although she did not want to disturb his reverie, she casually glanced at her watch, acutely aware of time.

"Come on," she encouraged gently. "I'm going to take you for a real coffee, then we're going to open that box."

Chapter 47

Ryan decided that sharing the content of the photographs was not productive at that hour of the night, although it now guaranteed him the absence of sleep as he contemplated their next move. Someone knew where they were and that they were together. They had not been careful enough; they needed to disappear. This was no ordinary organisation, like the Wheelers. This was someone else altogether. They were covert and skilful, traits not held in any considerable measure by the Wheelers. The photographs served their purpose; they terrified him.

Eve wanted to go and see some small-time ICT geek, Jamie Dawson, that she had helped to put away a couple of years ago. Her complete lack of insight into ex-cons and their feelings towards their prosecution barristers was unbelievable. Was she so naive to imagine that they would be fully accepting of her role and that "I was just doing my job" would merit an "It's okay, then, what else could you do?" If this guy was anything like the scumbags that Ryan had come across, she would be lucky to escape with all her limbs. He also questioned how trustworthy Jamie would be; after all, he was a criminal. Prison changed people in ways that Eve could not possibly understand. He knew this from his father. Tony was unrehabilitated having been through the system. He emerged from his "visits'" with little sense of recrimination, a sentiment echoed by the Wheelers. They deemed his punishment a badge of honour, part of an initiation into their inner circle. Once you were in, you were family, and families stuck together, loyal to the end.

In his family, Ryan had been the smart one, the one who was going to break the cycle. Okay, he was not heading to Oxford to be a doctor, but he did well at school and had a promising future. Ryan had seriously considered moving away until his dad was arrested again. His mum was heartbroken. He loved his dad but resented him because he'd failed his mum again. Ryan was her protector and would not leave her on her own. If Tony got sent down again, she wouldn't cope, despite assurances from the Wheelers that she would be taken care of.

Although Ryan's mind was whirring, he eventually drifted off, and he was awoken the next morning by the sound of Eve fluttering about. She entered the room with a forthright intention, like a Girl Guide off on an expedition; nothing was going to slow her down. Her words spilt from her like verbal diarrhoea, her stride only broken by her need to breathe.

"Seriously, how can you be this awake this early? Is it really five thirty? Jesus Christ, Eve, it's the middle of the night!" Fee moaned as she stood dishevelled in her doorway.

Early rising was clearly not a part of her lifestyle. Fee ignored Ryan and proceeded to the kitchen.

"I couldn't lie awake in bed any longer. I only slept a little while. I kept running things over and over in my mind," Eve replied.

"I'll have a coffee if it's not too much trouble," Ryan called to Fee. He couldn't resist confirming that Fee's dressing down had not intimidated him. He was sure that his audacity to make demands of her would rile her to the core, knowing she could not tell Eve about their little tete-a-tete for fear of upsetting her. Before following them into the kitchen, he concealed the envelope under the duvet cover; he would discuss its content with Eve later, away from Fee.

Fee had barely poured the water into the kettle before Eve started again. "Right, we have to get moving. If they attacked us once, we might not be so lucky next time. We need to get to Jamie Dawson as soon as possible. We've got to get to the contents of this drive."

"I still think you are a lunatic. What on earth makes you think for one second he is going to help us?" Ryan reiterated. "He's going to slam the door in your face. What can you possibly offer him that is going to persuade him to co-operate?"

Eve turned to her best friend.

"Oh no. I know that look. I am *not* going to bankroll this ridiculous plan that's going to backfire and get us all in trouble."

"Oh please, Feefee—I promise I'll pay you back. You're my only hope! Please…!"

"God, I'm going to regret this." Fee looked at Eve, who was still smiling sweetly. "Come on, what else do you want? How else am I going to aid and abet you?"

"Well, I don't think going back to my flat is a good idea. Like you said, it's probably not safe. However, I can't log on to Blackwell's network without my laptop to see if I can find a last known address for Dawson. So..."

"All right, I'll find it for you, but you've got to promise that when you've found out what's on this drive, you take it straight to the police. You can't deal with this on your own."

Eve flung her arms around her friend, nearly knocking her over. "That's why you are a wonderful human being!"

"How much do you need? A thousand?"

"I was actually thinking more like five, just in case we have any unforeseen expenses along the way."

"You seriously owe me for this one. I hope you know what you're doing. Right, it looks like I'm heading to the bank, then."

Fee logged on to the system remotely, and Eve accessed her files through the server. Eve emailed the senior partner and explained that due to the circumstances surrounding Tony Taylor's death, she was taking some personal time. As the door of Fee's house closed, Eve turned to Ryan. "Damn, I should have asked her to get me some clean clothes from my flat. It's okay. I'll give her a call."

"No—wait. There's something you need to see."

Ryan walked over to the duvet and retrieved the envelope from underneath it. He could feel the dread building inside him. Taking a deep breath, he handed Eve the envelope; his hand was shaking.

"What is this?" she asked, her eyes wide.

"I didn't want to have to show you these, but they came while you were sleeping."

Eve's eyes narrowed as she cautiously reached inside the envelope and pulled out the photographs. "Oh, my God!" she whimpered, her hand over her mouth. Less than a second later, the air expelled from her body and she crumbled. The photographs fell from her fingers, scattering on the floor. Ryan was not expecting such a strong reaction. However, his arms guided her gently to the floor. At first, Eve was stunned, unable to utter a word, her skin ashen. Ryan lifted her face to his, only to see her expression change from paralysis to horror. She buried herself deep into Ryan's chest. He could feel her sobs vibrating through him; he wished he could have taken it back and not shown her the photographs. He held her tightly, stroking her head as she trembled like a terrified child.

Eve's sobs rang around the flat as he held her. Ryan had no idea of how much time had passed, but eventually, Eve's body calmed. He hadn't realised it, but he had mirrored her breathing, which now became slower and deeper. As he held her in his arms, he felt like her protector, moved by her vulnerability. Now less rigid, Eve melted into Ryan's chest, and he shifted into a more comfortable position against the sofa to support her body. With her head nestled against him, he reached out and turned the scattered photographs facedown; there was no need to reexamine the horror. They sat in silence, still. Single tears trickled from her eyes across her now-scarlet cheeks. A patch on Ryan's shirt was damp where they had fallen. Finally, Eve released herself from his embrace.

"Sorry." She sniffed, wiping her face with the palms of her hands. "Devastated doesn't quite go far enough."

"Who is it? I assumed it was someone you knew because of the photo of you and Fee in the background."

"It's Tom, my junior from Chambers. He must have been checking in on me. He's got a key to my flat. I sometimes need him to pick things up for me." Her tears began to flow again. "He didn't deserve this. He's dead because of me."

Ryan turned to face her. "Listen, this is not your fault, and you can't blame yourself for this." He could see she was struggling, and it wasn't her fault; it was his. "Fee's right. I shouldn't have dragged you into this. You should go straight to the police and let them handle it from here."

"You're right. I know you're right." She sighed, her eyes swollen and red. "Where did they come from? You didn't have them before we went to bed."

"They came in the middle of the night, but I thought you needed the rest. Someone pushed them under the door."

"Oh, my God! So they know we are here? What if they come for us now? We've got to warn Fee. What if they're following her?" Eve moved to stand up, but Ryan held her arms.

"Wait. They aren't going to do anything in broad daylight. The photos were a warning, but we need to get out of here, and Fee needs to go and stay somewhere else too.

She's now on their radar. Pack her a small bag, and we'll meet her."

Eve hesitated.

"Go—now!" Ryan commanded.

Eve stood and started to gather things for Fee. While she was distracted, Ryan collected the photos from the floor and put them back into the envelope. He leaned forward to check that Eve was indeed packing, then reached under the duvet and pulled out a photograph that he had separated from the rest. A photograph Eve hadn't seen. He carefully folded and concealed it in his pocket.

Chapter 48

The images of Tom's body sprawled on the floor were trapped in Eve's mind. They could never be erased. She had never experienced grief like this; her entire world was irrevocably broken within a moment. Like shattered glass pieced back together, but minuscule shards always missing. Despite trying to block them, the images replayed in her head like a slideshow, their brutality intensifying. No-one deserved to die as a result of being in the wrong place at the wrong time, especially not a decent young man with a bright future ahead of him.

Even the loss of her mother at a very young age had not evoked these emotions. Eve had few memories of her passing; she had always accepted the way things were. As she reflected, her stomach twisted. Tom's family! For the last half an hour, Eve had been so consumed by her own feelings, she had not considered Tom's family, who would be devastated. She detested herself for being narcissistic.

Eve believed her mission was to help serve justice to those who had suffered at the hands of others. She adored Tom, so she had to continue to find the perpetrators and do her job.

Eve stared in the mirror at her swollen red eyes. Enough, she thought. She had to do this for Tom. His death would not be in vain. It was time to grow up and focus. This was not a game. Eve managed to compose herself and buried her feelings. To her great surprise, Ryan had been a rock. He had become her protector—maybe he didn't hate her as much as she first supposed, but Eve was now anxious about Fee. She had dragged her into this nightmare, and Eve had to ensure that Fee's life was not placed in jeopardy. Eve would not lose her too—it would be unimaginable. They were different sides of the same coin. Fee was the only person who truly understood her and told her off when she needed to be checked. She would be losing a sister.

Eve emerged from the bathroom calmer, but the softness had diminished from her face. Her hair was scraped back, and she was focused.

"Right. I'm sorry for that," Eve said firmly. "It won't happen again. I'm—"

"Don't apologise. Seeing the dead body of someone you care about is probably the worst thing that can happen." Eve went to interject, but Ryan continued, "I have been thinking, and I know what we are going to do next. If we just—"

"Let me stop you right there," Eve said pointedly. "I didn't become a successful prosecution barrister without taking risks and growing a thick skin. I am perfectly capable of thinking for and looking after myself. Don't imagine for a second that I don't understand what we've got ourselves into here. For Christ's sake, I've been dealing with dangerous scumbags for years—even managed to put some of the parasites in prison!"

Ryan's face begrudgingly acknowledged her words. He replied with, "So what do we do now?"

"Well, for starters, we get rid of our bloody phones. Anyone that can track us and know where we are must be capable of using our technology against us."

Eve held out her hand and gestured for him to take his out of his pocket. He obliged and removed the SIM card. Before she did the same, she frantically took out a piece of paper and a pen and started writing down numbers.

"What are you doing?" he asked.

"Unless one of us is a savant, I suggest we write down the numbers we need because I know there's no bloody chance I'm going to remember them."

After they were both SIM-less and phone-less, they would exit the flat and lose the people following them. Then they needed to get new phones. Before leaving the flat, Eve called Fee.

"Listen, they know where we are. I can't tell you how, but you're going to have to go somewhere for a few days until this is all sorted out. Trust me, I do not want to put you in danger. I'll meet you in the place we always go to when we win, lose, or draw."

"Oh God, Eve! Are you okay? I don't want to leave you with him—you don't know him well enough. Just get here as soon as you can. I've got your money. Just stay safe!"

"I'll see you soon. And don't worry, I'm okay."

Eve disconnected the call, collected her bags, then turned to Ryan, her red eyes fixed on him. "Now we need to lose whoever is following us, and we need to do it fast."

As they left Fee's flat, Eve took one last look around like she would not be there again for a very long time. She felt like crying but took a deep breath and turned away. They walked briskly down the treelined avenue, a gentle breeze rustling the leaves as if murmuring, *Move faster.* Eve looked behind her but could not see anyone following her or inconspicuously sitting in cars.

"They aren't going to be obvious, you know. They won't be wearing black glasses."

"Thank you for your insight into the surveillance community," she said hotly.

He gently touched her arm. "Are you okay? We can stop all of this right now if you want to."

"Look, there's a cab!" she cried, deciding to completely ignore his question.

She ran towards the taxi, showing her athleticism despite feeling drained. The morning sunlight shone through the window, dazzling Eve as she clambered into the back seat.

"Where to?" the cabbie chirped.

"Victoria Embankment, please," Eve replied. Ryan regarded her with a look of surprise.

"Doing a bit of sightseeing?" the cabbie enquired.

"Something like that." She turned to Ryan, whose brow had furrowed. Eve was not going to reveal her intentions when she had no idea who the driver was. She then had a thought."Actually, can I change my mind. Please, can you take us to the tube station instead? There's a couple of stops I want to make first."

"Are you sure? I can get you there in no time."

"No, just the station, please."

Within minutes, they arrived at the station. Ryan stood with his arms crossed, huffing. "What the hell was that about? Why did we get out?"

"I couldn't be sure who he was. He could have been a cabbie, or he could have been one of them."

"Now you are paranoid. You've been watching too many films."

"Say what you like, but I'm taking back control."

Eve and Ryan looked at the map, and Ryan traced his finger over the District Line until it reached Victoria Embankment.

"Nope, we need to change at Notting Hill Gate." She moved his hand upwards towards the Central Line.

"I thought you wanted to go to Victoria Embankment?"

"It's where the Met is, but no, we aren't going there. That's where *they* think we're going."

"Okay, mastermind. Where are we going?"

Eve could see Ryan was getting exasperated as he rolled his eyes and shook his head. She moved his fingers over to their destination. "Right here!"

*

The cabbie drove away out of sight, pulled into a lay-by in a nearby street, then picked up his radio. "They're just about to get on the tube—they're heading to Victoria Embankment. I think they're going to the Met."

Chapter 49

"Well, you weren't wrong," Walker proclaimed. "That was the best coffee I've had in a week."

"You can't beat Parisian coffee. They know how to make it properly." Hunt and Walker were seated at a kerbside cafe, the plastic chairs and tables fixed to the floor, with large bi-folding doors opening to the street. Although not glamorous, it was simple and the ideal location from which to watch Paris wake up. The gentle hum of the traffic and ping of bicycle bells created the perfect early morning ambience; the aroma of fresh bread and pastries filled the air. Hunt and Walker indulged, although Walker was wearing half of the crumbs down the front of his jacket.

"Don't suppose you get much time to go on holiday?" he asked.

"I'm not a lying-by-the-pool sort of person. I get bored." She sipped her coffee with delight, savouring every delicious mouthful. "You know what it's like—you can't switch off. Even when you might get a couple of days, something always happens to bring you back in."

"I like the idea of time off," he replied, "but after a few days, I get restless. I'd rather stay at home than have to contend with the masses on some cramped, sweaty plane. However, Paris is turning out to be quite a revelation. Nature calls!" he said before rising and heading to the bathroom, leaving his jacket slung on the back of his chair. She could see that he still had half the pastry stuck to the front of it, so she started to brush it off, although it appeared to be tethered to the fibres. Gently sweeping was having no effect, so she picked it up and shook it to try to dislodge the flakes. As the coat rippled, his mobile fell out of his pocket. A message was waiting for him: *BQH 1600*. She had no idea what it was about, and perhaps it was none of her business. Recognising the familiar sound of his clicking heels, she covertly slipped the phone back into his pocket and replaced his coat on the chair. She had no time to process it now.

Hunt drained the last of her cup before wiping her lips with a napkin. "Ready?" she asked.

"*Oui.*"

"*Tres bien!*"

"All right, let's not get too excited."

There were numerous branches of La Banque Postale in Paris, many of which were small and used for everyday financial services and transactions. The branch Smith had chosen was called La Postale Siege Social—quite the irony, one Hunt was sure was not wasted on Smith. Its exterior, in true Parisian style, fused traditional architecture with modern engineering. An enormous glass structure stood adjacent to a beautifully constructed building surrounded by cast-iron gates, which created a timeless elegance. Standing on the pavement opposite the structure, they were dwarfed by its enormity.

"We need to get into this bloody box. The French can be a real pain in the arse, and I have no idea if they will accept our ID cards as collateral. We may need to play this one differently," Walker contemplated.

"I'll handle this. Just follow me."

"Okay, but we've only got one shot at this. We can't fuck it up."

"Calm down, I know what I'm doing. Right, sort your hair out, we can't go in with you looking like a complete tramp," she said.

He stooped down to check himself in a parked car's wing mirror. "Funny!"

Despite its impressive outward expanse, internally the foyer area looked like many other banks with its grey monotone walls and glass dividers. There was a line of counters to one side, with meeting hubs and internet facilities on the other. At the far end appeared to be a premier banking section with a member of staff on hand to deal with queries. Hunt knew this was where they needed to be.

"Over there. They aren't going to deal with deposit boxes over the counter," she stated, not waiting for his reply before striding forward. The attendant was a young man in his early thirties, immaculately dressed in a perfectly fitting grey suit, not a hair out of place. As the pair approached, his smile seemed to radiate from ear to ear.

"*Bonjour, mademoiselle*," he greeted.

"*Bonjour. Pourriez-vous m'aider s'il vous plait. Je...*"

"How can I help you today?" he responded with a head tilt as if to say, "I knew you were English when you walked in."

"Oh, thank you. We are officers of the British Police and Security Services. We need to access one of your safety deposit boxes as part of an ongoing investigation." As she spoke, both brandished their IDs and passed them to him.

He examined their cards. "I am afraid I will have to contact my superior to speak to you. Do you have the account number you wish to access?"

Hunt handed him a piece of paper with the account number written on it; she had been sensible enough to write it on a fresh piece of paper.

"Please take a seat. I will return shortly."

The air conditioning, even first thing in the morning, breezed through the foyer, sending a chill through Hunt. Neither uttered a word as they waited, taking in the hustle and bustle. The minutes passed at a snail's pace, and Walker was shifting in his seat. It was a good fifteen minutes before the attendant returned, this time bringing with him another gentleman. He was also well groomed but slightly older, his salt-and-pepper hair adding a certain distinction. He had an air of quiet authority as he glided towards them.

"Good morning, Agent Hunt, Detective Chief Inspector Walker. I am Monsieur Chauvin, and I am the manager here at La Banque Postale." He smiled, shaking each of their hands before returning their ID cards. "Please follow me, so we can talk with a little more privacy." He gestured to a private room set away from the main foyer.

They followed him down the hallway and stopped at the last door. In the centre of the room was a polished wooden table, the natural light from the window reflecting off its surface. Its walls were embellished with a collection of black-and-white framed photographs, each depicting significant landmarks in Paris, with the centrepiece the glorious Eiffel Tower. He held out his arm, signalling for them to take a seat.

"Now, concerning your request to access one of our accounts' deposit boxes, I must first share this with you." Hunt and Walker braced themselves for a lecture on legal protocols and their lack of jurisdiction to access the account on French soil.

Hunt interjected before he could finish. "I appreciate that this request is somewhat unusual, and I also understand that you will have established security procedures for opening the box of an account holder without their consent. However, it is a matter of national security that we examine the contents of that box as soon as possible."

"On the contrary, Agent Hunt, please listen to the information that I must convey to you," he replied calmly. "Monsieur Smith is an excellent client of ours and has been for many years. Approximately three weeks ago, he made a visit to this branch detailing a set of precise instructions. I met with him personally. It was as if he had predicted your request," he said, almost with amusement. Walker and Hunt turned to one another in disbelief. How had he anticipated that this was going to happen? Hunt wondered as Chauvin continued.

"He made his intentions very clear and asked me to personally handle his affairs. His instructions were to allow Agent Hunt access to the box, should she arrive, on one condition—that she must carry out the instructions contained within it at his behest." Chauvin smiled and paused, waiting for her response. Relief washed over her, as she was finally going to get to the bottom of everything that had happened. "Are you in agreement with the conditions, Agent Hunt?" he queried.

She turned to Walker, who simply raised his eyebrows.

"Absolutely," she confirmed.

"Then please follow me," he instructed. Walker and Hunt stood and made for the door.

"I must apologise, DCI Walker, my instructions were very clear. Agent Hunt alone must access the box. On this point there is no negotiation. You must remain here, or I cannot allow access at all." Hunt glanced at Walker, feeling guilty that he was not permitted to be in the room when the box was opened. Ever since their moment of intimacy, she had felt closer to him, and part of her did not want to go down alone. They had become partners.

Frustration etched on his face, Walker conceded. "Fine. I can wait." He gave Hunt a slight nod to tell her it was okay.

"Thank you for your co-operation. Can I offer you a drink?"

"Water."

"Not a problem. Agent Hunt, this way, please."

Chapter 50

Ryan leaned forward to check where Eve was pointing on the tube map. "Oxford Street? What the hell are we going there for?"

"We need new phones. We've got to get to a place that's swarming with people so it's harder to follow us. It's the busiest part of London," Eve replied.

"We need to move from here. We're blocking the way," Ryan said as he was nudged and pushed by apologetic travellers and huffing commuters.

"Just wait. We need to stay here because there's no CCTV in this small spot. I checked as we were coming down." She reached into her bag and pulled out a light jacket and two caps.

"Put this on. We've got to try to change our appearance." She handed him a baseball cap. Eve put on the jacket, then wound her hair under her cap. She did look a little different, not impossible to spot, but it might buy them a little time. As Eve stepped towards the platform, Ryan grabbed her arm.

"We need to split up. You go on the first carriage, I'll

follow after. But don't look at me. I'll get off at Oxford Circus and meet you in—"

"John Lewis," she said quickly.

"Fine."

Then Eve made her move, and Ryan followed a few seconds later, positioning himself further down the platform, minutes before the tube arrived. As they waited, the platform became congested. Eve made sure not to raise her head for fear of being caught on CCTV. She could feel the rush of adrenaline through her veins, sure that she was being watched. Eve tried not to make eye contact with anyone but felt as if hundreds of eyes were boring into the back of her head. Her cap nearly lifted off her head as the rush of warm air signalled the tube's arrival. The tinny screech of its wheels on the rails faded as the train came to a halt; the rapid pipping of the door chimes warned her to be ready to embark. As the swell of travellers advanced, she was carried along. She positioned herself by the door, her face pointed towards the floor.

Subtly, Eve's eyes searched for Ryan in the next carriage. He wasn't there. Damn! she thought. Panic then set in. Where the hell was he? God, he had suggested splitting up, but she hadn't realised it was because he wanted to lose her. Suddenly, her stomach hit the floor, and she thought she was going to vomit. Did he take the flash drive? Eve was about to start patting herself down when her sensibility kicked in; moving frantically would draw unnecessary attention. Her hand subtly moved to her shoulder, where she brushed the side of her breast. It was still in there, in her bra, where she had concealed it earlier. Eve closed her eyes, a wave of gratitude flowed over her, but the cogs were turning in her brain, formulating her next move. As she panicked about Ryan, she noticed a man in the next carriage move from the tube door. He manoeuvred past the Perspex panel into a vacant seat, then she saw Ryan standing in the corner. He was doing exactly as he said he would, standing quietly with his head down.

She felt guilty. How could she be so quick to condemn him? Since they had met, he had done nothing to betray her trust. He had gone along with her ideas and comforted her when she had learnt about Tom. Despite his father being heavily involved in organised crime, Ryan's actions had been honest. Although her senses were heightened, her body loosened a little, relieved that she was not alone.

Eve had never counted the number of stops to Notting Hill Gate until now. Claustrophobia was not something she suffered from, but the tight grip she had on the metal handrail told her otherwise. The station announcer gave enthusiastic instructions on how to change to the Central and Circle Lines as the majority of the other passengers rose to their feet. Eve could see Ryan advancing towards the doors, surrounded by people. They both stepped from the train and strode in the direction of the exit. The fluorescent lighting reflected off the alabaster-tiled walls, shining a torchlight to guide them to the Central Line to rejoin the tube to Oxford Circus. The throng shuffled to the Circle Line, where the next tube was waiting to depart. Once again, in separate carriages, they stood facing away from the cameras. Within minutes they arrived at Oxford Circus.

Like cattle, they herded towards the ticket machines to pass through the turnstiles. Eve had insisted they use cash to buy tickets. Oyster Cards could be tracked; she had used this feature before as a piece of evidence to convict. Eve inhaled sharply as she finally stepped outside, relieved to be in the open space, however busy it was. Fresher than the underground cocktail of smells, above ground, the air reeked of fumes from the never-ending flow of taxis and buses. Bike messengers weaved in and out of the traffic like mice escaping a chasing cat, dicing with their lives. Shoppers laden with bags trudged from one store to another, men stood outside Googling, checking messages, waiting for the torture to end. Eve could see John Lewis ahead and hadn't laid eyes on Ryan, but it was easy to lose him leaving the station. The last time she had been in Oxford Street was only two weeks ago when she and Fee had met in Harvey Nic's Champagne Bar for some post-retail therapy. That moment now seemed a world away.

Eve arrived on the pavement outside John Lewis. She walked through the sliding doors and made her way to one of the sunglasses stands, waiting for Ryan to appear. She could hear the pad of his trainers slightly squeaking on the floor as he arrived.

"Okay?" he said, touching her arm gently.

"Okay," she replied.

"There's a mobile phone shop just down the street," Ryan suggested as Eve nodded in agreement. "But hang on, how are we going to pay for this stuff if they're tracing your cards?"

"I've already thought of that." She reached into her pocket and pulled out a credit card. As he read the name, he smiled.

"If she knows you've taken her card as well as asking her for money, she's going to go mental," he warned.

"Fee and I have used each other's cards on numerous occasions when we've needed to. We trust each other with our lives. It's not going to be a problem—I thought you might have gathered that by now."

"Whatever. But I want it noted for the record, or whatever you lawyers call it, that I said this was a bad idea."

"Noted. I'm going to go to a cash point, anyway. It would definitely look weird if I paid for two new phones and SIMs that are pay as you go. I'll buy mine with the card, you can pay cash. Come on, we've got to get moving. We said we'd meet Fee to collect the money, and we're already going to be late."

Eve withdrew the cash they needed, then each purchased their phone separately. Eve was more at ease now that they had changed their phones and moved to a busy location. It was time to get to Fee, knowing she would be furious and worried because they were late.

Whenever Eve finished a case—or sometimes during, if it was particularly gruelling—she would meet Fee for solace and counsel at their favourite drinking hole. It was far enough away from the courts to avoid meeting their counterparts. Scarfes Bar in the Rosewood Hotel was their place. Its walls were embellished with caricatures of modern culture, their whimsical content inspiring debate and amusement for its clientele, who arranged themselves on elegant velvet chairs. Others positioned themselves next to the roaring fire, hypnotised by its dancing flames. Leather Chesterfields were furnished with plush cushions, with mahogany tables beautifully complementing the wood panelling and ornate bookcases. Eve's favourite position was in the corner. They would slip their shoes off under the table and lift their weary legs onto the soft grey sofa. From there, they could enjoy the spectacle of people watching.

As they entered the bar, Fee was in their usual spot. She rose from her seat and threw her arms around Eve, gripping her tightly. Fee was pale and looked like she'd been crying.

"Are you okay? You look awful." Eve looked into her best friend's eyes with concern.

"God, of course, you don't know, do you? The police were called to your house this morning. They found Tom in your flat. He's been murdered." Fee's eyes filled with tears. "I've had the senior partners calling me all morning trying to get hold of you because the police are looking for you. They want to speak to you for obvious reasons. I told them that you were with me all night, but this is serious, Eve. They'll be looking for you."

The photo of Tom's body flashed once again through her head, and a solitary tear rolled down her face. She reached out to the tabletop to steady herself. She glanced around the room and saw that the other patrons were starting to look around. Eve urged them all to sit.

"I know about Tom. I found out this morning," Eve

replied solemnly. Fee looked at her with confusion, but as she was about to speak, Eve interjected, "I can't tell you how I know, but you need to get somewhere safe. I can't believe I have dragged you into this. I've packed a bag for you. Go and stay with your sister for a few days."

Fee looked at Eve in horror.

"I know you hate her, but this is the only way you can be safe."

After wiping a tear away from her blushed cheek, Fee reached into her bag and pulled out an envelope.

"I would try and convince you to go to the police again, but I know there's no point." Fee sniffed as if the trauma of Tom's death had stolen the fight from her. "There's five grand in here. Use it wisely. You're going to need it. Don't use your cards."

"This is my new number," Eve said, handing her a piece of paper. "For God's sake, don't lose it. It's our only way of contacting each other. Please, will you call my dad and tell him I'm fine? You know he'll be beside himself."

"Are you sure you know what you're doing?"

"Not really, but I'm going to find out what the hell is going on." She reached over and gripped Fee as though she were saying her last goodbye. Eve kissed her sweetly on the cheek and whispered into her ear, "Thank you. I will never forget this."

Ryan, who had remained silent throughout, turned to Fee. "Thank you," he said with humility.

Fee glared at him. Eve knew Fee would never accept him after he'd dragged them into all this. Eve stood, wiped her face, then signalled to Ryan to move. She turned for one last look at Fee. Eve had a foreboding feeling that this would be the last time she would see her friend for a long time.

Chapter 51

Hunt felt guilty about Walker not being allowed access to the safety deposit box as she followed Chauvin along the corridor and through another section of the bank. The Private Banking Suite was a definite step up from the rest of the transactional counters, with luxurious decor and marble flooring. Through this area they accessed a staircase descending to a lower level of the bank. At the bottom was another corridor, although this one was shorter by comparison and had a door within view. Spotlights in the ceiling reflected off the shiny marble floor, and although its splendour was undeniable, Hunt couldn't help thinking that it would double as an alarm system. The gentle tapping of their shoes was almost in sync, the clatter echoing around the walls. Eventually, they reached the vault. It resembled something out of an action film, its brushed steel exterior edged with yet more steel, reinforcing its armour. The keypad to one side was the access point, and once authorised, a dense, cumbersome handle could be twisted to gain entry.

"Excuse me," Chauvin apologised, walking in front of

Hunt to approach the keypad, keeping his back to her. "For security purposes." Hunt nodded as he entered the code to unlock the door. After he tapped in what seemed to be a convoluted sequence, a small green light illuminated with a *bleep*, indicating that the code was correct. This was followed by two loud clunks and numerous clicks before Chauvin expertly launched into action, rotating the handles to release the lock. The door opened slowly, like Aladdin's cave, revealing the contents within.

The vault was surprisingly expansive, and despite being subterranean, strategically placed lighting that beamed from square panels above created a warm glow which served to eliminate any sense of claustrophobia. The opulent marble continued to flow, and each wall was stacked floor to ceiling with an array of different-sized nickel draw casings. Row upon row of metal caskets, differentiated only by their numbers but all adorned with their requisite keyhole. She mused about the thousands of secrets concealed within, the identity of its patrons as well as the unfathomable riches they protected. In the centre was a rectangular glass table. A soft white leather chair was positioned beneath its glaze. She followed Chauvin over to the left side of the room, where he arrived at one of the narrower boxes.

"May I?" he requested.

"Of course." She watched him enter the key into box number 528. She held her breath as the tiny *click* unlocked the slender cover before gently swinging open to reveal the internal metal case. Chauvin had clearly sensed her unease and turned to her with an empathetic smile as he carried the box carefully to the table.

"I will leave you now. Please, take your time. The door will be closed over but not locked. I hope you find what you are looking for."

"Thank you, monsieur."

And with that, he left the vault door ajar to protect her privacy.

Hunt stood for a minute staring at the box. Her mouth became dry. She had been waiting for this moment for over a year. She prayed that its contents would finally disclose the truth surrounding Nick's death. Hunt could not entertain any other scenario; it would be heartbreaking. As her fingertips grazed its lid, its chilled surface made her fingers retract. The climate control was set to maintain a cool temperature to protect any objects held within that would perish in warmer conditions. Biting her lip, she placed her hands on each side of the box before lifting the lid cautiously to avoid disturbing its contents. The lid hinged halfway back, exposing several brown envelopes. She removed the first, and to her amazement, her name was written on the front. This envelope was significantly thicker than the others and was more like a file than a letter. The second bore the word *Zoe*, and finally the third was labelled *Incidentals*. Without delay, she opened the enveloped earmarked for her.

It was bursting with papers as well as photographs. Clipped to the top was a set of handwritten instructions. His handwriting as neat and methodical as his work ethic.

Agent Hunt,

If you are reading this, then the time has finally come. You will have by now seen the three envelopes, and each has a specific purpose. I think, however, this one will be of most interest to you. I have asked Chauvin to take care of my affairs, and upon receipt of these instructions, I request that you pass to him the second envelope labelled *Zoe*. She is to be gifted all of the assets outlined, including all funds and properties in France and Manchester. This is a condition of opening the box, and I have confidence, judging by your integrity, that you will respect my wishes.

Within envelope 3 is a package of incidentals that you may find useful when you leave here. I have a distinct feeling that your arrival and departure will not go unnoticed. I have also left a little something in the rear of the box that might assist.

I have enjoyed our little game of cat-and-mouse. Nonetheless, it appears that somewhere along the line, I have finally lost. Whatever your opinion of me, know this. I am not responsible for Nick Hardy's death, nor would I wish harm on either his family or indeed you. I hope the answers you are looking for will be within these pages.

Regards,

Smith

Her reactions to Smith's letter up to the final paragraph had been circumspect until she had digested his last sentiment. She had been informed by Ashford categorically that Smith was responsible for Nick's murder. Had he lied? Thoughts ran through her head at a hundred miles an hour. Why would Smith lie? If Smith deemed himself to be dead at the point of Hunt reading his letter, Smith would have nothing to gain from exonerating himself if he were guilty—he felt no guilt regarding his other targets. Why would Smith be any different about this? She could feel the pressure in her head building. She needed a moment to process, so she opened the envelope marked for Zoe. This package was more straightforward, containing a collection of bank statements detailing various accounts held in his name. All told, the total amount was just over €20 million. Having not seen his body or heard about his demise, she was unsure whether he was, in fact, dead or alive, but she would undertake his wishes as outlined.

The envelope marked *Incidentals* contained money clips, each holding thousands in sterling, euros, and dollars. There were also several European passports with alias IDs that Smith probably utilised when travelling. She would cross-reference the names with the information on her wall to confirm links. Lurking at the bottom was an ammunition clip, but no firearm. Just then, she remembered his instructions—the box. At first glance, there was nothing, but as she pushed her hand further in, her fingers brushed something strapped to the lid. Delicately, she eased her finger under the tape, gingerly separating it from the box until she was able to lift it out. The Glock 26 was a perfect weapon for concealed carry. She had no idea how to clear security with it on her person; however, she would take it all the same. Hunt doubted Smith had hidden the gun purely for her use; she imagined that it was a defence strategy that he had in place. Had he visited the bank and felt vulnerable, he would be able to protect himself.

Hunt then returned to the envelope addressed to her, this time taking a seat. She knew this was not going to be a swift process. Its contents were more like a file, swathes of paper and photographs meticulously organised in sections for Hunt to attempt to make sense of. It was in two distinct segments: the first seemingly details of his targets and movements, the second she could not immediately decipher. Hunt placed the second section on the floor—she would deal with that later. Smith had created dossiers about every target he had ever assassinated, all filed in date order. Each contained a photograph, his fee, the date, and brief details of surveillance carried out before the actual hit. She imagined that this was a tiny tidbit of the real preparation that accompanied each target, but this was created for her benefit to timeline his eminent career. As she spread out the documents on the table, it was like a "Who's Who" of European and Middle Eastern scumbags, the vast majority of whom she was familiar. She mentally congratulated him as she recognised the faces of his targets for a job well done. Smith had rid this Earth of some of the evilest and most dangerous people she had ever come across. In some cases, one might argue that he had performed a service.

Then she started to notice something. She had not correlated a large number of the faces staring at her as Smith's victims. Throughout the intelligence community, these kills were presumed to be the work of foreign governments, and several had caused major diplomatic incidents, with countries blaming one another. Why was he given these targets, and how did these governments not know that it was him? Her blood started to run cold. Was this why Nick was murdered? Had he also learnt about these connections? Her mind flew back to Nick's laptop. Was this the information that he had encrypted?

She had to focus. As she examined the files on the table, it was clear that Britain would gain from all of their assassinations, either directly or indirectly. The deaths of these individuals led to significant shifts in high-level leadership in many organisations, the protection of oil and trade agreements, as well as maintaining defence. The strategic thinking behind this type of operation would require an exceptional level of knowledge and understanding of Britain's global interests—information held in the Foreign Office. This individual would have access to classified information and an abundance of funds and would be undeterred by the fact they were committing treason.

Eve leaned on the table, resting her head on her forearms. What had she got herself into? She now understood why Nick hadn't shared what he was working on; he understood the enormity of the situation and its implications. Hunt searched through the papers and noticed each one had the word *Amicus* scrawled or printed on it somewhere.

Amicus—what did that mean? And why was it on all of the documents? This had to be some kind of code or conduit that was used in his contracts. Hunt now understood the deception surrounding Nick's murder. Smith was an easy target to incriminate; after all, he was an active assassin, the perfect mark. Scenarios rushed through her head. Had Ashford been lied to by the person in control so he could close the file on Nick's murder—or was he involved too? He had taken great pains to dissuade her from investigating further, but was this because he was genuinely concerned for her well-being, or was there an ulterior motive? She needed to find out what Amicus meant and if she could trust Ashford. If Ashford was ignorant, he would be incensed to discover a Foreign Office puppet master.

As Hunt examined the lineup of Smith's victims, she noticed a photograph inadvertently attached to the back of the last target, which was Tony Taylor. It was a CCTV still of a man getting into a vehicle in what looked like an underground car park. The image was severely obscured, the identity and facial features of the subject indistinguishable. There was no other accompanying paperwork with this one, no dossier. She turned the photograph over, and written there were the initials *AB*, *EC*, and *RL*, all with a question mark next to them. Was this the playmaker?

Chapter 52

With the envelope of cash firmly secured in her jacket, Eve was ready to move. As they walked out the doors of the Rosewood Hotel, Ryan turned to Eve. "Right. What is this brilliant plan of yours, then? We need to get out of the open. We're too exposed."

"We are going to Jamie Dawson's, the IT geek I prosecuted for hacking into GCHQ. When he was released, it was a condition of his parole that he went back to his mother's house."

"He isn't going to help us, I'm telling you now. You put the kid in prison. He's not going to welcome you with open arms. Besides, he's probably barred from using technology and can't get his hands on a laptop."

"I know I'm not his favourite person, but if he can't work, then he's going to be desperate for money. And that is something we definitely have."

"Okay, but don't say I didn't warn you that he's going to slam the door in your face."

Eve scowled at him, then advanced towards the edge of

the pavement and hailed a black cab. Ryan opened its door and, holding out his arm, ushered her to enter first as if she were his master, to which she smiled sarcastically. She relayed the address to the driver before leaning back against the grey leather seats. For a brief moment, Eve relaxed. It was the first time in hours she had felt moderately safe. No-one knew where they were heading (apart from Fee) or what their plans were—which also included Eve herself. The last forty-eight hours had been a whirlwind of fear, uncertainty, and utter devastation.

There was also another element at play, one that she was only willing to admit to herself. Although her fear had manifested itself through the elevated levels of adrenaline pulsing through her veins, she felt strangely intoxicated by the ability to assert her will, engaging in actions that were entirely out of her comfort zone. Eve was not about to let herself be dominated by a man she barely knew who, at any moment, could turn on her. Despite her need for self-preservation, during the short amount of time in which circumstance had thrown them together, they had developed a mutual trust. However, their next course of action had to guarantee the safety of her father and Fee. Without them, her existence would be worthless. Eve had been dragged into this by Ryan, yet she had been the one to dictate their course of action, particularly since she had been mailed the graphic images of Tom's body. Understanding the information on the flash drive was the key to surviving this ordeal and the only means by which she might negotiate their safe removal from the situation.

As the cab snaked through the bustling traffic, a comfortable quietness ensued. Eve did not want to utter anything that could be repeated by the driver to a third party, so she let her head fall back to rest on the seat. Ryan, however, did not appear to be quite so relaxed. Eve noticed the seriousness in his face but chose to leave him with his thoughts.

Eventually, they pulled up to Alexandra Road in Camden, the registered address for Jamie Dawson's mother. Despite their construction in the late 60s, the rows of concrete flats had a more modern appearance than others from that period. They had a unique charm. Given a lick of paint and a few bathing suits dangling over its balconies, you could be fooled into thinking you were in Spain. Once smart with well-tended greenery, hay-coloured overgrown shrubs and bushes now languished in its place with flower boxes littered with weeds and takeaway cartons. Rising on each side of a redbrick path, the flats were arranged like a theatre with prime seats to watch the events that unfolded below.

"Which number is it?" Ryan asked.

"It's flat 32. I think the sign said this way." Eve marched towards the narrow staircase leading upwards. Ryan followed closely behind, trying to keep up. The solid staircase led to a corridor with lines of doors. As they arrived at number 32, Ryan reached out his hand, stopping Eve from moving forward.

"Are you sure you know what you're doing?"

"Yes, now come on!" she whispered. "We haven't got time to waste."

Eve stood resolute in front of the shabby brown door.

Then, taking a deep breath, she knocked three times, the sound bouncing off the walls.

"Christ, try not to tell the whole row we're here!"

"Sorry." She frowned, then turned back to face the door, waiting for it to be unlatched. There was no answer. Eve stood and stared at it, willing it to open, but still there was no response. She decided not to ask Ryan for his input or even glance in his direction, because she was not moving until the door was opened. She was going to be answered. Eve then closed her hand into a fist and pounded the door. Ryan mouthed "Oh, my God" to himself as he leaned against the wall. With complete disregard of who might be watching, she lurched forwards and peered into the peephole, hoping to spot someone moving. Eve could see Ryan shifting awkwardly in her peripheral vision. She was about to step back when something flashed across the peephole. She pressed her body against the door, trying to identify what had caught her eye. Before Ryan had the chance to stop her, she stooped down to the letterbox and pushed it open with her fingers.

"Open the door, please. It is not the police. I just want to talk to you."

There was silence. Ryan bent down to her. "This is not working, and it's bloody dangerous, we need to leave. Now!" he implored.

"There is someone in there, and I am not going anywhere until they open this door." Her fingers still held open the slat.

The occupant, obviously party to this conversation, also

decided that ignoring them was futile. Eve saw a pair of skinny jeans slowly walking towards them, then she gestured to Ryan that someone was approaching. She quickly stood up and straightened her clothes. The shunt and grind of heavy deadlocks being jolted and pushed indicated that this door was not easily or frequently opened. The final sound was the chain being latched as the door opened slightly.

"What do you want?" The voice spoke calmly.

"My name is Eve Blake, and I need your help."

The door immediately slammed shut, forcing her to take a small step back. She quickly bent down again and prised open the letterbox.

"I'm not trying to get you in trouble. I just want to talk to you." She waited for a reply but received silence. "I'm not going to move until you open the door," she announced, then let the letterbox slam shut. Ryan had resumed leaning against the wall and looked exasperated, his eyes on the ceiling.

In vain, she tried again: "I promise I will make it worth your while." She took £100 in notes from the envelope that Fee had given her and pushed it through the slot. The clatter of the letterbox closing was closely followed by the shuffle of feet to retrieve it. Eve once again primed herself for an invitation to enter. The door was slowly pulled open, exposing its chain; the pale face of the young man was partially obscured by the door. His head tilted as he surveyed Eve and Ryan, who was now standing beside her. The silence between them seemed to last an eternity.

"Please," Eve begged, "I'm desperate!"

The door promptly shut. Eve closed her eyes and huffed in resignation. Ryan placed a hand on her shoulder as if to guide her away when she heard the dull scratch of the chain sliding off its rail. The door opened, and finally, they were face-to-face.

Jamie looked like most young lads, wearing skinny jeans, trainers, and a hoodie that looked like it could put itself in the washing machine. He was slightly taller than average, but he tried to mask it by hunching his shoulders. His limp hair was tucked behind his ears, and his oily skin and acne were clear signs of a not-so-healthy diet. He stepped back to allow them to enter; Eve had to breathe through her mouth to avoid inhaling his sweaty odour.

"Thank you," Eve said with sincerity.

The flat was stuffy with a narrow cream-painted hallway decorated with photos of family weddings and children wearing forced smiles in school uniforms. The aroma of burnt toast and stale air hit them as they followed Jamie into the living area. It was a small room, made to feel cramped by the oversized sofas jammed against its walls. The kitchen area was to one side, and there were two bedrooms off the hall. As far as Eve knew, he only lived with his mother; his father had left years ago when he was very young. Throughout the trial, Eve had felt sorry for him. He was clearly a very talented young man, but his energies had been channelled in the wrong direction. Academically he was capable, but his absence of social skills made him a loner.

Jamie sat down on one of the garishly patterned sofas, and Eve and Ryan followed suit. Despite slamming the door in their faces, Jamie was not bolshy or cocky—he was awkward, avoiding uncomfortable eye contact. Eve did not wait for him to begin the dialogue.

"I just wanted to say, before I ask anything of you, that I made sure that you were prosecuted fairly. Unfortunately—" Before she could continue, Ryan interjected.

"We need you to decrypt a flash drive. We need to know what's on it, and we need to do it fast."

Without directly looking at them, Jamie said, "I don't do that anymore. I'm not allowed a computer. I haven't even got an iPod. So if that's what you've come here for, you might as well just leave, 'cos I can't do it."

"We're not here to make trouble, Jamie," Eve said. "I know the conditions of your parole. However, I'm sure if I had a really good look around, I could find something incriminating. I mean, what are those headphones shoved in your back pocket for?"

Silence. Jamie still did not make eye contact.

"Look, I'm not trying to trap you, and I'm not interested in turning you in. However much you despise me, I was only doing my job. I just need your expertise."

"We've got money," Ryan chimed in again. At this, Jamie's eyes lifted towards them. "We can give you two grand, but we've got to do it now. Think of your mum. I'm sure she could do with the cash."

Jamie paused. Eve watched him bite his lip as he considered their offer. His shoulders were rising and falling faster as his breathing quickened.

"Four grand and I'll do it. If the coppers ask you about

this, you don't mention my name or say you've been here, or I'll have charges brought against you for harassment."

"Done!" Eve agreed.

Jamie stood and trudged into one of the rooms off the main hallway. Eve and Ryan followed and watched him as he emptied the bottom of his wardrobe. Several pairs of jeans and joggers littered the floor, with old trainers flung to one side. Just when it looked like it was empty, Jamie climbed in and slid a panel from the back.

"Jesus Christ, Jamie. How the hell did you get your hands on all this stuff?" Ryan exclaimed as he took out a collection of devices and wiring.

"I know people now," he replied. "You make connections on the inside."

Distracted by Jamie and his haul of equipment, none of them noticed that someone else had entered the flat.

"Who the hell are you?" the woman barked. It only took her a few seconds to recognise Eve's face. She quickly flew forward, her arms stretched out to attack. Ryan had anticipated this and stepped between them, her nails scraping his face as he deflected her reach.

"God, Mum, just stop!" Jamie shouted.

"Don't say anything. You and you," she bellowed, pointing at Ryan and Eve. "Get out of my flat now!"

Chapter 53

Hunt looked at her watch. Fifteen minutes had already passed since she had entered the vault. She knew Walker would be sitting in the room upstairs, twiddling his thumbs, seething at his inability to access the material. Something troubled her. She thought back to the text message she had accidentally read on Walker's phone. Its coded nature bothered her. He hadn't mentioned it to her at all, but why should he if it were irrelevant? She had not disclosed every message she had received, so why should he? None of his actions so far had caused her to doubt him. Their liaison in the park had come out of nowhere, and Walker was clearly out of his comfort zone. Whatever her instincts, she was powerless in the vault, a dark spot for mobile signals. She compartmentalised her thoughts and redirected her attention.

Hunt meticulously collected the papers laying on the table, re-collating them into their date order, certain that it would prove to be advantageous at a later stage. However, this time, she placed the photograph of the would-be puppet master on the top, due to its significance. Moving this group of papers to one side, she lifted the second collection of documents she had left on the marble floor. These were different. At first glance, many of the papers were written in Arabic, with dates ranging over a long period of years. From what she could decipher, their content pertained to the locations and details of munitions caches, detention facilities, ammunition trade deals, and shipments of arms from Western organisations. The fact that these documents were in a safety deposit box indicated that their existence was not common knowledge. She desperately searched for any clue as to who these documents might belong to, then found a signature. It was difficult to make out at first, but then upon closer study, she saw that the person in question was Muammar Gaddafi.

Hunt was shellshocked. The information that lay before her could cause unimaginable global repercussions. Western countries would be desperately clambering to condemn one another for assisting the abhorrent dictator to maintain an iron fist over his people. There were pages and pages of damaging records that would bring a cloud of shame to rest on countries all over Europe and America. As if this were not enough to induce a coronary, she then discovered further documents separated behind. These were different, corporate in nature. They contained names of numerous companies and corporations, some with locations and details, others were just names. There were also bank accounts with statements attached. Banks that were located in a range of countries, a number of which were based in Switzerland. While reading their balances, her stomach lurched. There were not millions but billions of dollars. Then it hit her. Amongst the intelligence community, there had always been rumours that Gaddafi had hidden billions in accounts around the globe. He was said at one point to have been the wealthiest man in the world. There were murmurs that small amounts of the money had been located in accounts in Italy, but it was a tiny fraction of what was thought to exist. The remaining funds had been concealed with no paper trail to locate them until now. These were documents detailing where some of Gaddafi's funds had been syphoned. Holy shit! she thought as she sank into the leather chair. This information was going to get her killed.

This threw her relationship with Walker under the bus; she was not going to drag him into this too. Enough people had already died. She now understood why Smith had left her the Glock—he knew she would need it. If the existence of these documents were to be leaked, she might as well paint a target on her head. This information was for her and her only. Smith understood that and knew that by explicitly instructing Chauvin to escort her down to the box alone, she would understand his rationale. Hunt's next move would be critical to her survival. She planned her speech to Walker, then after they returned to London, she would have to disappear. There was one person she trusted implicitly in the Boathouse, above all others, who would never be compromised. Upon returning to London, Hunt would make contact.

Her head was spinning with the information she had consumed. Although she did not want to leave the safe haven of the vault, she had to return to Walker. She organised the documents back into their envelopes, ready to go. Chauvin had been lingering outside the room since she had entered, on hand to attend to any request. Hunt walked towards the armoured door, her shoes gently tapping on the marble. Just as she thought, an early warning system. Chauvin had already risen to his feet.

"How may I assist you, Agent Hunt?"

"I need to transport some documentation back to London, but I will need something a little more robust. I also need to leave some instructions for the remainder of the box's contents."

"Certainly," he replied. "I will make the necessary arrangements." He stepped back out of the vault, and she could hear him relaying instructions. In his absence, she divided the paperwork into piles, emptied the comestibles envelope, and wrote instructions for Chauvin as per Smith's request. Next, she split the contents into thinner packs to separate them. Chauvin was swift and returned with a collection of envelopes as well as an A4 black document wallet with a plastic security tag. "Perfect," she said. "I will only be a minute." He nodded discreetly and once again left the vault. Hunt worked quickly to place the relevant envelopes in the secure bag before activating the seal. This way, its contents could not be accessed until her return to London. The rest was set aside for Chauvin. Checking one last time that there was nothing else lurking in the box, she finally closed the lid. Hunt then invited Chauvin back into the room to direct him: "Please follow the instructions I have outlined, sending the content via a reliable courier. Mr Smith was very particular in his wishes."

"Of course. I will ensure it is done as soon as you have departed. Is there anything further that I can assist with? A glass of water, perhaps?" he questioned.

"No, thank you. You have been very obliging, and I do not wish to take up any more of your time."

"Not at all, Agent Hunt, it has been my pleasure. Please, if you will accompany me upstairs, we can collect DCI Walker from where he has been patiently waiting." His warm, honest smile instilled confidence that her instructions would be carried out definitively. Walker was indeed still sitting in the room where she had left him, the frustration and boredom evident through his lethargic posture. He looked down at the package in her hand but said nothing, knowing this was neither the time nor place. Chauvin escorted them back to the main foyer where they had first entered, which to Hunt felt like a lifetime ago.

"Once again, thank you for your help."

"All part of the service. I hope you have a safe onward journey." He shook each of their hands in turn.

As they left the building, she took out her phone and opened Google Maps. She quickly searched for an appropriate location. "There's a park just up here called Jardin Catherine-Labouré," she said. "We can talk when we get there." Walker made no argument. As they strode forward with Hunt leading the way, neither spoke. Hunt's eyes were wide as she searched the streets and pedestrians for any signs that they had another tail. Within minutes, they reached the jardin. Hunt's brow furrowed as she examined the park for a safe location to talk. The lush greenery and wide-open spaces were littered with people enjoying their peaceful surroundings. Old ladies sat on benches people watching while young families played in the park. Students lay on blankets reading and making notes in the warm sunshine. Hunt would have liked to have visited under more pleasurable circumstances, but they had no time for relaxation. Both surveyed the area and, after a few minutes, deemed it safe to sit for a moment and talk.

She placed the envelope on her lap, positioning one hand on top, fear fluttered in her stomach. Walker and Hunt were both transfixed by it as if it were to come alive or explode. "Are you okay? You look like shit," Walker said, staring at her pale face. "While you were downstairs, I got a call. They've found Smith's body along with the Ahmadis in some abandoned train station in Manchester. Woodside called me. Complete carnage by all accounts. They think he took out the Ahmadis and then finished himself off. So if he left you instructions about what to do if he was dead, he was spot on." Hunt was strangely affected by the news; a pang of sorrow hit her for the man whom she had relentlessly pursued.

"Seriously, what's in there? Are you going to tell me?" Walker asked.

Hunt sat for a second, organising the words she had planned to say. Walker moved to open the package. "Don't!" she insisted, grabbing his arm. "It's not safe to open this until we get back to London."

"What the hell is in there? You were down there a really long time."

"All I can tell you is that he didn't kill Nick, and there's a whole lot of shit going on that we have no idea about."

Walker turned to her, gazing directly into her eyes. "Look, we're in this together, remember. You can trust me." He touched her hand, the tone of his voice softer. She didn't expect to see his sincere side again quite so soon, but she felt reassured.

"It's not that I don't trust you," she replied. "You shouldn't get involved."

"Too late. Just tell me. What was in the box?"

"He left instructions for his bank accounts and properties to be transferred to Zoe, basically tying up his affairs. That was envelope number two. Number one had details of every hit he had ever done, with pictures, dates, and details of some of his surveillance. He was bloody organised, I'll give him that."

"How do you know he didn't kill Nick?"

"He wrote it in a note he left me."

Walker's face was the epitome of scepticism. "Well, if he wrote it down, then it must be true. Come on! He was a trained bloody killer. Honesty was not his strong point."

"Look, there are people in these files that he's assassinated that I knew about, and there were also ones that MI6 thinks were the work of foreign governments. Those kills caused massive diplomatic incidents. Smith has been used as a private vigilante—someone is running him, someone with a terrifying agenda. Someone with Foreign Office connections."

"What? Are you joking? You've read one file from a sociopath, and suddenly the Foreign Office are running amock!" Walker huffed. "Just think about it for a minute."

"I know this sounds like some ridiculous conspiracy theory, but just imagine for a moment that it isn't. If someone is making these moves, we have no idea of the level of corruption that exists or how far-reaching it is. Why do you think we were being followed?"

"Okay, just suppose you're right. Who do we take this to? If someone has this much influence amongst the top brass, how are we going to be taken seriously? The IOPC would have a field day. I'd have investigators crawling up my arse."

"I don't know. I just need to think. My head is pounding."

"Was there anything else in the box, any other piece of information that might help?" he queried.

Hunt hesitated for a moment, agonising whether to reveal the other information. "Just passports for his aliases and some currency. Nothing else of real importance." She watched his reaction closely in case he had any tell that revealed he knew more than he was letting on. There was nothing.

"Let's get back to London," Walker said, sighing. "I have a feeling this is going to be a long day."

Chapter 54

The white-knuckle ride in the taxi back to the Gare Du Nord did nothing to ease Hunt's splitting headache. The driver seemed to have an affinity for his horn, blasting it every five minutes and shouting expletives at the other drivers. She still had the Glock firmly in the back of her trousers, and every jerk of his steering seemed to jab it against her skin. Thankfully she had not needed it; however, Hunt knew she would have to dispose of it before heading through security. Handing the driver a €20 note, she had never been so glad to get out of a taxi before.

As they entered the station, she searched furiously for the ladies'. Once located, Hunt made her excuses to Walker and started towards the door to dispose of the Glock.

"Wait a minute!" Walker called after her. "You don't want to be taking that in there with you," he said, pointing to the document holder.

She hesitated for a moment. "Of course, you're right," she said uneasily, slowly handing him the holder.

"Don't worry, I'll wait right here for you," he said,

shooing her away with his hand. She nodded in agreement before moving quickly, not wanting to leave him alone too long with the documents. Her anxiety was a combination of her reluctance to leave him with the documents while at the same time being concerned about his safety in case they had been followed. Reaching the toilets, she moved quickly into a cubicle. In the corner was a sanitary bin. She carefully removed the Glock from her waistband, thankful that it was no longer irritating her back, then quickly ejected its magazine before wiping it down. Finally, she used a piece of tissue to cover its hilt and lowered it into the bin, then covered it. It would be a while until it was discovered, long enough for their train to have departed for London. Hunt hastily returned to where Walker had been standing, but he was gone.

She spun around quickly, frantically searching for him, her panic rising with every passing second. How could she have been so stupid? She knew she shouldn't have trusted him, Christ, all it took was a quick shag, and she had completely lost her edge. The crowds in front of her were moving in a blur. She thought she had spotted his coat and moved towards a man before realising she was mistaken.

"What are you doing?" Walker said from behind.

"Jesus! You scared the life out of me." She sighed with relief. "You said you weren't going to move from over there," she chastised.

"I *thought* a couple of these might sort your head out," he explained, passing her a box of paracetamol and a bottle of water. "And besides, the shop was only fifteen bloody yards from where we were standing. I knew I'd see you come back out."

"Thanks, I'm sorry. I just want to get back to London. I'll feel better when we're on home turf." She could feel her face flushing.

"Let's get going, then. The sooner we're back, the sooner we can open this." He brandished the document holder before handing it back to her. She smiled contritely, annoyed with herself for assuming the worst.

They moved through security and passport control, then located their seats on the train. Hunt offered Walker the window seat, but she would not allow herself to be hemmed in; she needed an escape route should it be necessary. She couldn't help but think that this had all come to pass far too smoothly, considering the contents of the package.

Shortly after taking their seats, the compartment filled. Brightly coloured holdalls and wheeled suitcases were noisily hoisted and shoved into the racks above. The dull rattle of crisp packets and bottles opening as feasts were laid out on tables, a couple in the corner cuddled amongst a sea of faces glued to mobile devices. Hunt and Walker surveyed their co-passengers, but none instantly aroused concern. Hunt was thankful when the doors closed and the carriage jolted; they would soon be on their way. Walker had picked up a free copy of the *Daily Mail* and was flicking through its pages, its news content clearly riveting.

"What?" he said with amusement. "I'm not reading it for the hard news, it's for the footy at the back." She hadn't really considered him to be a football fan—she hadn't considered him to be an anything fan. Now that she thought about it, and she could imagine him in the stands, hurling abuse at the players.

"Arsenal, before you ask." He didn't lift his eyes from the pages.

"Shame, and I was just beginning to like you," she teased.

Even though they were heading back to London, Hunt couldn't relax. Her headache still had not abated, so she decided to take the paracetamol Walker had given her. She threw back two of the tablets and consumed half the bottle of water, her brain willing her body to absorb them with immediacy. Having barely digested the water, her head began to spin, her eyes fighting their closure. "Walker..." she mumbled, trying to grab his arm.

It was too late. She was out.

Chapter 55

Following the initial attack by Donna Dawson, Jamie's mother, the brawl had calmed. After five minutes of shouting, along with crying and anger, Donna had conceded, in part due to exhaustion. Like a dog licking his wounds, Ryan sat holding a bag of peas against his cheek, the throbbing heat thawing them out. Donna scowled at him from the opposite side of the room, her son's arm wrapped around her, attempting to pacify the lioness. Eve had done her best and managed to make cups of tea, trying to make small talk to break the tension. Donna was a strong and proud woman who had not been dealt the best hand by life, but like many strong women, she had refused to be a victim and fought for her family.

Eve finally reentered the room carrying three cups of biscuit-coloured tea. Donna uttered a resentful, "Thank you," as she took the mug from her, placing it on a glass coaster on the oversized coffee table. Eve took her place on the sofa next to Ryan. She could feel him quietly seething. Jamie turned to his mum as she sipped her tea.

"It's okay, Mum. I'm going to help them, and they're gonna give me four grand. It's for you. I want to pay you back for everything," he said sincerely.

She put down her mug and took his face in her hands. "Listen, we will be okay. I don't care about the money. I won't let you end up back in there. I couldn't take it again. We can manage."

"I know we can, but I can do this, and I won't get caught, I promise."

Donna pulled him close and hugged him tightly. "If you think this is going wrong and you're going to end up in trouble, you stop, and they leave." As they drew apart, she directed her words at Eve and Ryan. "Whatever he finds or doesn't find, you pay us, and you never mention our name to anyone or ever show your faces around here again—understand?" she hissed.

"Absolutely, you have my word," Eve confirmed.

There was a silence as Donna and Eve locked eyes, their expressions echoing the sincerity of their feelings. Finally, after what felt like minutes, a tear rolled down Donna's face. She quickly wiped it away with her hand, rose from her chair, and muttered, "You'd best get on with it, then." She stalked into her bedroom and closed the door behind her.

Jamie exhaled deeply and proceeded back into his room, reestablishing the connections to his network and rebooting. Remembering where she had stashed the all-important flash drive, Eve turned her back to Ryan and rummaged around in her bra. This was particularly unladylike; however, it was a necessary tactic to ensure its safety. She was embarrassed when handing it over to Jamie and apologised for its warm temperature, a comment that compelled Ryan to wince.

As Jamie connected his equipment, Eve did nothing to hide her fascination. Just when all seemed to be ready to get started, Jamie shut his laptop and turned to face them, his arms folded. His expression was unyielding.

"Cash," he demanded. "Or there's no deal."

Eve reached into her pocket for the envelope of cash. She slowly counted out £2,000. Jamie stared at the pile of notes that were gradually building.

"Half now, and the rest when it's done," she said.

"Fine," he sneered, snatching the money and shoving it into his hoodie pocket. With that, he grabbed the flash drive from the bed and inserted it into the USB port. Eve calmly breathed out, trying to steady her pulse, which felt like a rollercoaster, having brief dips of calm before being hiked to the top. It wasn't long before he was tapping away, using multiple combinations of text and digits to hack the device. Both Ryan and Eve were transfixed by the screen, their faces lit by its luminous glare. The only sounds were the gentle click of the keys repeatedly compressing alongside the quiet hum of the electrics. Eve's eyes darted across the screen, watching him try different combinations of code, impressed by his speed and dexterity. Her mind wandered as she watched Jamie work; a sudden wave of contrition enveloped her. This young man clearly had talent, but it had not been nurtured or channelled in the right direction. He could have achieved great things instead of being stuck in a pokey flat with a criminal record—and his mother.

Eve could see that this was not going to take five minutes, and while she had a moment to reflect, she also started thinking about her father. She realised that she had not spoken to him recently, and with all that was going on, he would be beside himself, anxious about her safety. He was the only family she had left. It had always been Eve and her dad; her memories of her mother were few, and sketchy at best. When she was little, their house was full of photographs of ice cream by the beach and birthday parties, trips away, and their first Christmas. The big hair and 90s clothes, showing a happier, simpler time. Then the photos changed. They were mostly of Eve. The happy family snaps in the minority amongst images of a father and daughter, inseparable, drawing strength from each other through those difficult years. Without realising, her eyes had filled, and she felt an acute heartache, longing to hear his voice. She didn't want to endanger him by telling him her whereabouts or her plans, but she wanted to let him know she was safe. She reached for the phone in her pocket and started to dial his number.

"Got it!"

She was yanked out of her contemplation by Jamie's triumphant outburst. "Good lad!" Ryan praised; he seemed genuinely impressed by Jamie's expertise. For the first time since he had opened the door, Jamie's demeanour altered significantly. He was animated and excited; this was a young man who was in his element; his confidence exuding. "Now, let's see what you're hiding, shall we?" Jamie mused, talking to his screen.

Without thinking, both Ryan and Eve moved closer, desperate to discover why this tiny object was so coveted and worth killing for. Eve's brief moment of sombre reflection was over, and she had to concentrate on what was going on in front of her. Her emotions could wait.

The screen suddenly filled with files, a confusing jumble of numbers and letters. Jamie systematically opened them one by one, and Eve frowned as she tried to work out what the codes concerned. Then a document opened on the screen, and as he had done with all the others, Jamie was about to close it when Eve grasped his arm. "Wait!" she exclaimed.

"What is it?" Ryan asked.

"Look. This is a screenshot of a bank statement," she replied, tracing her fingers across the screen. "And these are sort codes and account numbers." She paused for a moment, trying to make sense of the information. "Just scroll down to the bottom, will you," she instructed. "There!"

On the screen were rows of digits. Eve's lips moved silently as she read the figures to herself. The initials *MG* appeared on some of the papers as well as *TA*, but she had no idea what they alluded to. As if experiencing an epiphany, her eyes widened. Eve had roughly calculated the totals, and they amassed not just millions but billions. They were in a world of trouble.

"Oh, my God! Oh, my God!" Her hands covered her mouth. "This is serious. What the hell has Tony done?" Both men turned to her, bemused by her comment. "There are billions on these pages," she blurted, pacing around the room, "and anyone with access to these funds has incredible power. No wonder they're looking for this—there's enough money in these accounts to influence governments!"

"Jesus Christ," Ryan uttered, echoing her sentiments. "Now I know why we're being hunted for this. Shit!" He threw his hands in the air.

"Fuck!" Jamie barked. "I knew you two couldn't be trusted. Now I'm definitely going to end up back inside! Get out—I'm done." Jamie's eyes were filled with fury.

"All right, I'm sorry. I honestly didn't know what was on it. We'll leave. Here's the rest of your money." She took out the envelope and counted out the rest of his fee. "I really am sorry. I had no idea."

"I don't care. Just get out!"

"Come on, we need to move," Ryan pressed, ushering her towards the bedroom door.

As she turned to retrieve the drive from Jamie, something caught her eye.

"What's that?" she asked, pointing at the laptop screen. "Is that a video file?"

"I don't give a shit what it is," Jamie retorted. "I said I'm done!"

"Please, I promise we'll go soon. We just need to see what's on that file."

Chapter 56

Eve's pleading worked. Begrudgingly, Jamie agreed to play the video file from the drive. From the resignation on Jamie's face, Eve knew he realised they would not leave until they had seen it. Ryan and Eve positioned themselves once again behind Jamie to look over his shoulder as he opened the file. The image quality was poor; its dark, grainy picture was accompanied by sketchy sound quality. The camera moved in and out before it finally focused. It appeared to have been shot from a strange angle, like the person filming it was concealed. In the background was an old warehouse or outbuilding; its concrete walls created the backdrop. It wasn't long before its subjects came into focus.

A man stepped out of a dark blue car and leaned on its bonnet with his arms folded. Unfortunately, his position had obscured a section of his number plate, so it couldn't be made out. He was a young man in his thirties, tall, with broad, muscular shoulders, wearing dark clothing. His body language showed no signs of fear or anxiousness. He was relaxed. Seconds later came the sound of another car in the background, its steady purr fading as its engine was switched off. The vehicle did not drive into the shot. Damn it! Eve thought. Her hope of finding something she could use to identify the individuals was dashed. The scuff of shoes against the ground denoted the arrival of the young man's contact, then another man sauntered into the shot. This man was older, middle-aged, with greying hair and heavy-framed glasses. His domineering stance emanated authority; the man resting on the bonnet stood up to meet him as if to show respect.

The interaction between the two men was calm at first, then rapidly deteriorated into heated exchanges, with the younger man becoming increasingly animated, waving his arms around. He steadily moved closer to his counterpart, who was trying to pacify him. The poor sound quality prevented them from hearing the argument. Still, it was clear the younger man was aggrieved, as he moved closer and closer to his counterpart until they were eyeballing each other. The tension appeared to build until the older man said something that exasperated the younger man, who then turned his back to him; his hands grabbed his head as he faced his car.

"Do you know who these two are?" Ryan questioned Eve.

"I've never seen either of them before," she whispered, her eyes hypnotised by the screen.

"Oh, Jesus!" Jamie gasped.

The camera jerked slightly. The person holding it was clearly not anticipating what had just happened. The greying man had pulled out a gun and shot his associate in the back.

The young man tumbled to the ground as his legs gave way, his face pointing towards the camera. There was a moment of stunned silence. Eve's hand covered her mouth in shock; Ryan and Jamie were motionless. The film seemed to pause, then, unexpectedly, the executioner slowly walked forward, his expression indifferent. He patted his victim down and removed his phone from his pocket as if he had performed the process numerous times before. He rose to his feet and glanced over his shoulder before leaving the scene. There was the faint clunk of his car door opening and closing followed by the vehicle's engine firing and accelerating away.

All three were speechless. The camera was still. Just when Eve thought the horror was over, the camera moved and approached the body. She was so engrossed, she had forgotten that someone was behind the camera. Eve grabbed Ryan's arm for reassurance. The picture bobbed and wobbled as it travelled over to the slumped body. Eve winced as the camera focused on the face of the dying man. Assuming he was dead, the camera started to move away when suddenly, the victim's eyes flickered. The shot moved erratically and shook, indicating that the person filming was not anticipating this resurgence. The man lying on the floor was gagging and struggling to breathe, his head bleeding where he had hit the ground. Eve and Ryan watched his eyes narrow as he looked closely at the person before him, then his eyes widened, perhaps after he had recognised the onlooker's identity. As he choked and coughed, he uttered his words.

"Tell h...h...her..." he stammered, "find a friend."

His words were final. His bloodshot eyes closed. The video ended, the last frame frozen on his pained expression.

A tear rolled down Eve's cheek. She was stunned. She had never seen such callousness, such indifference to another human being. The victim must have had a family who would miss him, but his executioner was devoid of remorse or contrition. Ryan said nothing.

The stunned silence was curtailed by the click of the removal of the flash drive. This time, without aggression, Jamie said solemnly, "I've done what you asked. Please leave. I don't want any trouble. I can't break my mum again."

"Thank you. I am truly sorry to have exposed you to this. I honestly had no idea."

Eve carefully took the flash drive from Jamie's outstretched palm and turned to leave. She stopped, desperately wanting to voice how sorry she was, but she couldn't find the right words to express her sincerest regret. Ryan placed his hand gently on the small of her back and guided her towards the door. She hesitated, then realised there was nothing she could say that would mollify Jamie. Eve clutched the flash drive firmly in her hand, its heat warming her flesh as if conducting evil from hell. They walked calmly towards the door, then as they left, pulled it lightly until the final click denoted its closure. Eve and Ryan had not made eye contact since the end of the video. Still unable to look at him, she pressed her lips together and started towards the stairs. Ryan reached for her hand and pulled her round to face him.

Eve's pallor was ashen, her cheeks stained from tears. She

felt disoriented, not yet able to make sense of what she had seen. She was like a butterfly in reverse. The vibrant, confident person was morphing into someone damaged, her colours fading. Eve's damp cheek brushed against his neck as Ryan pulled her into his chest. She could not bring her arms to extend around his body; instead, they came up to her chest in an automatic defence mechanism as her shoulders trembled within his embrace. They stood for a moment, still. Eve could muster no words; discussions needed to be had, but her mouth failed to oblige. It was like an out-of-body experience—she was watching this person who looked and sounded like her but could not connect the terror of what she had seen with reality. Her body had become immobilised. A resident leaving their flat forced her into motion as she released herself abruptly from Ryan's arms and wiped her cheeks.

"Let's move," she said solemnly.

They retraced their steps back down the narrow stairs to where they had been dropped off earlier.

"I need to think. I need to process," she said, lightheaded.

"Well, I need a bloody drink," Ryan said, his response surprising her and lightening the moment.

She paused for a moment, her mind racing. Then she decided: "I know the place."

It wasn't long before they were able to flag down a taxi. Eve and Ryan climbed in, exhausted and relieved to be out of Jamie's flat. She reached behind her to grab the strap of her seat belt, but after struggling to pull it towards her, she let it go with resignation, and the buckle banged against the plastic interior.

"Where to, darlin'?" the driver asked.

She closed her eyes briefly, as if wrestling with her decision. "The King's Arms, please."

It was only a moment before Ryan made the connection about where they were going.

"Are you fucking nuts?" he whispered. "We'll be walking into the lion's den!"

"I know what I'm doing."

"Really? Well, I bloody hope so. Otherwise, someone will be filming our murders next."

Chapter 57

Regardless of its regal name, The King's Arms was one of the most dangerous pubs in London. It wasn't a place you would just pop into for a swift drink after work if you were fond of to your kneecaps. They had a very distinct clientele with notorious reputations. It had a vast footprint beside the main road, larger than the average pub, which was befitting of its status. It was not somewhere you stumbled upon. You went there with a purpose. Its exterior, once imposing with its sturdy red bricks and a multi-peaked roof, was now shabby and neglected with faded graffiti brandishing the walls.

"Are you sure this is the place you want?" asked the driver as he pulled up outside the pub.

"I'm sure, thank you," she replied, handing the driver his fare. His eagerness to depart hastily was further marked by the squeal of his tyres as he accelerated rapidly in the opposite direction. They were on their own.

"Are you all right?" Eve asked, although not willing to change her mind about entering the premises.

"Yeah, I'll be okay," Ryan responded, his face flushing. "I

hope you know what you're doing,"

"Not entirely, but this is a different game now, and these are the players we need. We've got to think like them." Something Eve had never imagined she would ever do or say. She had spent her entire life on the right side of the law bringing people to face justice for their crimes. She had already broken numerous laws, and her ability to return to her old existence was rapidly diminishing.

Ryan entered one last plea. "Once we go through these doors, there's no going back, I just want you to know that."

"There is no other option," she replied resolutely. "I know it, and deep down, so do you."

Eve moved to grab Ryan's hand but stopped herself. She could do this. Holding onto a man would only show weakness, and Eve could not show any vulnerability, or her ability to negotiate would be lost. She placed her quivering hand on the brass handle of the old-fashioned swing door, pushing it firmly before striding in. It swung back behind her like a saloon in the Wild West.

The interior of the pub was marginally more convivial than its exterior. Ring-stained wooden tables filled the room whilst maintaining a clear path to the mahogany bar. Red velour seats lined the walls, their once plush comfort now giving way to sun fading and fraying. At the back was a pool table with a rack of cues, the flashing lights of the fruit machine to one side luring the addicts to try their luck. In the far corner was an area that was distinctly different from the rest of the pub. There were no ring marks on this table, and it was surrounded by plush leather seats. The pub looked divided into areas with different sections for different people. As Eve surveyed the room, it was evident that neither she nor Ryan would fit into any of the categories.

The landlord was an older man in his late sixties. The deep crevices and mottled texture of his skin were like a road map, showing the outside world the evidence of a hard life.

Eve and Ryan's entrance was announced by the clatter of the door as it fell back into place. The music in the background continued to play despite the hush of the patrons, who examined them with barely disguised interest. Eve's skin prickled under their gazes. As they advanced towards the bar, members of the party sitting in the posh area rose to their feet. Two bald-headed, burly young men wearing tracksuit bottoms and tight T-shirts paraded their broad shoulders and bulging biceps as if presenting their credentials. On the leather seats sat another man, engrossed in a phone conversation whilst smoking a cigarette; the law clearly did not apply in this pub. He was shorter than his associates, but his wide jawline and scar tissue along his cheekbone persuaded Eve that he was just as hard. Confidence oozed from his every pore as the room waited in anticipation for his reaction. Next to him was another man who shared his swarthy complexion and black stubble, which he stroked as he observed. They looked like brothers; their resemblance was unmistakable.

Eve's kneecaps shook underneath her trousers. She felt like she was watching an East End gangster film, with the scene unfolding in slow motion. Ignoring all but the barman, Eve cleared her throat. "I would like to speak to Mr Wheeler, please."

"Who's asking?" one of the muscle twins commanded.

Before Eve had a chance to respond, Ryan cut in. "Tell him Ryan's here." The Wheeler family had had a stronghold in the area, and it was widely known that The King's Arms was their headquarters.

The man in the corner had clearly been listening to the conversation and stood and strode over to Ryan. He held out his arms, gesturing for Ryan to approach. With a grave expression, Ryan slowly walked to meet him. The man wrapped his outstretched arms around Ryan, slapping him on the back before taking his face firmly in his hands, much like a father comforting his child, giving him a stern look and a reassuring wink before releasing him.

"I'm so sorry, boy. You know how much I loved your dad."

"I know, thanks, Eddie," Ryan replied solemnly.

"How's your mum? She all right?" He ushered them into his domain.

"Bit of a mess, to be honest. She's still in shock," Ryan replied as all three sat.

"Well, we've all found his death hard, haven't we, lads?" His crew of devotees nodded along in agreement but showed little sign of grief. Eve had been silent throughout the entire exchange, surprised by Ryan's composure.

"I just don't believe it. We got Tony out, which, believe me, weren't easy, then someone went and bloody shot him! I promise you, son, we're gonna find the bastards that did this. No-one takes out one of mine and gets away with it."

Upon hearing this tidbit about the Wheelers doing

something to "get him out," Eve wanted to know how the hell they managed it. She broke her silence. "Sorry, can I just ask what you mean by 'got him out'?"

Eddie Wheeler had largely ignored Eve up to now. His eyes fixed on her, and within seconds, a wave of recognition enveloped him, and his manner changed. "Ryan, what the hell are you doing bringing her here?" he bellowed, banging his fist violently on the table and spitting on the floor. The rest of the pub once again fell silent. The muscle twins, taking this as their cue, moved to flank them, a well-practised manoeuvre, while two other patrons moved to lock the swing doors from the inside.

"Eddie, listen, please. It's not what you think. We need your help. I would never go against you, you know that we're family!" Ryan pleaded. The air between them was tense, swirling with betrayal and anger. The only sound was the music pealing out of the speakers. Florence and the Machine's "The Dog Days Are Over" reverberated around the walls, pulsing like the blood racing through Eve's veins.

"So what do you want?" Eddie demanded as he sighed.

"We're in trouble, and we can't do this by ourselves," Eve said. "Someone's killed one of my colleagues, and they've been following us." Eve took the photos out of her bag and passed them to Eddie, who examined them quizzically before handing them back.

"Jesus, what a bloody mess—this isn't just someone having a go at one of my lads. What the fuck is going on? What aren't you telling me?"

Ryan touched Eve's knee as a signal not to speak. "Dad

stole a laptop from a hotel. Really bloody stupid, but he didn't realise that in the laptop case was a flash drive. Now we don't know what's on it, and we don't want to either, but someone wants it back, and they're willing to kill for it."

Eve was proud of herself for not reacting during Ryan's explanation, although she was annoyed at him for assuming she would have told Eddie everything. She wasn't stupid. She was just about to interject when her phone rang.

"Sorry, I have to take this," she said, pacing over to the other side of the room. "Fee, are you okay? This is really not a good time."

"Eve, listen. They've got your dad, and they want to exchange him for the drive."

Chapter 58

Amicus had collaborated with Ashford on many occasions but had never used his people to run an operation before. It was clear from their growing list of incompetencies why she preferred to use her own team. Up until now, their arrangement had been mutually advantageous. Ashford identified the targets and settled her fees, and she arranged for the contracts to be undertaken. This had worked to their reciprocal benefit for years, but the Ahmadi assassination had changed the game. Ashford wanted him taken out. He was deemed a threat to the stability of the new Libyan regime after he betrayed the rebel forces and the British government. What Amicus had not foreseen was the information in Ahmadi's possession. Smith had travelled to Tunisia to locate and kill him. It was only afterwards when searching his lifeless body that he recovered the drive concealed within his clothing.

Amicus received the drive from Smith, not realising the intelligence and power she held in her hand. Only after Butler had decrypted it did Amicus understand the connotations of the information at her fingertips. She designed a plan to realise its potential and, if it was followed through successfully, she would never be underestimated or ignored again. Amicus had been foolish not to have stored it securely; however, that mistake was now being rectified.

Ashford knew nothing of the material on the drive, and Amicus had no intention of revealing its contents. He assumed he was tidying up the mess that had been created. Amicus had informed him that the drive contained a video file that would cause irreparable damage if exposed. It was, therefore, in his best interest to secure it. Amicus was understandably anxious about the role played by Ashford's people, but in the absence of Smith, she had little alternative. Her private jet was ready to transport both her and Butler back to Geneva the following day, and she had no intention of leaving the country without the drive. A pivotal meeting had been arranged that had taken months to arrange. If the opportunity was squandered, it would never be offered again.

"Where are we up to?" she demanded, expecting that after their last conversation, Ashford would address her with contrition.

"Blake's father has been taken to a secure location. She will be contacted to arrange the drop, and the drive will be recovered. I will personally deliver it to you. All will be taken care of," he responded, his tone neutral.

"Good. Once Blake has handed over the drive, disorient and abandon her father somewhere. Enough people have already died. My jet is on the tarmac, and I will be leaving tomorrow at six p.m. I expect to have the drive in my possession. Do *not* fail me." As she turned her head, she could see Butler waiting to ask her a question. "Keep me informed," Amicus continued. "I want to know exactly what is going on. There is no room for mistakes." And with that, she hung up, her comments directed at both Ashford and Butler.

Amicus could see Butler waiting for her to complete the call. Her expression still contrite, as if trying to demonstrate her self-reproach for her earlier actions. "Everything is arranged. The meeting will go ahead at the requested time with all requisite parties in attendance."

"Good. Have you set up everything from our end to facilitate the transaction?"

"We are ready to proceed. All we need is the drive."

"This bloody lawyer had better comply. My trust in Ashford's people is rapidly deteriorating based on their current performance. As soon as we know her location, I want eyes on her."

"Understood," Butler replied. The meeting had taken Butler months to organise, and Amicus was not going to see it jeopardised at this late stage. What Butler did not realise was that she was Amicus's "team." Yes, she had used contractors for specific purposes, but Butler and Smith were Amicus's constants; she had chosen both of them specifically for their skill set and their reputations. As much as losing Smith had hurt, he was replaceable. Amicus could not lose her right-hand woman, whom she trusted with her life. All was now in place, ready to progress, but then without warning, Butler's pocket vibrated.

"Hello…Yes, when? Oh, okay, thank you." She faced Amicus, her expression grave. "They've found Smith and the Ahmadis. They're all dead."

Chapter 59

Eve's chest tightened as she absorbed the news of her father's abduction. She pressed her hand to her chest, trying to alleviate the pain; however, she then struggled to breathe. She spun around to look for Ryan. He was immersed in conversation with Eddie Wheeler; then he spotted her. She held the phone to her ear, but she couldn't focus on what Fee was saying. Ryan sprung to his feet and rushed to her side. He took the phone from her limp fingers and pressed it to his ear. "Hello?" he said. "What's happened?"

Ryan then proceeded to listen to Fee repeat the information. Eve stood beside him, hands covering her mouth, eyes focusing on a spot on the floor to steady herself. As he took in the information, Ryan lifted his hand, grabbing the back of his hair in exasperation before turning to Eve. He held her waist to stabilise her as she wobbled.

"Is he okay? What do they want? Okay, call as soon as they contact you." Ryan hung up in annoyance. He gently took Eve's cheek in his palm and stared directly into her eyes, forcing her gaze to meet his.

"We're going to work this out, I promise," he said.

She could only think of her father, terrified. He was an honest and decent man, an innocent victim who had never done anything in his life to deserve this torture. He was all she had left. Ryan took her hand firmly and led her back to Eddie, who had been carefully observing from his corner. Eve followed without argument, holding onto his arm, steadying herself.

"They've taken her dad," Ryan told Eddie. "They want to exchange him for the drive."

Eddie paused for a moment. "If you don't know where he is, there's nothing I can do about it. My best advice is give them what they want, then walk away. They ain't gonna mess around, sweetheart."

Eve stared at the floor. Without handing over the drive, it was hopeless. She hated herself; everything was her fault. She could now only hear muffled sounds of conversation.

*

Ryan could see Eve was becoming catatonic and knew he would have to take over. It was the first time he had directed their actions since this entire thing had begun. Eve had largely lead the way, but he could see at that moment, she was not capable of any clarity of thought.

Eddie drummed his fingers on the table, then knocked back the remainder of his drink that had been patiently waiting.

"Right, here's what you're gonna do," Eddie declared, returning his glass with a dull thump. He grabbed a well-thumbed newspaper that rested beside him and ripped a piece from its corner. "Pen!" he demanded, clicking his fingers. One of the muscle twins obliged quickly without hesitation. The erratic scraping of the pen on the thin paper jerked the table as he wrote. "Go to this address. You can lay low until you need to move. Mandy will see you right until you need to make the exchange. Do not give them the drive until they let your dad go," Eddie said to Eve, "otherwise he's as good as dead. These people don't mess around. You're gonna need this."

He signalled to muscles number two, an unspoken language between them. He walked over to the bar and stooped behind it before retrieving a rectangular box. He then placed it on the table in front of Eddie, who lifted its lid and brought out a small handgun. Ryan and Eve stared at it as Eddie expertly handled it.

Ryan was no stranger to weapons; his father had kept a gun in the house, concealed at the back of his wardrobe. He had discovered the unloaded gun whilst playing as a child, but he was never brave enough to touch it. When he became older, that changed. One evening, while Mum was out, Tony had caught Ryan looking at it. Although angry at first, Tony relented and taught him how to engage the safety and ready the weapon before finally allowing him to squeeze the unloaded trigger. Ryan had never handled live ammunition but had watched his father load the firearm.

Ryan could see Eve's eyes bulging as she watched what was unfolding. Eddie offered it, flat on the palm of his hand. Ryan subtly squeezed Eve's hand before taking a step forward to take it. It was heavier than he remembered, but all of the things his dad had shown him came flooding back. Taking the gun was unavoidable, he told himself, it was for their protection. They could not walk into the exchange without any form of defence against professionals who would think nothing of slaying them in cold blood.

"Huh! You're a natural," Eddie remarked as he watched Ryan handle the gun. "Your dad would have been proud. When this is all over, come and see me. We've got some things to discuss."

"Course," he replied with conviction, having no intention of having anything to do with this family again. He took the gun and placed it with some ammunition in the bag that Eve had been carrying, but this time, he took charge of it. They looked like they were ready to go when Ryan stopped. "I just need to go to the gents', okay?"

"Fine, just be quick," Eve said.

Ryan placed the bag on the floor and headed through a swing door behind them. Eddie turned to Eve and gestured for her to sit.

Ryan knew he did not have much time, and instead of going into the gents', he strode straight past and through a second door into an alley behind the pub. Its prison-like high wall bolstered by barbed wire warned him that this was not somewhere with which he wanted to become familiar, however much the Wheelers wanted him to. Ensuring that he was hidden, Ryan took out the photograph he'd kept hidden from Eve. His blood ran cold. He read the instructions written on the back, took out his phone, and quickly tapped a message. He paused for a brief moment before pressing send, torn by what he was forced to do. He had no choice. Message sent. He replaced the photograph in his jacket and headed back into the pub, where the tension between Eddie and Eve seemed to be reaching a crescendo. Eve had appeared to have come round and was beginning to be more animated.

"How does it feel to be on the other side?" Eddie sneered. "Lines get a bit blurry when things don't go your way, don't they?"

"This wouldn't have happened if Taylor had been sent down like he was supposed to be. How did you manage to get him off? I'm confused!" she retorted.

"Why? Because someone like me has got influence and contacts within the police?" He looked at her expression, which with every word was growing with disdain. "Yeah, there are bent coppers in your precious Met, a shitload of them who would be only too happy to assist. But that's another story, and not one I'm in any rush to share with you."

"I suggest you take her out of here," Eddie directed at Ryan, "And don't ever bring her back." His eyes were thick with fury.

"Don't worry Mr Wheeler, I have no intention of returning." Eve hissed.

"Thank you," Ryan said to Eddie, taking the piece of paper from his hand with the address on it. He didn't need the address; he knew full well where Mandy lived, he had been there before.

"Show them out, lads."

The muscle twins once again obeyed the commands of their master and flanked Eve and Ryan as they ushered them towards the door. Taking their cue, the locals, just as before, moved to the doors and opened their latches. It was darker outside now than when they had arrived and surprisingly peaceful—the cool breeze providing refreshment against the humidity.

"Are you okay?" Ryan asked.

"Fine." She shook her shoulders and head gently, as if re-centring. "We need to get to this place and call Fee. I can't lose my dad. I just can't."

"You're not going to."

Chapter 60

Stunned by the events of the last few hours, Eve and Ryan travelled to the address provided by Eddie Wheeler. She didn't trust Eddie, but out of desperation, she had no option.

The house was unremarkable, a carbon copy within the row of houses it occupied. The streets were crammed with cars desperately trying to park outside their own homes. It was an ideal safe house location because of the constant bustle of the road; there were people and cars all around, and it would be difficult to determine anything out of the ordinary. They paid the taxi driver and stood on the pavement outside the paint-flaked front door.

"It's late. I hope this is okay," Eve murmured.

"It's not that late, not round here, and believe me, Mandy is well compensated. There's no need to worry about it being inconvenient."

Eve knocked on the door politely, raising her heels nervously in anticipation. It was like a déjà vu—this was the second strange door she had knocked on in the last twenty-four hours. As they waited, Eve was overcome with a different type of sadness. She was worried and anxious about her father, but this was the first time she had admitted to herself that it was unequivocal that she would never be sanctioned to practise law again; too many laws had been broken and lines crossed. It was ironic, the people she had spent her career despising and prosecuting were the ones whose help she needed the most. Astoundingly, but not without condition, they were willing to assist. Her moral compass felt out of balance. Her actions were now driven by survival, not ethics. Now *she* was standing in the shadows, not in the light or the dark, but somewhere in between.

Moments later, the door opened. A middle-aged woman with tightly curled hair and a blunt expression stood before them, one hand holding the door a quarter open, the other pressed against the wall. The heaviness of her makeup did nothing to smooth the deep crevices of her wrinkles. She stood for a moment, taking them both in. Eve smiled apologetically with Ryan alongside. She looked past Eve and took the measure of Ryan.

"You Tony's boy?" she demanded.

"Yeah, I am."

She paused for a moment, analysing his response. "You look like him—you got the same eyes. Loved your dad," she said, her voice softening. "He was always a decent bloke. Come in, then." She stood back against the hall wall as the door opened widely. The dated living room was dominated by leather furniture and a large flat-screen TV; it was furnished with high-end products designed to amuse its guests. Mandy's interior design skills were firmly stuck in the

90s with gaudy-patterned wallpaper and an array of tacky ornaments. It was a modest two-bed terrace with its living room to the left of the entrance, a flight of stairs leading to the bedrooms, and a kitchen to the rear. They followed her into the kitchen, where she promptly filled the kettle. Eve had expected a barrage of questions; however, Mandy was disinterested—either that or well trained not to enquire about their business.

"You hungry?"

Eve realised they hadn't had anything to eat since that morning, and she was suddenly ravenous. "Yes, actually," Eve replied.

"Right, I'll bring you something with a cuppa. Come on, I'll show you upstairs." She strode past them and headed up the staircase to the bedrooms. The stairs were steep, but Eve's weary legs seemed to make a harder job of it.

"Bathroom is here, and your room is in there." She paused for a moment, waiting for them to move into the bedroom. "I'll bring you a sandwich in a while." Closing the door behind her, not waiting to hear Eve's faint "Thank you."

Eve sat on the edge of the bed, the soft mattress lowering under her weight.

"We need to call Fee back now. I want my dad released as soon as possible. I don't want to think about what they're doing to him. This is all my fault." She started to cry as she searched for her phone.

"Stop. There's nothing we can do. We have to wait for them to make contact. Your dad might be battered and bruised, and probably scared out of his wits, but he'll be okay. Christ, if he's half as bad as you, he'll be running rings round them!" He looked into her eyes earnestly as Eve let out a half-sigh, half-laugh. He was right. Her dad was no pushover; he could definitely handle himself.

"The best we can do is try to rest, and eat," Ryan continued. "We've not had anything all day. If you can't think straight because you haven't eaten or slept, that will be worse for your dad." She could see the concern in his eyes. Having a meltdown now would not be good for anyone. She lay back, sinking further into the mattress, the fatigue more intense than she had imagined. Ryan moved towards the door.

"Where are you going?" Eve asked disconcertedly.

"The loo—is that okay?"

"Sorry, I'm just on edge. I can't stop thinking about Dad."

"Well, just be grateful that yours is still here," Ryan said pointedly, before closing the door behind him.

Eve thought for a moment. They had been together all this time, and she hadn't considered that although they were in danger, Ryan was hurting too. Tony had been murdered in one of the most brutal ways imaginable, and Ryan hadn't once talked about how he was feeling or shown any emotion. The guilt made her stomach churn even faster than it had before. A few minutes passed, then Ryan returned. He lay down on the bed next to her, both of them staring at the Artex ceiling.

"I haven't even asked how you're feeling about your dad.

I'm so sorry." She gently took his hand in hers. To her relief, he responded, and the warm pressure of his skin calmed her a little.

"He always tried to protect me, but he couldn't stop, he couldn't help himself. It was the only life he knew. Plus when you're in with the Wheelers, that's it, there's no getting out again. Loyalty is everything. He was doomed from the start."

"It doesn't mean you didn't love him, though?" Eve turned her head to meet his eyes.

"I hated what he did, but yeah, I loved him." He rolled onto his side and brushed her cheek softly with his fingertips. He lifted her chin, her eyes slowly closed, inviting him in. His smooth lips pressed softly against hers, lingering, enveloping. Her skin tingled at his touch. As they separated, their eyes gazed at one another, and then as if a sudden thought had struck him, Ryan moved his head to the side, sighing deeply.

"Are you okay? What's wrong?" Eve fretted.

"I'm sorry, I—" Ryan was interrupted by the door being rapped, followed immediately by Mandy barging her way in with a tray holding a plate of sandwiches, mugs of tea, and glasses of water. They rose swiftly from their lying position as she slid the tray onto a pine chest of drawers opposite the bed. She turned on her heel and brought over a glass of water.

"Drink this. You look like you need it." She stretched her arm out, thrusting the glass at Eve.

Ryan turned his back towards the window. She took the glass, thanked Mandy, and proceeded to drink.

The water was refreshing. Eve had not realised how dehydrated she was. She poured the cold liquid into her dry mouth, her body rejoicing at the replenishment. Over half the glass had been drunk, then her head began to spin, and the tumbler slipped from her fingers. Her legs gave way, and she hit the floor, the deep pile of the carpet softening her landing. Her vision blurred, and the only sound she could process was muffled conversation, although it felt more like shouting. Through the fog of her consciousness, she saw Ryan drop to his knees. He attempted to rouse her before the room was suddenly occupied by two figures dressed in dark clothing, manoeuvring Ryan to one side. She knew she was being manhandled by the two men, but her last memory was of Ryan's feet walking away, slow-motion abandonment when she needed him the most. In her head, she screamed his name, but her mouth emitted no sound. In defeat, she yielded to her poison.

Chapter 61

Eve's limp body was bundled down the narrow stairs, then lugged through the kitchen into the concrete yard at the rear of the safe house. Beyond the yard, over the wall, was a service lane. A black van was parked adjacent to the wooden gate, its sliding door open, ready to receive its passenger. Eve slipped in and out of consciousness; her brain was unable to process events. Her unresponsive limbs made no argument, and her mouth was powerless to communicate her outrage or demand release as the potent concoction surged through her veins. Thrust roughly through the open side of the vehicle, her body sank into its cold metal base. The van's engine vibrated underneath her as it started to edge forwards. Her nausea built rapidly as the rocking motion and sudden jolts slid her from side to side. She screwed her eyes shut to prevent herself from vomiting.

After a while the terrain radically changed; the van slowed as it hit potholes, accompanied by a scratchy rhythm of dings, like the sound of tiny stones and grit bouncing off its chassis. The van stopped, and the two men who were sitting in the front launched the door sideways, revealing Eve wedged against a wheel arch, her loose hair draping her face. They gripped her under the arms and dragged her from the metal bed, then approached a flight of stairs heading underground. After being dragged along a corridor, finally, she was thrown to the ground. Her body craved sleep; her eyelids refused to stay open for longer than half a second, and she was out cold.

*

Eve had no idea how long she had been unconscious or where she was. Her arms and legs were in an agonising position, both shackled together to restrict her movements. They had dumped her in a dark room with a row of tiny windows at the top of the external wall. The lack of natural light told her it was still night. Gradually, her consciousness began to return and with it the excruciating aftermath of her toxin, followed by the migraine from hell. The pressure in her head felt like her eyes would pop from their sockets at any moment, and her arms were sore and tender from being dragged. Despite finding herself scared and alone and in the dark, her overriding emotion was anger. Ryan had betrayed her. He'd walked away while she was taken, not even trying to protect her. His kiss—like Judas. She chastised herself for her weakness. How could she have been so stupid? Eve had fallen for his charm and become blinded by her emotions. From the very beginning, *he* had dragged her into this. As a result, Tom was murdered, Fee had to leave her home, she had consorted with criminals and participated in illegal acts, and the worst of all, her father had been abducted.

Time slowly passed as Eve lay in the dark. Then came the sound she had been dreading, the dull thud of approaching footsteps. She remained on the floor, unable to get up, waiting in anticipation. Light streamed in from the corridor as the door swung open; the fluorescent tube above flickered but failed to light. The two men from earlier lifted Eve onto an old wooden chair placed in the middle of the room. After swearing at the light strobing above, one of the men left the room and returned with a large torch that he shone in her face. Like a vampire seeing the sun, she twisted her head as far away from the light as she could; the bright bulb burned her eyes. They seemed to be waiting for something or someone—they were like guards flanking their victim in case of escape. It wasn't long before a third man appeared, but with the light shining directly into her eyes, she couldn't make him out. He stood in the shadows.

"Where is it?" the man standing out of view demanded.

"Where is my father?" she hissed. One of the heavies stepped forward and backhanded her face, the force nearly sending her chair backwards.

"We've not got time for this. Tell me where it is, or your father is dead."

"I'm not telling you anything until I've seen he's alive and you give your word to release him."

The heavy stepped forward, his arm ready to strike her again, but Eve did not flinch. Her eyes glared at the shadowy figure. She heard him walk out of the room. Moments later, he returned, handing a mobile to her guards. The phone was thrust in her face; she strained her eyes to see it. It was FaceTime. The picture was dark, but in the centre was a man slumped on the floor, his back pressed against the wall, his face bloodied and pained.

"Dad?" she cried. "Are you okay?" Her eyes filled, relief that he was alive.

"Eve? Where are you?" he replied wearily, his eyes searching for her. "I'm fine, don't worry about me. Just do what they say and..." The phone was removed from her vision and returned to its owner.

"I believe that was my end of the deal. Now where is it?" the man bellowed.

"If you untie my hands, I'll get it for you."

The heavy turned his head, waiting for authorisation before undoing the binding on her wrists. The returned use of her shoulders and hands was a huge relief. She rubbed her wrists before reaching inside her bra for the drive. She hadn't felt it since she had passed out, but she put that down to the fact that her entire body was numb. It was missing from where she had concealed it. She frantically patted her upper body in the hope that it had become dislodged and slipped down inside her T-shirt. Dread twisted in her gut. It was gone.

"It's not here," she protested. "It must have been lost when these bloody idiots took me from the house."

"Bullshit! They patted you down before they took you. You were too out of it to notice. Don't fuck with me. Where is it?" The tone of his voice now filled with fury. "Choose your words carefully. Your father's life depends on it."

"*It's not here!*" she shouted. "I haven't..." All of a sudden she had a flashback: Ryan had fallen to his knees when she hit the floor, and Eve had assumed he was trying to help her, but he must have been stealing the drive. She had been too disorientated to realise.

"Oh, my God. He took it from me!"

"What are you talking about?" The stranger was getting impatient.

"*He* took it—you know, Ryan, the one who set me up! He must have grabbed it just before these two dragged me down the stairs!"

"Don't lie to me!" He signalled to one of the men to do his worst. He lynched her by her T-shirt, then backhanded her again and sent her flying, the wooden chair breaking beneath her as she fell on top of it. He did not stop. As if taking a free kick in a football match, he swung his foot backwards before landing a blow directly in her stomach; she wailed in pain as his boot struck.

"I'm not lying to you. He's taken it. I don't know why, but I haven't got it!" She cried in agony, rolling and clutching her abdomen. "Why would I lie? I want you to let my father go," she rasped, warm blood trickling from a gash in her head, her cheek beginning to swell from the impact. The stranger marched forward, grabbed the torch, and shone it directly into her eyes. The light was so bright, it blinded her, obliterating her ability to identify him. He grabbed her by the hair and pulled her upright so he was sure she could hear and understand.

"If you *are* lying to me, both you and your father are

going to meet again very soon—on the other side!" he threatened, throwing her back down to the ground. "Fuck!" he muttered to himself as he passed the torch back to his henchman and strode over to the doorway, then took his phone from his pocket. "She hasn't got it...No, I don't want you to tell Amicus yet. I'm handling it! Just do as I say, tell her I will bring it to her. Where are you flying from?...Biggin Hill, right, I will be there at four to personally hand it to her."

He turned to his operatives. "Keep her quiet for a couple of hours while I straighten this out. I'll be back for her later."

Eve had been listening intently to his conversation, knowing she would need to remember it. Her captors approached her from behind, and a large hand went to her throat. Her windpipe constricted, her body fought for air before surrendering. Then once again, darkness.

Chapter 62

Present

Eve could feel her body being gripped as she lay still on the concrete.

"Open your eyes. It's okay!" Ryan cried. "I shot the guy chasing you. You're not injured."

Injury or not, her body was still trying to recover from being beaten and drugged. She listlessly lifted her head, trying to make sense of what had just happened. Ryan took hold of her shoulders and propped her up so she was sitting upright. He moved to touch her face, but she fiercely swiped his hand away.

"Don't touch me, don't you dare touch me!" she ordered. Ryan backed away, contrition flashing across his face. Eve managed to push herself from the ground, her arm stretched out, warning him not to approach. She turned and hobbled over to where her captor lay. This was the first time she had seen a dead body up close. Although distressing to witness, having seen the image of Tom sprawled on her floor and knowing these people were probably responsible, her level of sympathy eroded. She was numb. Ryan moved next to her, his face solemn as he looked at his victim.

"We have to move quickly in case any others come back," he said.

"I'm not going anywhere with you! You left me when I needed you the most. How could you take the drive knowing that my dad's life depended on it?" she roared. "Because of you, he's probably dead, and I will never forgive you for that. Get out of my way!"

"You don't understand," he pleaded. "I had no choice."

"Of course you had a choice, but you just left me. Christ, it was probably you who asked Mandy to drug me."

His failure to respond told her everything she needed know. She barged past him, heading for the van that had transported her the previous day. "Just wait!" he demanded, grabbing her arm and swinging her around before pulling out the photograph he had been keeping in his pocket. "Look!" he ordered, pushing the photograph into her hands. She held it for a moment, trying to process what she was looking at. The grainy, monochrome image had been taken in the dark. It was of a bedroom with a wardrobe to one side and curtains drawn behind. In the foreground was a bed with what appeared to be a woman asleep, facing the camera. In the immediate foreground was a figure dressed in black, pointing a gun towards her head. Her body language suggested that she was in a deep sleep, blissfully unaware of the intruder in her room. Eve turned the photo over, and written on the back was *Get the drive—09457 260806.*

"That's my mum." He shuddered. "I was in exactly the same position as you. They were threatening me too."

"Why didn't you tell me?" she hissed, his confession not serving to pacify her. "If you had, maybe we could have done something about it earlier, instead of ending up in this bloody mess. You've been lying to me for days!"

"I'm sorry. I was scared. I didn't know you a few days ago, and I didn't know if you would help. I have already lost my father this week, and I wasn't prepared to lose my mother as well."

Eve was torn. She understood his motives, but she couldn't forgive him.

"I left when I did to move her to somewhere safe. I packed her on a train, and now she's out of London. I took the drive in case I needed leverage. I was always going to come back for you. Look, it's here! I brought it straight back to you," he protested. She could barely look at him, her heart and her head struggling to conciliate. Eve snatched the drive from his open palm and started towards the van, tears spilling from her eyes. He grabbed her again, spinning her around and kissing her with both hands clutching her face. She fought off his advances, pushing him away with all the strength she could muster.

"Please," he pleaded.

She wiped the tears with the heels of her hands, pulling herself together, finding her stoicism. "Don't!"

"Where are you going?"

"I heard them when I was being interrogated. I'm going to find this Amicus at Biggin Hill, wherever that is, and give him the drive myself. Don't follow me. We are done." She turned her back on him.

"Wait!" he urged. She did not turn around, so he ran and stood in front of her. "If you insist on going, you're going to need this." He handed her the gun that Eddie had given them in the pub with the envelope of money. "Thank you," she said coldly.

"I am so sorry. I really do—"

"Enough," she interrupted. "Before you lie to me again." Eve barged past him without making eye contact. She strode over to the van whose keys were still in the ignition. She started the engine and, as she checked her wing mirrors, saw a sombre Ryan before she slowly pulled away.

Her tears stung her grazed face as she tried to focus on the road ahead. The last few days had been the most terrifying of her life, but she had also never connected with anyone in the way that she had with Ryan. Their whole relationship had been based on lies; she would never trust him again. Her thoughts were consumed by the fate of her father. She had no idea if he was alive or dead, but she had hope and had to believe that all was not lost. The figure in the shadows had acknowledged that she still had a purpose, wanting her to be kept alive to obtain the drive. Surely this meant her father had also been granted an all but brief reprieve. Eve now had nothing else to lose, her life as she had previously known it was altered beyond all recognition. The actions she had taken had been unlawful and dangerous but also bold. Her moral compass felt like it was spinning, unable to centre. The value she now placed on life itself alongside loyalty and trust could not be purchased with any amount of money.

The building she had driven away from was by the Thames, and it was essential to find somewhere far enough away to examine the contents of the van. There had to be something useful, something that could help her. Pulling off the main drag into a quiet side street, she opened the side door. At first glance, the van contained black bin bags, a crowbar, duct tape—your basic henchman's toolkit. Then she spotted it. It was upside down and covered in dust and grit from having been thrown around in the van, but it was her bag. Her captors must have taken it when they removed her from the safe house. Eve grabbed it. She riffled around, taking out the spare clothes and finding the paper with Fee's number on it, then—bingo! A phone! Its power was waning with less than 20 percent left, but it was enough. Holding it up she checked the signal. London had its faults, but for connectivity, it was brilliant. She opened a browser and Googled Biggin Hill. The back of her neck prickled as she stood beside the van's open door. She was exposed. She climbed back into the driver's seat and instantly felt more secure, knowing she could leave at any moment.

The search results returned quickly. Biggin Hill was a small commercial airport located twelve miles from London city. It was specifically for business travellers with private jets, a discreet method of transportation, allowing its patrons not to have to rub shoulders with the masses. Her recollection was sketchy, but her captor said he was going to rendezvous there at 4:00 p.m. It was 11:34 a.m., so she could take a breath; there was plenty of time. The next few hours would be best used to eat, freshen up, then drive over. She could safely watch from a distance, then plan her next move. Her father's life was at stake, and she was not going to jeopardise his safety because she had been reckless.

As Eve checked the mirrors, she leaned closer to look at her face. The reflection was almost recognisable. Gone was the well-groomed, confident professional. She had been replaced by a grey and dour pallor. The dark circles under her eyes aged her, her expression now hardened, her body exhausted. Eve knew that she could not go to confront Amicus in her present state—she would be dismissed as fragile. She resolved to find a chemist and purchase makeup to clean herself up. Before setting off, Eve downloaded a map to get her from her current location to Biggin Hill. Taking a deep breath, she pulled out of the side street and headed back onto the main road. The countdown had begun.

Chapter 63

Despite never having driven a transit, Eve was handling her new vehicle with relative ease. There was a part of her that enjoyed having a large van; other cars made way. Her attitude on the road matched her resolution within; she refused to be pushed around. The streets were busy, as it was approaching rush hour. She saw numerous branches of Boots as she passed parades of high street shops. However, it was almost impossible to find somewhere to stop and park, her frustration evident through her road rage. Her temperature started to rise as she desperately searched for somewhere to stop, but then she saw it. Up ahead was a retail park with the usual host of stores. "Thank you, God," she hailed silently as she pulled into the left-hand lane and entered the estate. A vacant space waited towards the middle of the car park, one that she could drive into and out of—reversing the van was not something she wanted to attempt right now. Before accessing any of these shops, she had to clean up her face.

The dried blood in her hair and on her clothes would attract unnecessary attention. She looked around in the van for anything she could use to wipe her face with, but there was nothing. In her bag, she found a hair bobble. Using her fingers as a brush, she lifted her dank hair and managed to conceal the blood by creating a messy bun at the back. The blood was like superglue, matting and hardening her hair. With nothing to wipe her face, she used her own saliva and the edge of her T-shirt to clean the thin stripes of dirt on her forehead and cheeks. She covered up the bruising that had appeared on her throat by lifting the collar of the jacket she took from the bag. It was not perfect, but it would do.

Eve removed the keys from the ignition and took her phone and a handful of notes from the envelope. As she crossed the car park, something caught her eye. There was a gym. On its billboard, it promised no monthly membership; it was more like pay-as-you-go. Perfect, Eve thought. She would pay for a session and use their facilities to shower and clean up. First stop was Boots.

She strode through the doors with her mental shopping list. She needed an array of toiletries; it had been days since she had seen a shower. As Eve placed the items in her basket, she felt a small sense of relief that she would soon be clean; her skin crawled. Strong paracetamol and medicines would help to numb her pain before she proceeded to the makeup counters. Eve always purchased luxury makeup brands; Fee had educated her when she first moved to London. All of that now seemed a world away. She collected what she needed to disguise her bruises and cover her dark circles, then paid at the self-service counter. Next stop was Marks and Spencer. She headed straight for their sportswear department and purchased a full set of activewear as well as a towel, new trainers, jacket, and fresh underwear.

Eve was about to go to the gym when she thought about her phone. Its lack of power would be an issue, although 20 percent would be enough for now. What if she needed it later? She decided to purchase a portable phone charger from Curry's.

Finally, she was ready for the gym. Walking into the foyer laden with carrier bags did not scream "ready to exercise." Heading back to the van, she decided the black bag would be more appropriate. She transferred her purchases into the bag, all except the trainers and jacket, which she put on.

The glass doors of the gym swished open as Eve approached. A long-haired, tanned woman was standing behind a desk. She wore a tight-fitted polo shirt which accentuated her athletic figure. A man came in after Eve whom the girl seemed to recognise. She said a friendly "Hi" to him as he swiped a membership card and walked through a turnstile which led to a set of double doors.

"Hi, can I help you?" she chirped, her name badge stating her name as Katie.

"Yes, I'd like to pay for a session, please."

"Have you been to us before?" she questioned politely.

"No, no, I haven't. Is that a problem?"

"Not at all. I just need you to fill in this form with your details, and we can get you started." She smiled, handing Eve a clipboard with a form and pen attached. Eve stood at the counter and completed the paperwork, then passed the clipboard back to Katie along with the fee.

"Right, Miss Saxon, that's great. Tim, who usually does our inductions, is off today. He's got the tummy bug," she said apologetically, handing her the change. "I can get someone else to show you around—"

"It's absolutely fine. I know my way around gym equipment," she lied. "I'll be fine."

"Okay, then, it's just through those doors. The showers and changing rooms and sauna are to the left. You'll need a 50p for the lockers, and the gym suite and equipment are further up on your right. There are plenty of instructors around to help you if you need anything."

"Thank you," she replied as she walked through the turnstile that Katie had clicked, granting her entry.

The locker room was open with shower cubicles and toilets to one side. Eve opened a locker, then placed the phone inside hooked up to its new charger before taking her bag into a cubicle. After dropping down onto the small wooden bench, she rested her head wearily against the wall. She was exhausted and her body and her brain were working on overdrive. The cascade of hot water soothed her skin; however, the cleansing was rapidly replaced by a burning sensation. A pink river flowed to the drain as the dried blood in her hair was released. Her nourishing shampoo smarted as her fingers traced the gash within her hair which had clotted and sealed. She washed her face and body repeatedly; she didn't feel clean. No matter how much she scrubbed, she couldn't wash away her heartache.

The amount of bruising on Eve's body was extensive, a stark reminder of the importance of getting to Amicus before her father met the same fate. Dressed in her new clothes, Eve was fresh and energised. The makeup she had selected largely covered her bruising and fatigue, but her reflection felt different. There was only one thing left to do. Refuel and hydrate. A large coffee, an enormous sandwich, and a banana later, Eve was ready to go. The battery life on the phone was 80 percent, and Google Maps was primed and ready to give directions. The time on her phone read 1:37 p.m., just under two and a half hours left. Pulling carefully out of her parking space, she headed south.

Chapter 64

Hunt's eyes stung as they opened. Her arm stabbed with sharp pain, and her head pounded as if it had been bludgeoned by a hammer. Her eyes searched for any clue as to where she was. Her stomach heaved at the pungent smell of cleaning solution, and as she began to move, she saw the cannula in her arm hooked up to a drip. The foam mattress she lay on and itchy blanket rubbing against her skin were standard hospital issue. Light streamed through the window next to her bed, and a curtain was drawn on the other side. Hunt had no idea how long she had been there or what day it was.

"Ah, you're awake," announced the nurse as she appeared from the other side of the curtain. Her smile wrinkled her nose as she moved closer to Hunt's bedside. "Now, please don't worry, you're safe here. Let me make you more comfortable," she said as she adjusted her sheets and pillows. "My name is Debbie. Can you tell me what your name is?" The nurse waited a moment, allowing Hunt to process the request.

"Hunt," she uttered.

"Have you got a first name, my love?" Debbie urged.

"Jo. How long have I been here?"

"They brought you in yesterday, late afternoon, and you've been asleep since then. Can you tell me what happened, Jo? Take your time."

"I had a splitting headache, and..." she slurred, trying to remember exactly what had happened. "Then I felt worse, and my head started to spin and...Walker, where's Walker?" She tried to get up, searching for him, but he wasn't there.

"Steady on, Jo, you are still very weak," Debbie said as she guided her back onto her pillow. "Is Walker your boyfriend? Would you like us to call him, Jo?"

"No!" she snapped as she gripped the side of the bed to hoist herself up. Debbie stepped in to support her as Hunt struggled to shift up the bed.

"You need to rest, Jo. You need to get your strength back. I'll call the doctor to come and check you over. He's doing his rounds."

"I need to go." Then Hunt remembered. "Where are the documents?" she demanded as she lifted her blankets and scanned the small cupboard next to the bed. Her voice was rough, her throat dry and aching.

"You were found by yourself, Jo, nothing and no-one else around you. The other passengers said you had been on your own for the whole journey."

"No, he was sitting next to me!" she insisted, falling back into the large pillow behind her with a loud sigh before ripping the cannula from her arm. "He's taken the envelope.

Oh, my God!" she seethed. "He really did a number on me." Her hands held her head in despair.

"Who did? Are you okay, Jo? Is there anyone we can call? We've done some blood tests to find out what caused you to black out."

"I know exactly what it was. The bastard gave me Rohypnol!"

Debbie regarded her, her face solemn. "Has this happened before? The police can help you, and we can keep you safe."

"It's not me that's going to need protection. I'm fine, but I need to go," she assured Debbie, whose expression was a mixture of bemusement and concern.

"I can't force you to stay, but I strongly advise that you at least see the doctor and get him to check you over."

"Okay, please go and get him. I need to leave as soon as possible."

Relief flooded over Debbie's face as she left the cubicle.

Hunt waited a minute, listening to the squeak of Debbie's shoes growing distant. She threw back the covers to reveal a blue cotton gown, but she was still wearing her underwear, although her bra had been removed. Hunt carefully dropped the side railing of the bed and swung her legs around until they were flat on the tiled floor. She leaned over to the cupboard next to her and opened its door to reveal her clothes neatly folded inside. To her amazement, when she unfolded them, her phone was tucked inside and remarkably so was her passport.

Hunt pushed herself into a standing position, and despite swaying a little, she managed to centre herself. Her head was still splitting, but she would deal with the pain later. She needed to leave and find Walker before the documents got into the wrong hands. A jug of water had been left by her bed, and she was confident that this time it would provide the hydration that she needed. Once dressed, she moved swiftly out of the ward and headed towards the door. A beeping noise from one of the beds in another room kept Debbie and most of the other nurses preoccupied while she slipped out.

She looked at the time on her phone. It was 2:00 p.m. Walker had plenty of time to leave with the documents completely unnoticed. He could be anywhere by now. Her instincts confirmed it—something was not right. Had he engineered their liaison to disarm her? There was no time for self-recrimination or analysis of her actions; Hunt needed to focus. The Rohypnol had not only given her a dry mouth and stinging eyes but also a fuzzy head that was still aching.

As Hunt was about to leave the hospital, she was distracted by a mirrored window. The reflection that greeted her was washed out and exhausted, the shine faded from her hair. She dived into the adjacent toilets and splashed cold water on her face, and her skin prickled as it awakened. She dried herself and re-adjusted her disheveled clothing before once again looking in the mirror. Although she still looked exhausted, her reflection had changed. The fortitude behind her eyes was manifesting. Hunt had a fire in her gut, ready for whatever was coming.

Walker had been playing a long game, waiting until he could get his hands on the documents. He had been calculating and manipulative, but now it was her turn, and she was about to change the game. Hunt had no idea where he was or who he was working for, and trying to work this out at this late stage would be futile. The only thing she could do was decipher his message and attempt to head him off at the pass. The message had read *BQH 1600*. That was unquestionably 4:00 p.m., but where? She Googled the initials. The first site in the list was a company called BQH, who were quantity surveyors in New Zealand. This was highly improbable, so she continued down the list. Eureka! BQH was the airport code for Biggin Hill, London. She had less than two hours. According to Google, it was just short of twenty miles and would take just over one hour and twenty minutes to get there. There was no room for hesitation so she headed to the cashpoint just next to the hospital shop. Hunt raced out of the front entrance and jumped into a taxi. The smiling cabbie turned to her as she counted £100 into his change receptacle. "Get me to Biggin Hill Airport in one hour, and I'll double it."

Chapter 65

"What's going on?" demanded Amicus, her rage building at the lack of communication from Ashford.

"When I spoke to Ashford, he said he was going to personally place the drive in your hands at four o'clock," replied Butler.

"I will never again be at the mercy of others, particularly those who are completely incompetent!" She glowered, pacing around her hotel suite. "Where are they holding her?"

"He wouldn't tell me, and even if we knew, now that we're a man down, I'm not sure any of our secondary contacts would be able to get there fast enough."

"Bloody hell! If we don't get our hands on that drive this afternoon, we can say goodbye to our meeting. Everything we have worked for utterly decimated in one fell swoop." Amicus's chest began to tighten. "There is nothing that we can do but proceed as planned and trust that Ashford will deliver. He fully understands the consequences of his failure." Amicus saw Butler's eyes widen, her comment echoing her earlier promise to deliver consequences. There was silence between them for a moment. Amicus held the solitaire diamond of her pendant between her fingers as she thought, and then she turned to Butler. “Phone ahead to Biggin Hill. I want to be able to take off as soon as I have the drive. We are not waiting a moment longer. Do not take no for an answer. Pack everything up, we are leaving.”

Butler nodded, then returned to her room.

This was an easier task for Amicus than Butler, who had a bank of laptops and technology that had to be carefully packaged and stowed before their departure. Travelling by private jet ensured that Butler didn’t have the plague of hand baggage allowances, which meant that the equipment could be with her at all times. Butler had a room that was much smaller and located on a different floor. Her accommodation only needed to serve as somewhere to sleep and freshen up. Amicus had packed most of her possessions and was almost ready to go. She was used to packing light, as her life was spent travelling to meetings.

Amicus dialled the concierge and ordered brunch to go, accompanied by an abundance of coffee. Her mother had ingrained within her the importance of food, water, and sleep to stay level-headed and alert. Amicus would not embark on a journey with her body wanting, and neither would she have Butler operating at less than 100 percent, particularly in light of what was about to transpire over the next few hours.

Chapter 66

Google Maps had given Eve a convoluted route to Biggin Hill Airport. After becoming totally confused, she pulled into a Waitrose car park and looked up the "How to Get to Us" section of their website, which was more concise. Once she had navigated the dreaded M25, it was not far off junction 6 and, according to their map, was well signposted. Despite this, her journey took over an hour due to roadworks and a broken-down coach causing chaos on the hard shoulder. When she finally arrived, Eve could see the car park directly in front of the main terminal building. Space was at a premium. It did not appear as if it could accommodate more than 250 cars, and parking a huge van would be conspicuous, sandwiched amongst the Range Rovers and Bentleys. Eve decided to drive a mile further down the road, where a winding lane led off towards what looked like a farm in the distance. It was not ideal, but there was no other option.

Eve's mission was to get to the airport and locate Amicus. She placed the phone in her pocket and switched it to silent, then took some cash from the envelope. She concealed the drive once again in her bra, then reached under the passenger seat. Tiny grains of grit and dirt brushed against her fingertips before she found what she was searching for. Eve dropped down to her knees and extended her arm further under the seat to grasp the wrapped handgun. Terrified of it firing, she manoeuvred it from under the seat with the utmost caution, then placed it on the seat next to her. Eve unwrapped it anxiously, her heart in her mouth as the heavy cloth unfolded to reveal the grey sculpted metal. As Eve examined the gun, she noticed three horizontal lines scratched along its barrel. She had no idea why, and at that moment, she didn't care. Its unused magazine underneath its grip gave her a sense of certainty that she was not about to put a hole in anything or herself. Eve took a deep breath as she placed it in her palm, the adrenaline making her lightheaded. She had never handled a gun before, and although Ryan had briefly explained how to use it, it filled her with panic.

The handgun was small enough to conceal on her person; however, Eve would be sure not to click in the magazine until she had identified where Amicus was. She would not jeopardise her safety by being rash. After one last look around the van for anything useful, Eve pulled down the sun visor, then stuck the keys between the visor and the roof. The display on the phone showed 3:17 p.m., just over forty minutes before the handover. She was determined to negotiate her father's release. There was no time to hesitate.

The return journey on foot to the main terminal

building, with heavy legs and growing fatigue, took longer than Eve realised. Replaying the image of her captured father, his words echoing in her head gave her the surge she needed to advance. It had taken fifteen minutes to walk to the terminal building; she had to find Amicus, and fast. Walking into Biggin Hill would not be like entering Heathrow. Eve would be spotted instantly, and without a clear idea of where she was heading, she would be promptly escorted from the premises. Standing back out of view, she took out her phone once again to examine the plan of the airfield. The interactive map detailed two main terminals as well as numerous private jet operators who managed their own hangars. Her gut told her Amicus was not going to be travelling through the main terminals; if he knew what was on the drive and was prepared to go to these lengths, he would be travelling incognito. Eve just needed to discover which hangar. Just then, a black E-Class Mercedes rolled past her and indicated one hundred yards down the road. Scrutinising her map again, she surmised that the car could be taking a passenger to a private hangar. This was it.

Eve carefully moved along the road, treking through the row of trees standing to attention. A disinterested security guard appeared to be manning a barrier, jumping to attention to allow the Mercedes to pass, then waiting for it to be out of sight before returning to his phone. This was clearly not a position that required a great deal of hard work. His apparent lack of concentration indicated that he had a minimal workload and seemed well practised in appearing to be alert. The sound of an engine might pique his interest, but he seemed to be utterly oblivious to everything else in the surrounding area. He occasionally gave a cursory glance to his left and right when he sipped from his mug, before he returned to what looked like some kind of game. His face smiled and grimaced as his fingers moved frantically across his screen. As much as she wanted to, Eve couldn't merely commando roll past his guard box and hope he was too preoccupied to notice—there had to be another way.

Remaining under cover of the trees, Eve continued along the road, following the line of wire fencing; she desperately searched for another way in. As the road curved around, the fencing became buttressed by swathes of wild bushes and brambles; visibility from the road diminished quickly. It was 3:46 p.m., less than a quarter of an hour. After scanning the trees over her shoulder, Eve dropped down onto her hands and knees to examine the fence. There, ten feet to the right, was a section of wire that had become disconnected from its post.

The fence had been weakened by the sprawling bushes and undergrowth wrapped around it, like a boa constrictor choking its victim. Fending off scratches and nips from brambles and thorns, Eve crawled towards the fence and laced her fingers within its holes to take a firm grip. Her hands like claws, she yanked the wire, using her body weight as power. She rocked back and forth trying to weaken its fixings, until after a minute of sweating and heaving, it loosened enough to create a gap high enough for her to crawl through flat on her stomach. As she crawled forward and through the opening, the jagged edges of the wire dug into her skin as it pulled and ripped at her hair and clothes. Finally, she was through, but not without injury. There was nothing to be done about it now; she wasn't bleeding to death, and she had been through worse.

Eve crouched down until she could again conceal herself within the trees on the other side of the fence. Once hidden, she removed the debris on her clothes in an attempt to once again make herself presentable. From her vantage point, she could see the rear of two hangars; it had to be one of them. In a moment of panic, Eve grabbed her chest to check that the drive was still in her bra. It was still there, but her relief did not last long, the gun was missing.

Chapter 67

The black E-Class slowly pulled into the hangar, where it delivered Amicus and Butler to their waiting jet. Having prearranged a specific time before their arrival, the border control agents were ready to attend to them. Their inspection was efficient and brief, all paperwork satisfactorily reviewed and cleared for departure. As the agents exited, their footsteps were amplified by the enormous steel walls and roof of the hangar. It was wide enough to accommodate three jets, but Amicus had arranged the privacy she needed, ensuring hers was the only aircraft parked. Also in situ were the waiting ground crew, whom Butler directed. Within minutes, their luggage had been efficiently loaded, and their aircraft prepared for departure.

The aircrew had served her for years. They understood that confidentiality and discretion were of the utmost importance; their service and loyalty were always rewarded in considerable measure. Ex-RAF Officer Henry Dalton was their pilot alongside the ever-attentive cabin manager, James. Butler instructed them to wait in the cockpit with the door closed, understanding their departure would be imminent. One of the benefits of Biggin Hill was that there were no runway slots; passengers could have a little more flexibility in their departure times.

Checking her rose gold Rolex, Amicus saw that the time was approaching 4:00 p.m. "Where the hell is Ashford?" she snapped. "If he fails to deliver, I—" She stopped dead. From the oval window next to her cream leather seat, Amicus watched as a slim figure dressed in black crept quietly through the front entrance of the hangar. Amicus could tell it was a woman from her body shape; she also knew she was not a professional, as she was awkward in her movements. By this time, Butler had moved over to her side of the plane and was also watching intently.

"What do you think?" Amicus probed quietly.

"I think we need to find out exactly who it is and what the hell they are doing here." Butler was also not threatened by this mystery woman, but she was perturbed by her presence. Butler glanced at Amicus, who lifted her head in agreement.

The figure froze when she saw Butler descending the aircraft stairs and glaring directly at her.

"What are you doing here?" Bulter snarled.

"I'm looking for Amicus. Is he here?" the figure replied.

"Who are you? What do you want?" Butler demanded.

Chapter 68

Eve stood opposite Butler, who had emerged from the plane; both eyeballed each other. Butler did not flinch at Eve's question about who Amicus was at all. Eve knew she was in the right place. Eve took a few steps towards her, willing her knees to stop shaking under her trousers. Eve tried to prevent Butler from reading her panic. They both glared at each other, neither willing to show weakness.

"I want my father to be released—now. He has nothing to do with this," Eve ordered. For a second, she could see the confusion on Butler's face as she processed her words, then, moments later: "You're Eve Blake. What the hell are you doing here?"

"I've come to exchange the drive for my father's life. If you want it returned, release him immediately."

Butler's reply was interrupted by another woman as she emerged from the jet. "So you're Eve Blake. You have caused me no end of trouble."

Eve regarded the elegantly dressed woman with confusion as she slowly descended the stairs to join Butler on the tarmac. Eve subtly peered to see if there was anyone else on board, but they seemed to be the only passengers. Then it hit her: *Oh, my God—Amicus is a woman.*

Eve's jaw tightened as Amicus strutted towards her like a lioness stalking her victim. The heady aroma of her perfume intoxicated Eve's senses as Amicus moved closer. Everything about this woman oozed sophistication and poise. She had never imagined that Amicus would be a woman—but why not? Why should it have been a man? Women were indeed as strong, driven, and ruthless as men; she had prosecuted enough of them during her career. Amicus was unlike anyone she had ever encountered.

"I believe you have something that belongs to me."

Eve opened her mouth to speak, only uttering a syllable when a black Audi Q7 roared into the hangar, forcing Eve to veer out of its path. The vehicle squealed to a halt, and Ashford leapt from the driver's seat, enraged at the sight of Eve standing there.

"Is this what you call delivering into my hands personally?" Amicus sneered at Ashford. Eve stared at him, his voice and his physicality familiar. This had to be the man in the shadows.

The jet's cockpit was pointing in the opposite direction; therefore, the crew couldn't see what was unfolding. "This has been a complete fuckup from the beginning to the end," Amicus said, glowering. "So where is it? I have wasted enough time."

"Just wait," Ashford replied, his mouth tight with fury. He took out his phone and FaceTimed a number. The person at the other end answered immediately, as if primed for his call. "Show him," Ashford directed into the phone, then turned the screen toward Eve. She moved forward a few steps so she could see the image clearly. Eve could see her father slumped in the same place, weary and exhausted, but alive. Relieved, she closed her eyes for a brief second, then reached for the drive. Holding it between her thumb and fingers, stretching out her arm, she demanded, "Now let him go!"

Ashford's eyes narrowed. "That offer expired this morning. Shoot him."

It was almost instantaneous. The deafening roar of the gunshot shattered the silence. Eve collapsed to the floor like a puppet whose strings were cut. She lay on the ground gasping for breath, the deep, barking moans of her lungs the only sound as they fought for air. Tears streamed from her eyes, obscuring the sight of Butler running to her side.

"What the hell are you doing?" Amicus yelled at Ashford. "I told you to let him go. How dare you defy me!"

"I've had enough of your bloody orders. Once this is over, we're finished," he retorted. Eve could feel Butler's arms supporting her as she remained on the ground. Ashford's rage continued as he flung open the rear door of the Audi and reached inside. He dragged someone from the boot and threw them on the tarmac. Eve could see the bewilderment on Amicus's face; she had no idea what was going on or who this individual was. Butler had managed to help Eve steady her breathing, but when they both lifted their heads to examine who it was, Eve's breath quickened again.

His face swollen and bloodied with his hands tied behind his back, Ryan had taken a severe beating. His body was sprawled in front of them; Ashford displayed him like a trophy of his handiwork. Ashford then pulled out a firearm, stood over Ryan, and pointed it at Ryan's head. "Now hand over that drive, or you're going to lose your boyfriend too."

"Don't!" shouted a voice from behind the plane. They all turned to see a woman carefully edging around the jet from the opposite side, her gun poised. She had entered undetected, apparently listening and watching from the other side of the hangar.

"And who the hell are you?" Amicus demanded, throwing her hands in the air.

"She's one of mine. Jo Hunt," Ashford muttered. "Why are *you* here?"

"Cut the bollocks. Where's the envelope?" she demanded.

"What envelope?" Ashford snapped.

"The one Walker took from me after he slipped me the Rohypnol."

Ashford paused for a moment, then sighed sarcastically. "Well, *you* fell for that one. I used to think you had a promising career until you slept with Nick and fucked it up. Then you went and did the same thing again with Walker—practically a stranger! A quick shag in the woods and you lose all your instincts. You made it too easy."

"Will someone explain to me what is going on?" Amicus screeched.

"My partner was Nick Hardy. He was murdered a year

ago, and Ashford told me that Smith was responsible. I've been tracking your little operation since then, trying to work out what was going on. Smith led me to a deposit box in Paris filled with detailed records of every target he has terminated, including dates, times, and surveillance information, for the last five years."

"And what does that have to do with me?" Amicus shrugged incredulously.

"Your name is written all over the papers. It's all linked to you."

Although still in a state of shock, Eve still needed to be mentally present for what was transpiring. Something was bothering her. She repeated the name *Amicus*, *Amicus*, *Amicus* in her head. Her eyes closed, willing her brain to function. Latin, it was Latin. It was the least favourite subject that her dad had taught her, but it was useful all the same. She desperately tried to remember what it meant.

"A friend!" Eve shouted in realisation. They all looked at her, utterly perplexed. "The dying man on the video said, 'Tell her to find a friend.'" Eve pushed herself up from the ground. Her mind still busy. There was something else. There was something about him. She closed her eyes again, trying to remember. Then it came to her. Eve turned and glowered at Ashford. "It was you!"

Chapter 69

Hunt edged over to where Butler and Eve were standing, her fingers tightly wrapped around her gun. Ashford maintained his position, his weapon pointed at Ryan's head. As Hunt drew closer, Eve noticed her firearm—three scratches. Hunt had found Eve's missing gun. It had been missing since Eve had crawled through the fence. Her jaw clenched, Eve slowly moved her arm against her pocket to check that the ammunition magazine was still there; despite her impressive bluffing, Hunt would need it. Eve thought quickly. She stumbled in Hunt's direction so that she would catch her. As Hunt grabbed Eve's arm, she fell towards her and artfully whispered close to Hunt's cheek. Hunt's glare revealed that she understood.

"It was you," Eve repeated, turning back to Ashford. "I saw you on the video. You shot him in the back, then left him there to die." Eve remembered the video as clearly as if she had seen the events live; her horror was still as vivid.

"Shot who?" Hunt questioned.

"I have no idea what you're talking about. Now stop

stalling and hand over the drive, or you'll be responsible for the deaths of two people today," Ashford warned as he kicked Ryan.

"You killed him!" Eve shouted. Her cheeks flushed; her nervous energy was making her pace as she explained. "He was, er…young, tall, athletic build. You argued first, then…he turned his back, and you shot him. He fell right in front of his…oh, what colour was it? Dark blue! His dark blue car. He must have been important. Why else would someone film it?"

As Eve spoke, Hunt's eyes suddenly bulged as though she had been stabbed with a sharp knife; she appeared to recognise the details Eve had recalled. And then Hunt erupted. "You piece of shit!" she shouted at Ashford, now pointing her gun at her boss. "You shot Nick in the back and left him to die like scum. Nick was like a son—he would have done anything for you!"

"Anything apart from following instructions to keep out of it," Ashford snapped. "He brought this on himself. I couldn't let him jeopardise our whole operation. Besides, it wasn't my call," he said unapologetically.

"So whose call was it?" Hunt demanded. "The man in the photo?"

"Not at liberty to disclose. You know better than to ask."

Amicus had observed the entire altercation, threats and insults hurled from each side like a singles tennis match. The current score was deuce. "Well, although this has been mildly entertaining, I've had quite enough. Hand over the drive and the envelope. I have waited far too long. You can resolve your differences after I've gone," Amicus dictated before turning to Butler. "Tell the crew to start the engines. We're leaving."

With Ashford's attention distracted by Amicus, Eve's eyes shot to Hunt. Eve hastily passed the magazine to Hunt, who promptly locked it into place and released the Glock's safety catch.

Its sound alerted Ashford. "Brilliant!" He laughed. "It wasn't even bloody loaded. You really are a complete joke, Hunt. Why did I think for a second that you had potential? You should have stayed as a copper with the rest of the girls."

Eve could see Hunt's eyes narrowing and her mouth tensing as Ashford continued to hurl abuse. "Hand it over!" he shouted; the noise of the engines began to whirr.

"Let him go!" Eve said defiantly. Ashford looked at Amicus. "Now!" Eve barked.

Ashford stepped forward and kicked Ryan. "Get up." Ryan struggled to his feet and stumbled over to Eve, who then positioned him behind Hunt. Eve then slowly advanced towards Amicus, who also moved towards her, their eyes fixed on each other. Eve uncurled her fingers and held out the drive in the palm of her trembling hand. Amicus leaned forward and grasped it, not breaking eye contact. "Under different circumstances," Amicus consoled. Eve turned her back on her and quickly returned to Ryan, who was trying to sit upright on the floor. Taking his face in her hands, she examined his injuries. He winced as she touched his wounds.

"Quite the reunion we've got here, haven't we," Ashford snarled. "The whore, the scumbag son, and the disgraced lawyer. Make the most of it, because it's not going to last long. You see, I can't let you three go around shouting your mouths off about my arrangement. There are bigger elements at play." Ashford slowly edged forward, not breaking eye contact with Hunt. Eve rose to her feet. Her whole body fizzed like a sparking dynamite fuse, ready to explode. Amicus's eyes darted between Eve and Ashford, her expression serious. "Stand down, Ashford, don't be a bloody idiot," Amicus warned.

He ignored her and continued his tirade at Eve and Hunt. "I have spent most of the last fucking week trailing after you two," he said. "You have caused the deaths of innocent people." He waved his gun in Eve's direction. "That poor young boy in your flat whimpered as he struggled for his last breath. Then there was your pathetic father, and you couldn't even manage to come through for him, could you? And don't worry, as for your lawyer friend Fee, we'll be dealing with her next."

In one swift motion, Eve grabbed the gun from Hunt, aimed, and fired at Ashford. The bullet pierced his chest, sending his body cascading to the floor. Blood quickly saturated his clothes as he lay on the ground. Ashford was now the one who gasped for breath and struggled for his life. None rushed to his side to assist; they stood paralysed, witnessing his agonising demise. Ashford's last moments left him gagging on his blood as it spluttered from his mouth.

The sound of the engines had largely masked the gunshot, but it was Amicus who broke their stupor. "We've got to move him. Put him in the back of the car," she commanded, looking at her watch, her brow furrowed. Eve was rigid. She stared at Ashford's body, unable to blink or avert her eyes. Hunt bent down and released Ryan from his restraints. He stood shakily, then followed Hunt and Butler to where Ashford was lying, helping to drag him round to the boot of the Audi.

Eve was still standing with the gun in her trembling hand, which she pointed to the floor. Her body had reacted without the permission of her brain, like an involuntary reflex. Her ears rang as she tried to focus. Eve would not let Ashford murder her best friend or Ryan; he had already taken Tom and her father. There was no other way of stopping him. Eve had to kill him; it was necessary. This was the only way she could rationalise it in her head. Ashford was evil, and his death, although brutal, had saved the lives of the people surrounding her.

Shifting a dead body the size of Ashford's was arduous for Hunt, Butler, and Ryan. Their heavy breathing and grunting were evidence of the effort involved. It took three attempts to raise him high enough into the Audi; Ashford's limbs were flailing as he was lifted. His blood smeared their clothes, his last act of contempt. The clunk of the boot closing shattered Eve's stupor. She watched as Butler gingerly opened the passenger door, her coat wrapped around her hand, before she retrieved the envelope containing Smith's files that Walker had stolen from Hunt.

Amicus nodded to Butler as she held up the envelope and began to stride towards her jet. Eve's head spun as she rocked on her feet; this time she dropped the gun. Ryan wrapped her arm around his shoulder to steady her. Amicus suddenly turned on her heel and faced Eve. "I could use someone of your talents. Your tenacity and resourcefulness have really been quite something, plus that legal mind of yours would be of great use to me." Once again, Amicus slowly circled her like a vulture. "Consider it. Are you willing to throw your life away? To suffer the consequences of ridding the world of that disgusting excuse for a human being?" Eve was dumbfounded by her offer. Of course there would be consequences, and she would be convicted of murder. Eve also understood that none of them would be stepping forward to expose the truth of what had happened and corroborate her story. But she was a barrister; it was within her moral code to seek justice within the law. How could she go against everything she had ever believed in and fought for? How could she consider not calling the police and ending this all now? Immobility set in as she tried to decide her fate. Now she was the judge and jury of her own life.

"What about me?" Hunt questioned. "I could be an asset to your organisation."

"I don't think so. At the first opportunity, you lost the information that I needed. Your lack of judgement nearly led to the exposure of highly classified documents."

"You mean the documents about Gaddafi's billions?"

Amicus regarded her with cynicism. "I have everything I need in this envelope. Ashford did not thoroughly look through all of the paperwork. Otherwise, he would have seen those documents."

"On the contrary, 'those documents' are not in the

envelope. When I was in Paris, I requested them to be mailed elsewhere. I suppose my 'lack of judgement' had not kicked in by that point because I had the foresight to separate them and send them somewhere secure. Ashford and Walker had no idea of their existence. I refused to discuss them with Walker. There are only two people who know where they are, and right now, I think you might need to ensure their location remains secure." The three of them stood facing each other, three points of a triangle, an unholy trinity.

"Eve, don't do this. You can't. I will stand by you. We can get through this together," Ryan begged.

Breaking away from the others, she turned to face him. "I don't know whether I can ever trust you again. I know you had your reasons, but you lied to me from the beginning. How can I be sure you aren't lying now?" Eve's eyes filled with tears. Ryan had betrayed her in the worst way possible.

"Because you know me, and you know how I feel about you." He took her face in his hands and kissed her softly. Her lips responded, feeling the tenderness in his fingers, the sincerity in his eyes. But it was too late; the damage was done. She didn't trust him and never would again. Eve stepped back from him, unlocking his arms from around her, releasing from his embrace.

Amicus looked down at her watch. It was time to leave. "One mistake, and you're out," she cautioned Hunt.

"This could be the beginning of a beautiful arrangement." Hunt smiled wryly as she followed Butler up the aircraft stairs.

Both Ryan and Amicus had positioned themselves in front of Eve. "So what's it to be?" Amicus demanded an answer to her proposition. "Freedom or justice?"

Chapter 70

Eve fastened her seat belt and stared out the window. On the ground, Ryan drove away in the black Audi, the body of Ashford laid out in its boot. Eve's head fell backwards onto the headrest as she closed her heavy eyes. She could not have imagined how her life could change beyond recognition within a few days. The decisions she had made, the people she had consorted and built relationships with, the grief that was yet to come as her mind found the space to process what she'd lost. But her decision was made, and whether it was right or wrong, her life was about to change again. Eve had no idea whether she would still be standing in the shadows or finally be stepping into the light.

Get Free *Standing In The Shadows* Bonus Material

Building a relationship with my readers is the best thing about writing. I will occasionally send newsletters with details about new releases and other bits of news relating to Standing in the Shadows.

Upon signing up you will receive additional information about the main characters and places that have inspired the book.

You can sign up by clicking here.

Enjoy this book?
You can make a big difference.

Honest reviews of this book will help bring it to the attention of other readers.

If you have enjoyed this book I would be grateful if you could not spend just five minutes leaving a review (it can be as short as you like) on the book's Amazon page.

Thank you very much.

About the Author

Karen L Worsfold is the author of Standing in the Shadows. She makes her online home at www.karenworsfold.com. You can connect with Karen on:

Twitter @AuthorWorsfold

Facebook at www.facebook.com/karen.worsfoldauthor

Instagram @karenworsfoldwriter

Printed in Great Britain
by Amazon

20534987R00205